The Jaguar

ULTAN BANAN

Cover design by Ultan Banan © 2025
Editing by Seminal Edits

ultanbanan.com

ISBN: 978-1-914147-26-5

'I am only concerned with what is not mine.
Law of Man. Law of the cannibal.'

'Our body is, after all, only a society constructed out of many souls.'

The Jaguar

Part One

London, March 1849

I

a bed for the wicked, the wrecked and the raw

I am the soft lustre on the horizon. Too the grave meniscus; the scutch of the meadowgrass. The interminable radius of the rogue star and the worn bed of the dead mother. The hollow of the scallop shell, the moon dog, the parhelia. A veil on the still-warm body of the deceased child. The knowing physic, the blood's tonic.

I am the velvet slough of ocean.

Across these seas, this soft light, slivers of darkness intrude.

A finger pokes at my ribs.

'You go now.'

I open my eyes. He's over me, the boy. His face yellow in the light, black his eyes. They show no emotion, these Orientals. He speaks through the grasping fog of my slumber.

'Go now, you go...'

'No,' I say. 'One more.'

'You no money. You go.'

I slide a hand in my pocket. He's right. I had silver. Now I do not. A simple economy, mine. Bankruptcy is a daily humour.

'Go now...'

'Yes, yes.' I sit up.

Time within these walls there is not. Hours flee on the satiate breeze of the pipe. I never know where I am when my repose ends. Here I find myself again, ghosts of my night travels departin me, roused from the

1

clutch of my vigil. This room where I take flight, and where I revive; morning upon morning, I am thrust again into the black streets.

Outcast.

The boy watches, waitin for me to move. How can you wait in a place with no time, I wonder? Maybe he lives outside time. He's not waitin, only observin.

I stand up. Mechanical. All I need do is follow my clock. Sure as day and night are one, it'll lead me back here in twelve hours' time, where I'll take my repose and come alive again. Until then, I need to put silver in my pocket. I step towards the door, the boy's eyes followin. Men lie around, still in the immortal slumber. I look at their faces and know their ecstasy. I envy them, but soon again it'll be me... I'll lie down and cross the boy's palm with a coin and he'll hand me the pipe, I'll suck on it and imbibe the holy poison. The air sickly with it, I inhale as I tread a penitent line to the door. The boy at my back. He darts out ahead to slide the deadbolt and I step through the curtain. Outside, the delinquent light of London. Light enough. Mornin perhaps. Who knows what drab edge of the day I've stepped into?

'You go,' I hear as I step across the threshold. *I'm already gone, boy. See you in a half-turning of the sun.* I turn to peer at his unknowable face but the door is already shut.

I've come to hate the daylight.

I stumble down the alley. Down the end, where the alley meets the street, a voice hearkens.

'Alright sweetheart.'

'Lizzy?' I say.

'Oh. It's you. Kick you out again, did he?'

'It's all *céad mile fáilte* when there's silver in your pocket, but when you're fleeced they show you the door in a heartbeat.'

She leans back against the wall. 'Didn't keep a coin for a handjob, my love?'

'Bit early for trickin, innit?' I say. 'What shade of the clock are we?'

'Gone six already. Waitin on a boat.'

'Indiaman comin in?'

'We'll see. You doin a bit o'work today?'

I cough, the black air catchin in my throat. 'Aye. Need to scratch up some coin.'

'Save a penny for me tomorrow, you fool. I'll pull your peter for ya, half price.' She giggles.

'You're a born romantic, Lizzy. See ya.' I walk out into the street.

'You see any sailors, you send em right over 'ere. And stick your head in a bucket of water – you look like living shit.'

Her cackle follows me as I cross the street.

Sibylline ghosts nip at my heels then slip away. I cut down the Causeway onto Fore Street. Front door's open when I get there. Lynn's ballin out her auld fella from the kitchen out back. First thing in the mornin and he's already gettin tore a new one. I sit on the porch and roll a smoke, and wait for it to die down. I know better than to get in the middle of it. Lynn has a tongue like a lash – would tear lumps off a man. So I smoke and wait. I hear Barney roarin, nothin but the song of his retreat. Barney's all bark. His boots sound on the stone floor and he appears behind me and steps over my shoulder into the street, slumps down the wall with a sigh. I hand him the tobacco.

'You in the doghouse?'

'Never feckin out of it,' he says.

'Late one?'

'Five in the mornin.' He grins.

I shake my head. 'Some stamina you have. You workin the day?'

He nods. 'Ten. If she'll give me peace for a couple hours' kip. You comin wi' me?'

'If there's work.'

'Aye, there'll be work. We'll have a bite then rest our heads for an hour before we head down.'

I hear Lynn out back, pots bouncin, foul words still pourin from her. With no one to swear at, she'll rant at the cats, the back door, the air if needs be. Never a woman to waste a good rage, Lynn.

Barney pinches the butt and slips it into his pocket, a hacking cough tearin at his lungs.

'You brave enough for it?' he says.

'Aye. Let's give it a shot.'

We get up. Barney leads the way. A black tabby pauses in the hall, eyes me. The fucken cats in this house. Couldn't bear children, the pair of em, so she filled the house with cats instead. Probably why Barney gets no rest.

He walks sheepishly into the kitchen. I adopt a similar pose and follow. Lynn hears us come in and turns.

'Aw, the fucken pair o'yis,' she shouts. 'One auld piss-drunk fool and one moocher. Yis'll get no welcome here. Piss away off.'

I know the routine. I sit at the table and let it play out.

'Aw, love,' Barney says, 'ya know I love ya, and if I get carried away sometimes it's only to let off a bit o'steam. Can't deny a man that, can ya?'

'Five in the mornin? You good-for-nothin streak o'piss!' She pulls the filthy dishrag from off her shoulder and flings it at him. I've been struck with that foul rag first thing in the mornin before. Ain't pleasant.

'Now love, don't be like that. Tell ya what, how about this – today when I get paid, I'll pick up a bit o'that nice shinbone you love, eh? That always puts a smile on your face, eh?'

Lynn marches over, smacks him around the head, snatches up her rag and smacks him with it again. For good measure.

'Sit down, you waster,' she says. She looks at me. 'Look – the moocher at the table already. That's all you bring into this house – moochers and tramps. Tell him he's payin for his breakfast. Tell him I wanna see coin.'

'Lynn,' I say, 'I'll fire a cut of the wages Barney's way when I finish today. Promise, hand to god.'

She turns, stabs the wooden ladle in our direction. 'Not a penny between the two o'yis. You with the drink and him with the other – never saw two bigger wasters in all my life.'

The cats are gathering at her feet. Lynn, their hefty queen, giver of sustenance, fiery deity of the tenement felines. She kicks at one with a missing eye. It leaps across the floor.

'I swear, Lynn—'

'Aw, clamp it.'

We fall to silence, share a look then suppress a giggle. Mirth would be the end of us: no breakfast, no kip... we'd be wanderin the streets for three hours then goin to work on an empty belly. Done it before, ten hours lumpin maize or flour and not a scrap of food in the stomach. No fun at all. No way for a man to put the day in. So we suppress the nervous laughter. Barney turns to look out the window. I watch the cats circle the goddess of destruction and the giver and taker of life: Lynn of Limehouse, known and feared city wide.

The things a man'll suffer for a bowl of oats.

Lynn thumps and clatters and swears and blows, and soon there's a big steamin bowl dropped – no, slammed – onto the table in front of us, two spoons pulled from the pocket of her apron and shoved into the thick mess. It's eatin, I'll say that for it. We mutter tentative thanks and prise the spoons from the sludge, and shove it into our waitin bellies. She's even remembered the salt. Too much of it, to be fair, but we'll be sayin nothin. Lynn has very particular skills, and she's a crack shot with whatever's at hand: rags, knives, pots... she'll hurl it. She's even been known to toss a cat or two about the place. Lethal woman.

'Fine stuff, Lynn,' I say. 'Marvellous.'

She grunts, not turnin to look in our direction. That's it now. We'll be ignored til we get up to leave. Then we'll have to suffer another tongue lashing, just so Lynn doesn't feel like she's being robbed. What Lynn doesn't take in silver she'll extract in flesh. She'll take payment some way.

Soon we've the food down us. Only way to eat it is fast. Barney's first off his chair.

'Smashin, love,' he says.

She turns. 'Like two dogs yis are, only come to eat and shit then piss off again, plates left at your arse.'

Plates are stayin right where they are. She'd murder us if we took a step near the basin.

'Go on, get out of it,' she says. The bowl in front of me is snatched up off the table. I wait til she turns her back then I slide off the chair. I'm already makin for the door.

'Magic, Lynn,' I say.

More grunts. I slip out with Barney followin, a grovelling thanks on his lips as he backs out after me. We go in the other room and close the door.

'Jesus Christ, save me,' he says. He makes the sign of the cross and lies down on the bed.

I laugh and stretch out on the floor. There's still a bit of warmth in the hearth. 'Some man ye are, Barney. You must have all the saints at your back, bless ya.'

'One of these days I'll learn to be a man,' he says.

'Wake me when that day comes.'

We are awoken. Lynn rouses us from slumber by launchin a great kick into Barney's head.

'Get up and get to work. And tell that moocher I want sixpence at the end of day for his breakfast.'

We waste no time. We're up and out. Rainin now, we head down Fore Street in the direction of Limehouse Dock. The air is soot-heavy, the streets awash. The boots on me are in need of repair. We tramp along the wet footpath, two men with the day come ugly upon em. Heads bent outta shape and no kinda rest, off to work we shuffle. Barney nods at men passin in the street, heads down and collars up, a damp pipe hangin from the lips, heaviness in their gait, the slap of water underfoot. Not a day for singin. We walk in silence til we hit the dock. Three or four riverboats are tied up, two men on each, lumpin sacks or heaving carts. Or back-bent, shovellin grain. Barney stands and watches.

'Where are we?' I say.

'Right on time – look, there she is now.' He points at a barge comin down the Thames, stern-end throwin out to take her into the Cut.

'Come on. He'll be waitin for us other side of the bridge.'

We head up Linton Place and cross the bridge, comin down onto the bank of the Cut. There's a row of riverboats tied up and waitin. A big barrel-chested man on the dock beside her, hair plastered to his face. He lights a pipe as we near.

'You see her come in?' he says.

'She's just turnin into the Cut now,' Barney says. 'My cousin, Ryan,' he adds, pointin at me.

The man nods. 'Have a smoke then grab yoursel' a shovel.'

After six hours lumpin we hop a skiff goin downriver and get off at the Hole pier. Barney takes me over to the Antigallican. I'm no man for the drink, but he insists, so we settle in and order an ale and a pie. The place is rowdy with workin men all filled with a thirst from a day shovellin or cartin or humpin, men who'll drink til they fall then crawl home on their hands and knees to fat violent wives just like Lynn, women whose only resort is to torture them mentally and physically so that the cycle is repeated continuously and with a tragedy so inevitable it's comedic. Me, I've no such life, no such wife – I live day to day but go home to no one. My only responsibility is my nightly salve. My escape, my sanctuary. My habit. Even now the urge is on me. It carries me through the day, the relentless tick under my skin, beggin me to scratch.

'Oi, traveller...' Barney's clickin his fingers in my face. 'Did ya hear me? Did ya hear what I said?'

'Aye. Lynn, aye,' I say.

'No, ya clown – I asked if you wanna go over to Peruvian Wharf with me Monday for a couple days' work.'

'Peruvian? Lumpin guano?'

'What else?'

I shake my head. 'The smell'll be on me for a week.'

Barney shrugs, crams the pie in his mouth with his fist. 'Four shillings for ten hours' work. Don't tell me you're gonna knock that?'

'You remember what Lynn said last time you came home with the stink of guano on ya?'

'Aye, how could I forget.' He shudders. 'Well, just you leave the missus to me.'

'Now Barney, don't let on like you got any kinda clout over the missus.'

'Aw now, she's only a big softie. If I telt ya the things she has me do to her at night, *ooh-wee*... She's a big teddy-bear.'

'I've heard enough.'

I've barely touched the pint in front of me. I get up and push my way out back where I piss against the wall. When I go back in, there's an old waterman next to Barney. Bent crooked, cap on him and the pipe hangin from his mouth, big muttonchops plastered on the side of his face. Hoary auld fella, spinnin some yarn. I see my chance and catch Barney's eye.

'I'm off, then.' I throw sixpence on the barrel. 'For Lynn. Don't drink it.'

'Off? Where you off to? You haven't touched your ale.'

'Need some air. I'm away to clear my head.'

'You gobshite, you gonna leave m—?'

But I'm already out the door. My destination is already written – Jamaica Street. My mistress awaits, in that place she will always be. Time to lay in her bosom and hear her melody. Sweet she is, and joyful her song. Aye, she'll hold me all evenin and whisper in my ear, seductive golden whispers to make a man melt. And all she wants for it is silver. I finger the coins in my pocket. Two whole silver shillings, enough there to keep a man happy the love-long night. I'll put the evening away in her embrace and wake up in the mornin a man renewed.

Day and far night, Joon Sing's is always open. I cut down the alley to the burgundy door and hoof it inside, shuttin out the day's remains behind me. Light does not follow here. I step through the black curtain, the acrid hum of chandoo thick on the air, a curtain woven of the stuff of dreams. Only got a sniff of it and already I'm comin over all poetic.

The boy emerges from the cloud. He nods and leads me to a mattress. I sit and place a shilling in his hand.

'I'm here for the night.'

He palms the coin and disappears through the haze. I wait. As if time mattered now. Men of my ilk lie around on cots, men hazy on smoky serenades. What comes to them in their sleep, I can only surmise. Visits from such as who live on the wing, sprinkling strange wisdom down from the sky, a celestial night music borne of strange melodies and mad arrays, shoeless street urchins high on beauty, fuck-clusters of stars weeping in the black whisper of night...

My heart quickens in anticipation. I take my boots off and pull my foot into my lap in the Hindoo manner. It's a strange contortion but somehow comforting. Queer enough it all is, me an Irishman in the heart of the British Empire, in a Chinese lounge waiting for some Hindoo opium. A brave new world, and me only returned from Buenos Aires. Not gone thirty and seen it all. Haven't got more than a couple shillings to rub together but I've two eyes in my head and boots on my feet, and what more does a man need?

The eyes become smoke-heavy. One man is whisperin to himself, shadowy sweet-nothings of pure joy... I can hear it on his lips, his repose upon him, the song in his ears: *O gentle men, let me tell you a tale of soft solaces, exuberant beds filled with safety and mirth and the slumber of the discontent, of them that suffered but have healed and found delight in the silver pipe oriental. Heed ye the stories of its revelations! Listen that I may rouse ye to its plentiful charms, for tis only a little black pill one needs to chase away the ghosts of poverty and hunger. Know ye that bread is unnecessary for the contentment of living? Lie with me, and let me show you wherein hides the delectable nourishment...*

I wait still. Where is the boy?

Pray ye, be patient, soon ye shall hear...

Never was a man for the drink. Even at home, years before, never took to it. Pithy comfort in it – a poor man's pillow. The chandoo is a finer tit to rest one's head, the best tit for suckin. Give me that mystic nipple any day of the week and I'll suck it dry. *Lord, I'm thirsty for it.*

The boy reappears. I feel the ache of centuries upon me. I wonder is it even real at all. Who is this boy, gatekeeper, guardian? How is it he's the one who unbuttons her corset and feeds me the holy tit of succour? The boy is timeless. I could come here in a hundred years, and it'd still be the same boy, unchanged, feedin men the same holy tit.

He takes his time, floats across the room, eyes lowered. The boy sees nothin and the boy sees all. Still I wait. When will he float on over here?

I'll rise from my slumber and converse with the boy. I will understand his words. I will be gifted with the knowledge of his tongue, and I'll tell him about whales and headless men and strange, beautiful urchins, and he'll relate the secret of the holy mistress, the wherefore and why, the aeons across which she nourishes us with her strange music.

He kneels in front of me. I look in his eyes. They tell me nothin.

'You lie,' he says.

I lie on my side. He holds the grain in his tongs. I take up the pipe and wait for him to place it over the flame. The light dances over his face, his eyes, his lips... *Why you, boy? Why you?*

The grain begins to bubble, I place the holy nipple in my mouth. He transfers the grain to the pipe. I inhale.

Golden music.

I awake in the bed of gentle music. The boy is gone. Men have died around me and been reborn; I hear the song of their awakening. We listen together through the fog of forgetting and the waters of memory; all things return in one's repose. Somethin calls me and I sit up. I stand and walk among my fellows. Their contentedness leaks from them like a guppy wine.

I walk through fog, guided by my inner compass. It takes me to the door and into the street. Black London, night upon us. Many things can be heard in the city night, even for them who haven't supped the delicate poisons. I hear bird and man and sleeping and sickness, and rats and dogs and the angry drunk; boys and girls in troubled dreams I hear, the mother's woe, all things that keep a man awake nights, and all of it, yet, sweet music on a dread eve. There is no darkness only slumber. Sadness is only for the unhappy.

Alone on the street. I turn down the cold cobble thoroughfare, my compass guiding me waterward. All my life I was on, going to, or running from, the water. Never could escape it. Tried, but it always called me back. Seaman, riverman, born on the water and tied to her, prisoner to her too. No love affair there, only a tremulous tale, but who's the man can flee such a mistress? Such a one demands loyalty. I have tried, yes, but she won't let me go.

I meander the mad dark of the street. Candleless windows, drawn curtains and silence. No moon above. Twinklers up there: *Star light, star bright, first star I see tonight, I wish I may, I wish I might...*

Like eyes above, I feel their gaze. Is it they have roused me from slumber?

I chance a whistle, softly at first, testing the night air, seeing how it dances. Down on the river they hear it, I know. Old rivermen hear all, they've been listening to her the life everlasting. River song, night eddies, cold whispers. *Hear me now, sweet Laraine, word-whisperer, whistle with me and let's lay together...*

I stop at the junction and stand in the middle of the street. City's far gone tonight. I can smell the river now, the hum off her. I try to do a little jig in the middle of the road but I've no boots on me.

That's what happens when you go night-wanderin, boys.

At the quay now I hear her louder, the warble, the consonance. There are men about too. I don't see em but they're there, lost in fogs of pipe smoke and sorrow, men like me who've been captive all the life and come to know the beauty of it and are blessed. I hear them, for my ears are their ears.

The Hole pier. Behind me the factories, the warehouses. Other places of worship, too – the watering holes. But I sing for a different mistress. I go down to the wharf and lie next to her. I peer over the edge into the quick moraine; all what she carries with her, brick and iron and cleat and bottle, flotsam of industry, the clogged intestines of empire. Still, she's the one we follow, the one we steer our ships across, the compass of our broken souls.

I see a flash across her integument, a flit over the eddies. I roll onto my back and look into the sky. Imagine, I do, another out on this night. A heron, perhaps. Perhaps it's her called me from slumber to go traipsin. Put into port in Athens once, worked a day and a night on the *Erodios*. They told me the heron was a messenger from the gods. Circlin, could be, above. Watchin.

Maybe it's time to get the head down for the night.

I get up and go back up the narrow street. Alone again. None watchin now.

I head up Spread Eagle Street, and on Gun Lane I find the night's only companion, hugging the street corner.

'Well, fuck,' she says. 'Where are your bloody boots?'

'I had em before,' I say.

'Well, now you don't.'

Right enough, the ground is cold underfoot.

'You trickin?'

She laughs. 'I never lay down with a barefoot man in my life, and I never will.'

'If I buy you a bit of fish for breakfast, will you take me home?'

'You better 'ave more than a bit of fish,' she says.

I dig around in my pocket and pull out a shilling. I hold it up and smile.

'Fine,' she says.

'Wait here,' I say. 'I'll go get my boots.'

Mad yelling wrenches me from sleep. I feel hot breath on my neck and turn. She's there next to me in the bed, a hand on my chest, our legs entwined. Other side of the wall, a pot is thrown. How do people live with each other at all?

Lizzy stirs next to me in the bed.

'Mornin, sweetheart,' I say.

'Facking 'ell,' she says. She gets up and beats on the wall. A lull, then shouts flare beyond. Lizzy gives em an earful. I turn away. A man like me isn't made for mornins such as these. It seems my eternal misfortune that it's often how I wake.

'I'm thirsty,' Lizzy says.

'I'll get ya somethin. What do ya want?'

'Put the kettle on.'

'Aye.' I throw my legs out of the bed and go light the stove. I put water in the kettle. Then I get back in the sack.

'Don't fink you'll be getting a mornin court'sy,' she tells me. 'You used up your coin last night.'

'Not even a cuddle?'

'A cuddle? I can feel that filthy fing pokin my thigh... what kind of cuddle is it you's finkin of?'

'I'm just waitin for the kettle to boil, love,' I say. 'Kettle don't boil if you don't stoke the fire...'

I grab at her and she wriggles away. Then she kicks me in the shin. I roll back outta the bed and stand up. The boyo is pokin out at ninety degrees from my belly, like the ensign on a merchantman sailin downriver with a blow on. I peer down at it.

'You gonna leave me like this?' I say.

'Unless you got another shilling in your pocket, you can go and pull your Larry til he goes back to sleep.'

Aye, nothin in this life's for free.

'What about that bit of fish you promised me last night?' she says.

'Fish?'

'Yes, lover boy. Fish. You promised me breakfast.'

'Did I now? Well I best go get it then.' I pull on my trousers and jacket. The prick on me is still half-hard so I tuck it into the belt and pull on my boots. 'I'll be back in a jiffy.'

'Make sure you are. The stomach on me is growlin.'

'Shame something else isn't growlin this mornin,' I say.

She throws a pillow at me as I stumble out the door laughin.

It's dry out. I take Three Colt Street down to the pier. I find an auld biddy hawkin fish from her basket and pick up a few fillets of sole. She wraps em in newspaper and I take it back.

Lizzy's still in the sack when I get in. I drop the fish on the counter and pour the tea. I take the fryin pan down from the hook.

'Don't you dare touch my pan,' she says. 'I'm not havin you make a balls of breakfast.'

I put the pan on the stove and hold up my hands. 'By all means.'

I take my tea and sit down at the small table, and pick up a newspaper. Four days old, but I have a gander at it nonetheless.

'Where'd you get this?' Lizzy says, unwrapping the fish.

'Down the pier.'

'Mmm... fresh. From the widow Clara?'

'Some auld one,' I say.

She drops em in the pan. The fillets sizzle and spit. The smell of fish fills the tiny room.

I open the paper at a random page. Tales of Ireland. Tales of famine and illness and dyin. 'A hundred dead in a single week in the same workhouse,' I say, readin out loud.

'You what?'

'I said there's a hundred dead in one week in the same workhouse. Donegal.'

Lizzy's busy at the stove. 'What's Ireland got to do wi' me, love? Sure they's droppin dead like flies right next door. Them two you heard screamin at each other earlier, they just moved in. Last family in there took ill, started shittin themselves and didn't stop. Forty-eight hours later, dead. You don't need to go to Ireland for dyin, love. Plenty of it 'ere.'

Talk of dyin and shittin is spoilin my appetite. I close the paper and put it on the table. A little silver glint from below the sideboard catches my eye. 'Aye, true enough, Lizzy,' I say. I nip down onto my hands and knees and reach under, and pull out a shilling. Lizzy turns around and I close my hand.

'What you crawlin around on your knees for?'

'I'm sure I dropped a penny, love,' I tell her.

She laughs. 'Ain't no coins on my floor, sweetheart. I'd know about it. And if there is, it's mine. Like where the Queen goes and sticks a flag in, it's hers. You're in my kingdom now.'

I sit down, slippin the coin into my pocket. Lizzy comes over with two plates and puts em on the table.

'Here. Eat.'

'Good woman you are, Lizzy.'

Good fish it looks too, with a few bits of fried potato.

She sees me lookin at the plate. 'Don't you be prayin over my food.'

'I'm not much of one for prayin,' I say.

'Good. Then eat.'

We eat and wash it down with tea. When I finish, I get up off the chair to go.

'You workin today?' she says.

I shrug. 'Dunno. If there's work goin. I need to go see Barney.'

'Yeah, well. Might see you around later, might not.' She lifts the plates from the table.

'Might do,' I say. 'See ya, I mean.'

'Fuck off, then,' she says.

I laugh goin out the door. Some woman.

In the street, a tinge of regret hits me about palmin the coin off her floor. Couldna been hers, though. Like she said, she'd know about it. Had to have been from a trick, spilled from his pocket when the two of em stumbled in drunk. I pull it out and look at it, turnin it over in my hands. I slip it back in my pocket and turn up Jamaica Street.

Born on the water I was, popped right outta my ma on the boat from Raghery, a week premature. My da was takin her to Ballycastle to see the doctor when I poked the head out. Fair mess I made on the boat, I'm sure, but I survived, and I been on, near, or by the water since. There wasn't a place I lived wasn't near the ocean or by the river. I was wed to her thereafter. The father was takin me out in his boat since I could stand on two feet, and didn't I find it easier to stand on a boat than on land, for with my two feet on the ground I was all over the show, with bloody knees and scratched arms and broken skulls, but put me on the boat and I knew my bearings. I knew the rhythms of her. Afternoons, we'd come in from an afternoon's fishin off Ushet or Sroanderrig, and when we'd cleaned the nets I'd get back in the boat and lie there in the gentle bob of the sea and listen to the sweet *leuleup* of the waves against the harbour wall, or if she was howlin, by Christ, and sometimes she howled, I'd sit under an upturned skiff and watch her, the far-flung fury of her, and I'd feel at peace. Her tumult put my heart to quiet, and didn't I love her for it. I'd sing to her, because I knew she liked it, and sometimes it would even calm her, and I thought, *Aren't you the man, Ryan, can calm the seas with sweet lullabies.* Still to this day, I know she hears.

I open my eyes and see the boy with the pipe, realising I'm far from Raghery, but I know soon as I close my eyes I can go back there anytime fella, so I pipe up and inhale and lay my head down, and wouldn't ya know, I feel her under me, even there on the Chinese bed, I feel her soft undulations, so close to the river, see, don't you know you can feel her even through the ground and the earth? One like me who's lain with her the whole life knows, can tell she's near. Put a bag over my head and carry me to any corner of the earth, and by Christ I'll find the shortest road to the water. Funny how the pipe makes you keen to her.

Back in the boat now, I sail on out, my mind back to Lizzy and her quare charms, never knew the girl like her back in Ireland, no sir. A fine pair and a wayward stare, and a mouth like a stir-gone sailor clean off the boat. Lips that rip, make a man all coy like, make him wanna get in the boat and feel the reel of the water, all soft and bubbly, lyin there in her gelatin squeeze. *Aren't you the poet, son...* aye, whispers there are in the Chinese pipe that give a man sweet words. But let's be straight fella, the old poisons from Bihar – *Bee-harr...* now there's a place a man could sail to, where they cultivate the stuff of woven dreams. And what does a Mick from Rathery know about Hindoos? What does he need to know? Haven't you sailed all over, been even down all south of the known world, Río de la Plata, silver rivers and dark men, and guachos and caudillos and yerba maté, and Guaraní and Mazorca, and what did you know about all that before you went, save a few misguided notions and four palabras in the Spanish tongue? *Gracias, señora...*

Hindoo... no bother, son. I'll learn four words of the Hindoo and smoke til I'm blind, wouldn't that be the way to go, out there in the baking sun, malaria they say, but I'm sure the pipe cures it too, I'll just keep on smokin til I'm back on the sea, any sea, and that's alright with me. *Bee-harr. Pat-nah. Colcatta, Ben-gal.* Sail away, Sean. Perhaps I'll take Lizzy wi' me. How'd she be in the Orient, hoistin up her skirts and openin her legs, sure I'd love her just the same. I'd buy her a parasol and we'd walk through mad streets that smelled of indigo and raw silk, and all things a man from the blunt shores of the Irish sea knows nothin about, save he knows the ocean is there if he only desire. Me and Lizzy on the boat together, I'd get her on the pipe so we could lie together in the gentle tremble of the rolling lee, *leuleup!*

Chinese beds, Hindoo beds, seabeds, a whore's bed... s'all a man wants, an auld bed to lay his head:

A bed for the wicked, the wrecked and the raw,

A man in a quandary, what does he want more?

A pillow, a tit, a reliquary of sorrows,

And have a man such, need he think of tomorrows?

Sing lad, and be done with sorrow. Think only of a warm chuff and a plate of fish, and a hearth and a fire, aye, just a walk along the shore and a little boat moored there for the man of no sorrows. Yes sir. There it is, that's all, and it only took the pipe to see it. All golden river, I'll sail on down it til I find that little cottage, I'll know it, I'll know it from the smoke in the chimney and the smell of fish, and the shawl hangin on the back of the door and the bangin of pots – is that my windbreaker over the chair by the fire to dry out? Yes – a home. A man knows it when he sees it, and a seaman knows it more, cause he can smell it before he hits land, smell the pine and the bitumen and the barrel of porter, and the fierce hum of dung and sweet spring blooms, apples too, and the tang of the slaughterhouse, even the dinner on the kitchen table and the smell of his woman's hair. A sailor smells all these and more when the ship draws near. Here on the bed is a sailing of sorts too. Adrift here on gentle tides, and hell if I don't get all the good smells, even here with the thick fog of the pipe and the odour of men asleep for days, all of it right under my nose. We're in a land of the senses, and what truth other is there really? Forget the heart. Forget the mind. It's in the fingers, on the tongue... that's where you find it.

A memory comes back to me of the boat from Buenos Aires: A hand in an elegant green glove turnin the page of that great book... what secrets within? What truths those fingers found? Hands that have prised open what was hitherto closed, fingers that've clawed into a few truths, like opening an overripe pomegranate, the seeds to spill like little ingots into the waiting palm. Yes, those hands know.

Once again she comes. In and out of my dreams she flits, now here and now not, a fleeting heron in my sky. Or perhaps she's the lighthouse to an old sailor like me, the flash of the radiant nightbeam which turns to dark again. But she always returns. Don't you know now? How long since you stepped off that boat and she placed the silver in your palm, and didn't she dig the nail into your skin as she closed your hand, drawing blood? She took somethin from you. Marked you. Ever since, she been a-callin when you sleep, tappin on the high window of your reveries, and maybe there in your nightmares too. Those you like to forget.

I feel a hand on my shoulder. *No, it is not yet time*. I push the hand away but it persists. When I open my eyes there is no slant-eyed boy. There's another, a white man like me. He shakes me.

'Oi, Paddy...'

Slivers of darkness across the soft light of my seas. A ghost at the sullied window of my reveries.

II

what is sometimes spoken in dreams

Time has flown from me. He sent his personal secretary yesterday with another invite; I may have been shortsighted in not accepting sooner. Given his position, he may be of use. My caution was sage, yet I can't continue to hide in the shadows. Eventually my father will find me. That consequence I'll deal with when the time comes. Anyway, It's time I expanded my social circle in London beyond the walls of this house. I must put myself out there, regardless of where it leads. My cover will hold, so long as the Foreign Secretary keeps his tongue in his head.

I'm not one of these women who sees the villain in all men and victim in my own sex. The cold truth of the world is that we are vicious all, men and women alike. Women have one advantage, though, in which men are lacking: memory. We recall. We collect and recollect. We treasure. We memorialise. Often, our memories are enshrined in our possessions. Here, in my study, I have only to look around to remember...

My bookshelf: I know where each book comes from and what it contains. An athenaeum of collected wisdom; it's no exaggeration to say that among these books, my soul lingers. But not only in my books. The urn on the fireplace – in it, the ashes of my *abuela*. She too possesses a piece of my soul. The portrait of me by Pueyrredón, it has captured and imprisoned a part of me. It's not that I let myself be picked away at by the things I possess, but a soul such as mine must be allowed to roam free, to extend beyond the confines of the body. My soul is greater than the sum of its parts. Greater even than these possessions of mine. It cannot be contained. It is monstrous.

I stop in front of the mirror. I wear a dress the shade of deep jade. The cloth from Cairo. I'm sure there isn't another like it in all of London. It's not my intention to impress, but I do like to leave an impression.

I had certain expectations when I sailed to London, but it turned out not as I imagined. London is a pit, the trough of civilisation. A trough at which I will have to take a seat. I liberated a chest of silver from my father before I left, but my resources are limited. With the purchase of a house and the procurement of staff, the coffers are fast depleting. The time has come to get my hands dirty.

There's a knock at the door. Constancia enters.

'Sorry I'm late, my dove. I was daydreaming. I'll be right down.'

'Si señora.'

She goes out and closes the door. I marvel at the changes in my little bird since our departure. She's a different woman. If only I could marry her off, but I fear she's past her best. Once my finances have been restored, though, I could always buy her a husband, couldn't I? She's not yet on the discarded pile and she cleans up nicely. I'm sure there's a man in London who'd wed her if I bought them a little house.

I fight the protests of my hair. It doesn't agree with this foul English weather. Every day is a struggle. Clips are my saving grace; I pin the hair in a dozen different directions. With a hat on, no one will notice.

Downstairs, Constancia looks anxious.

'Mi amor, what's the matter?' I sit down.

'Look at the paper, señora.' She comes and sits next to me. 'Page two.'

I lift *The Times* and open it. The reason for her anxiety is immediately clear.

'Negotiations between Moreno and Palmerston…'

'That's why he wants to meet you, isn't it?' She digs at a fingertip with the nail of her thumb.

'I suppose it is.'

'What if they relent? What if they give in?'

'And my father gets his way? Are you afraid?'

'Will he find us?'

I put the paper down and take both her hands in mine, and look her in the eye. 'When you agreed to come with me on this adventure, this new life, didn't I promise to watch over you, to protect you always?'

She nods.

'And I meant it. I'll never let anything happen to you, I swear.' I kiss her on the hand. *My sister, my songbird.* 'Don't worry. No harm will come to us.'

She gets up, reassured. I can't stop her worrying, but I'd never let anyone hurt her. She's precious to me.

I eat a quick breakfast then Constancia meets me at the front door.

'Come and put my hat on for me, mi amor.'

She places it on my head and fixes it to my hair. 'So what will you say to the minister?'

'Supongo que esperará que le bese el culo. No puedo garantizar que lo complazca.'

She smiles, then her face turns serious again. 'Will he protect us?'

'We can't rely on his protection. But I'll do my best to ensure his discretion.'

'Don't make him mad. You can be very... direct.'

'I'm practical. I do what we need to survive. That's all we can do right now. Soon, it will be easier.' I stand up and kiss her on the cheek. 'I'll be back shortly after three.'

She walks me out the door. His carriage waits outside. I squeeze Constancia's arm. 'Keep the tea warm.'

The trip takes less than ten minutes, and at a quarter to two, we're outside his residence on Carlton Terrace. A footman meets me at the door and leads me up the stairs and inside. After taking my overcoat, I follow him to the drawing room, where he leaves me.

I sit. Before me on the wall is an enormous portrait of my host. Portraits can be deceptive. I know this from experience. Usually portraits show only what the subject wishes.

Outside in the hall, footsteps approach. Female. Soon a woman appears in the doorway.

'Ms. Azul?'

'Yes.' I get up and approach her. We meet in the centre of the floor and shake hands.

'I'm Lady Palmerston,' she says pointedly.

She's protective of him. She's here to read my intentions.

'A pleasure, Lady Palmerston.'

'When my husband told me we had a guest from Argentina, I was extremely curious. I hope you'll forgive my intrusion.'

'No intrusion whatsoever. I'm a guest in your home, after all.'

'Shall we sit?' She indicates the chairs and we take a seat. 'My husband will be along as soon as he can. He's a very busy man.'

'I have no doubt. I'm sure it's no small affair running the foreign affairs of a country such as Great Britain.'

'Indeed.' She does her best to maintain decorum, but her curiosity causes her to cross the line from polite conversation to errant intrusion. 'But my husband didn't mention why exactly you've been invited... I must admit, I'm at a loss.'

A question too far. 'I'm afraid I have no idea. My family have business interests in Buenos Aires. Perhaps it has to do with the blockade.'

'How terrible. Are you long in the country?' Her eyes search for more.

'No.' I grow tired of her questions. 'I wonder, m'lady, has your husband recovered?'

'Recovered?' She frowns.

I point at the painting on the wall. 'I mean, he was clearly ill when he was captured for this portrait. Tuberculosis, was it?'

'Tuberc—?'

'My dear – you've met our guest.' The Foreign Secretary appears in the doorway. 'Forgive my tardiness, ladies.' He approaches and holds out his hand. I get up to shake.

'Ms. Azul?'

'Yes.'

He kisses my hand. A habit I've always despised.

'Please, come with me. We'll talk in my office.' He turns to his wife. 'Excuse us, dear, but time is pressing.'

'Of course.' Lady Palmerston watches us leave the room.

He leads me across the hall to his office, stopping to address the footman outside.

Inside, he closes the door. Before we sit, he stands in front of me with mock importance. Hands behind his back. 'So, Ms. Azul, may we dispense with the charade? May I call you by your proper name?'

'You may call me Ms. Azul.'

Taken aback at my abruptness, yet he nods. 'Very well. Please sit down.'

I sit and look around the office. The man has testaments to his own greatness on every wall. Such men are the easiest to manipulate.

He takes a seat and sighs. 'I suppose you can guess why I've asked you here, Ms. Azul...'

'Because my father is running rings around your blockade?'

'Not quite.' He looks at me across steepled fingers. 'Perhaps you overestimate your fath—'

'It seems you have *under*estimated my father's position, sir, since it's been four years now and you've gained nothing from your charades. Indeed, it would seem you've only harmed British and French business interests in the region, hence your summoning me here, to see if I might appeal to my father for a swift resolution to the mess. You may be frank with me, Lord Palmerston. I'm not someone who cherishes circumlocution.'

He's silent for a moment. 'You're not at all as I expected, Ms. Azul.'

'What were you expecting? A wallflower? I didn't spend my days in my father's palace studying carnations, sir.'

'No, quite...' A knock at the door interrupts us. The footman enters with a tray, setting it on a table next to the desk. He pours us a tea.

'How's the tea in Buenos Aires?' the Foreign Minister asks.

'We grew up drinking something very different.'

'Ah. Jungle tea, I expect. This is something of a different class. Assam. I prefer it to the Chinese. It's a good deal more refined.'

The footman holds up a sugar cube. I shake my head.

'Leave it on the table,' Palmerston says.

'Anything else, sir?'

'Thank you.'

The footman leaves.

I pick up my cup. 'It's something you British have a real appetite for, isn't it?'

'Shall I let you into a secret, ma'am? Well, perhaps it's no secret, more of an inconvenient truth. You see, for years Her Majesty's government was alarmed at the damage being done to the Crown's coffers by the import of tea into this country. All the gold and silver in our vaults was being shipped to China merely to sustain demand – most of it for tea, but sugar costs the country a great deal too.' He drops a cube into his cup and stirs.

'And how is that, sir, when you don't pay for it, but merely grow it on stolen land and harvest it with slave labour?'

The corner of his mouth twitches. 'Do you know how we offset the drain on our coffers due to the tea?'

'Enlighten me, sir.'

'Opium. We flooded China with opium and took back all the silver we'd poured into it to satisfy our demand for tea. In a word, madam, *trade.*'

'I'm sure the Chinese will be forever grateful.'

'Madam, you're no fool, so I won't dance around you with niceties. Here's the inconvenient truth of which I speak – the British Empire was built on three things: slavery, sugar and opium. We're the most powerful empire in the world by virtue of trade and the free flow of capital, and any peril to these very staples upon which we built the empire is seen as a grave threat to our national security. This is the wherefore of your coming here today, madam.'

'The most powerful empire in the world, sir, yet you are finessed by a handful of ships in a "backwater" all the way south of the *civilised* world. Explain that to me, please.'

'Yes, quite...' He holds the cup in two hands, peering at me across the brim. 'I'm getting the feeling, madam, that your trip here today will be of little advantage to me.'

'I'll be as frank with you, Lord Palmerston, as you've been with me. As much as I find your manoeuvring tactless and desperate, I have to be straight with you. You see, I have absolutely no contact with my father, nor do I plan to in future. And if your hope today was to entice me to appeal to his better nature, well, I'm afraid I can be of no assistance. You are, as they say, on your own. But who knows, sir, maybe the solution is very simple. It might just be a matter of packing up the troops on Las Malvinas and sending them home. In that case, my father would probably give you what you want.'

He clears his throat. 'You know as well as I do, madam, that the British cannot, nor ever will, give up claim on the *Falklands*.'

'No, of course not. In that case, I wish you the best of luck sir.'

I take a sip of the rancid tea and put the cup in the saucer.

'Well, I can only thank you for coming to see me today. I'm sorry our meeting was not more fruitful.'

'I'm flattered to think that the British Secretary for Foreign Affairs saw fit to invite me to his home. Perhaps our meeting may not turn out to be so *fruitless* after all. I have a question for you, sir, if you don't mind.'

He nods. 'Please.'

'How long have you known about my presence here in London?'

'Since your boat docked, madam. British intelligence is the finest in the world.'

'I see. And is Mr. Moreno aware of my being here in the city?'

'If he is, he didn't hear it from us.'

I smile and stand up. 'I'll take my leave, then. Thank you for your time.'

He gets up and comes around the table and takes my hand. This time he does not kiss it. 'Myself and my wife are fond of entertaining, madam. We like to have the occasional soiree. Perhaps you'll join us some evening?'

'Maybe I will.'

'Our guests would be thrilled to meet someone of your... allure.'

'Thank you sir. I look forward to it.'

'Shall I have the cab brought to the door, or will you stay for lunch?'

'I'll be leaving, Lord Palmerston.'

'Very well. Let me see you out.'

This is a man used to getting his way. I've devoured many like him. I don't foresee he'll be any different.

After I've returned home, I call Constancia. My little bird needs distraction. 'Let's go shopping,' I say. 'There's a new store just opened in Knightsbridge. We'll take the morning and do something nice for ourselves.'

Her face lights up. I know I shouldn't – I can ill afford the expense right now, but soon I'll have an income.

'Tell Winters to ready the carriage, then go and get dressed. We'll leave at one.'

'Si señora.'

She hurries off. Constancia is easily pleased. I wish I were a creature of such simple tastes. That's why I love her so – she's delightfully devoid of complication. How happy she'd make some lucky man. Yes, I'll buy her a home and set her up with a husband. She's given my family a life in service, and I will repay her. It will be my final gift to her – freedom and her own life. Even if it'll break my heart for her to leave my side.

I flick through the paper as I wait. The British East India Company has defeated the Sikhs and Britain annexed Punjab. I don't know why, but the article stirs something in me. That name: 'East India Company'. My instincts are triggered. I've learned to listen to these twinges. I know something will come of it later.

When I meet an excited Constancia by the door, I take her by the arm. 'Let us sally forth,' I say, in my new English tongue. She smiles.

In the street, the smell hits one immediately. There's no street in this city that's not ankle-deep in horseshit. We had no such problems in Buenos Aires. Our streets were clean, our air clear. How is it that Britain, for all its power, wealth and reach, can't keep on top of the shit?

'Morning, m'lady.' The driver doffs his cap.

'Good morning, Winters.'

We climb into the carriage, Constancia sits opposite. I spray the air with parfum. She still looks distracted, but when Winters cracks the reins and we take off down the street, a little smile crosses her lips as she gazes idly out the window. Some parts of her are still a mystery to me. I know her as one woman may know another, but only insofar as our lives have been intertwined for as long as I can remember. It's true, I can lay bare the hearts of men, but I've never gazed into Constancia's. I wouldn't; I love her too much. Her secrets are hers, and they're buried far from my prying eyes. I have captured many souls, but hers remains unto her.

She looks at me and I smile. She was truly beautiful, ten, even five, years ago. Before the war.

'I'm going to treat you today,' I say. 'Let's get some new curtains for your room. The ones you have are so ugly.'

She gives an enigmatic little shrug. She will not tell me what she wants. I'll have to drag it out of her.

'Where are we going?' she says.

'Knightsbridge.'

'Yes, but where?'

'A new store. It's the talk of the town. It's called Harrod's.'

She turns to look out the carriage window.

'Are you still worried?'

She shakes her head. 'I feel safe with you.'

I'm taken aback by her candour. She rarely speaks with such openness.

'Well, I'm pleased you feel that way, mi amor.' *My little bird flies higher every day.*

I feel a sudden surge of love for her. I have never felt such way for a man.

When we pull up outside the store, we look out the window at the grand building. Winters struggles down from the cab and opens the door. We step out.

And what do you know? Here in Knightsbridge, they have clean streets. They have men to shovel the shit.

'Thank you Winters.'

Constancia takes my arm and squeezes.

The doors to the store are opened for us. Inside, the air is heavily perfumed. The place is bustling. I feel Constancia's excitement through her fingers. Yes, I'll be good to her today. I'll have to be attentive and watchful, to see what takes her eye. And then I'll need to convince her it's perfect for her while she pretends she doesn't want it. 'It's too fancy for me', she might say, or, 'I could never wear such a thing'. Such are her ways. But we'll play her little game.

'Oh look,' I say. 'Let's look at the Parisian fashions, will we?'

Her grip tightens. Like this, through her fingers, I'll read her desires. I stop at a mannequin to admire a dress.

'Beautiful,' I say.

'Too much lace,' she says.

How you make me work, my little bird.

How easy it is to make us happy. All we require is the security of our possessions. Nice things – that's all we need. When we've returned from Knightsbridge, I force Constancia to model her purchases for me. She resists with a display of false modesty, but soon she relents and we get silly and display our new clothes. And for an hour or two, we are delightfully and childishly content. All for the price of a few pounds. And what of possessions, must they be expensive? No, they must not. Possessions become so in the *act of possessing...* value is added in the owning of it; it makes no matter for how much it was purchased.

I'm not referring to sentimentality – I'm talking about *endowment*. Value is acquired in the personal relationship one develops with one's possessions. Owning lots of things does not make you rich – the wealthy individual is the one who knows the worth of what one owns, a worth that increases over time, a worth born of engagement and appreciation. Many have no understanding of acquirement. It's money that deadens one to appreciation. The poor have a strong relationship with their possessions, if only because they have so few. Others, like me, know the worth of objects. Why? Because I've seen the suffering of those robbed of all they own, and know the pain of being severed from everything one holds dear.

But what of people? Are they also mere possessions? Of course, but it isn't always so. Do I own Constancia, for instance? Well, yes. She was purchased by my father many years before as a maidservant. Since then, I've come to learn her value, a relationship that has transcended mere acquisition; the love I feel for her required me to reassess my ownership of her, so that she has evolved in my eyes from mere possession to something akin to a cherished sister. And because of this, I renounced my deeds of ownership. I will set her free when the time is right.

And what of men? Are they possessions too? Naturally. Men are a different breed, and cannot fill the place in a woman's heart a sister can. Men cannot be loved, not in a pure sense. They can only be seized, occupied, subsumed. Possessed. It's a trifling thing, but men have no depth. A man can kill a woman, but a woman can *destroy* a man, wholly and irrevocably. I've done it. Even now, here in this strange land where I know no one, I am the possessor of countless men; when I care to, I hear them whisper in the vast archipelago of my being, their echoes a feeble lament, souls with no substance, existing only because I possess them. Not that these souls don't have their uses. Would I keep them around otherwise? All souls have use, and I'm the possessor of innumerable souls. All I need is to summon them and they come. They're at my disposal day and night. Their value appreciates over time as I come to discover the variegated complexities of their forms.

Souls are fickle and tempestuous. Souls are troublesome. But they are mere possessions, after all, and I am adept at their acquisition.

After we've had our fun, we have dinner then I retire to my study. Constancia knows I'm to be left alone evenings. Evenings, I require no company. After nightfall, solitude is a requisite. I take my evening enterprises seriously. It's a time for growth and learning. *Evolving*.

One thing I do not lack is will. Will drives me to push myself day after day to rise higher, reach deeper, grow stronger. My education is not for the faint-hearted. Only those with the strongest constitution can do what I do. Men have no concept of what a woman is capable of. They make assumptions based on the values of our day. Women are no less to blame, pandering to established standards: the fragile, the coquettish, the obedient. But I am no such woman. It's perhaps unfortunate I was born into the family I was. Had I been born the daughter of a provincial caudillo, I'd have been among the *montoneras*, a guerrilla, with my foot in the stirrup and a rifle on my shoulder. Yes, I'd have been on the walls of Montevideo, or on the hills facing the mercenaries that tear apart my country. I may dress in lace and silk, but I have a heart that is capable of much darkness.

But for all that I was born into the aristocracy. I grew up within the confines of my father's crazed dominion. As much as he tried to shield me from the reality of it, I knew. I came to the knowledge late, but I discovered the truth of it nonetheless. Some nights I took a carriage around the city – I saw the square and knew what it represented. I saw the bodies on the street. At first I was horrified, but later, when I came to align it with the essence of my nature, I was only saddened for my country. Some men deserve to die. Many do not. It's an inconvenient truth of war that those most deserving of death often escape it. This is the painful reality with which we must learn to live. To some extent, I've learned through time how to restore balance. But those secrets of mine I do not divulge easily, for my knowledge is hard won.

I take a volume from the bookshelf and carry it to the desk. I have many curiosities on my shelf, but this one... this is the prize. Brought here from my country, carried there by a Franciscan monk a hundred years previous. The book is a testament to man's search for hidden knowledge, and the men who compiled it had no idea it would end up in the hands of a woman. The old shaman knew its potential, and perhaps his ancestors too. That's why I killed him. For there can be only one; such power leaves no room for company or competition.

In the large steamer trunk in the corner of the room, I have my medicines. I take out the *caapi* I brewed the night before. My own variation, adjusted to my requirements. There are many formulae; over the years I played with them all, imbibing, testing, finding the balance I required, and with a few of my own additions perfected the medicine. It's a conduit and a pathway, a door to realms shut to those who are not seekers of true knowledge. Fortunately, I was shown the door when I was young. My teacher was ruthless and pushed me beyond even my own capabilities.

I sit, and lower the lamp. When I sip the brew a nervous excitement fills me. I know where the *caapi* will take me but I don't fear it. A woman without self-control has no business doing what I do, but I've had years to calm my baser instincts.

After twenty minutes, the medicine begins its work. It invades the capillaries, pumped by a heart that registers only the thrill of the impending crossing... At this moment, I have a heightened sense of my own makeup. There's an increase in blood flow to the amygdala and insula. I become aroused. Dormant emotions rise; I fight to keep them in check. Many are overwhelmed by the *caapi*; one must be resilient. The increased blood flow to my brain stimulates the cortex. I'm assailed by memories of my mother... they come upon me in waves: her hand on my cheek and the ring on her finger, a tiara in her hair, the smell of vanilla on her neck, the fullness of her breast... the sadness of her song and the loneliness of her nights. I feel it now, years later and a world away. Anger too, at senseless death and dying, for even though she was my father's greatest supporter she saw the blood of Argentina and her people and felt the silent rage of a continent. It comes to me in flashes, sadness and pain and joy and bitterness, and no sooner is it there but it dissipates. I move on, for this is not memory but travel. Soon darkness subsumes me. My heartbeat slows. Time slows too and soon ceases altogether, for time is not a concern of the *karai*. As long as time is present, vision is not possible. One must banish time in order to truly see.

First the dark, then heat and humidity. Low sounds, animal. The smell of moss and bark. The earth under my feet. I reach out and touch a vine, grip it, and when I open my eyes I'm in the dark jungle, the jungle of the psyche, the mind eternal, the memory of all things lost, the place of all forgetting. Here all things gather; everything may be known here by she who searches.

In the centre of the clearing, the smouldering remains of a fire. There are many souls which haunt the deep realms. Some hide when they sense I'm near. It's true, I instil fear in those who are a part of me. Their shyness is amusing, since it's only through me they still live. I approach the centre of the clearing. By the fireside, a severed arm, half-eaten. The Old One has been here, feasting on the dead. Gods have healthy appetites and within us there are many. As long as we lack power and will, they are never sated. I press a hand into the fire. Green sparks fly. When I remove my hand, fractal patterns glove my skin momentarily, then fade, traces flickering up my arm. There is much to engage oneself with here in the deeper realms. The lichen underfoot; if I draw close and whisper to it, the light of my words is carried across the jungle floor, a vast endoscopic network that transports messages to the far reaches of consciousness, as the tributaries of the Amazon cross the continent. It's beautiful. I leave the clearing, following my inner spirit, her I've come to trust: my guide, my light. Through ivy and guaimbé, I make my way to the small hut. I smell the smoke from the shaman's fire carried through the trees.

Birds announce my arrival. The *karai* will be there, smoking his pipe. Drinking. His is a heart agonised by imprisonment. Such is the path of free spirits in captivity. His hut has fallen into disrepair. The old man is not what he was, but he may be of use yet. Outside the entrance a pot sits over a cold fire. I open the door and step in.

—It's you, he says.

He squats in the darkness. The glow of his pipe illuminates the contours of his ailing face.

I sit on the ground and place the book on the table in front of me. I open the cover. Inside, inscribed in a faded hand: *Divina Metamorphosis.*

—How are you, old man? I say.

Getting information out of the old man is like pulling teeth. Perhaps that's what I'll have to resort to. Old shamans are stubborn as wild mules. They don't take kindly to being broken. Nor should they. Every human is entitled to freedom, but there are conditions under which one relinquishes those freedoms. War is one. I went to war with the old shaman and he lost. After that, he belonged to me. But still he fights and resists, denying me the knowledge I need to unlock the mysteries of the book. It's only a matter of time, but time is not a great concern. He'll come around, one way or another.

I am an age below in the depths of my being. Coming around is an ordeal.

Back in the heavy density of the room, a sigh escapes me. I gather myself, then get up and put the book on the shelf. I am discreet with my peculiarities. Constancia has been around me long enough – she knows my ways, is used to the proliferation of strange occurrences that follow in my wake, and is accustomed to the ominous paraphernalia gathered in my study. Even in Buenos Aires, the aroma of strange elixirs would fill the air at all hours of the night. She has never asked, and I don't feel obliged to explain to her. For that I'm grateful.

I leave my study, locking the door. Constancia is downstairs in the drawing room with a needle in hand. She's a simple woman, with simple habits.

'Put that down and come lay with me on the divan,' I say.

'You've been studying, señora?' she says.

'Yes mi amor.' She knows I crave human touch after hours at my 'studies'. I need it to 'come back', so to speak. It's not easy having a foot in both worlds: the inner and the outer, or, more correctly, the material and the transcendental. Having crossed over, one is like a shadow upon return. Constancia helps me touch earth.

She sets down her needlework and comes to lie with me. I wrap my arms around her.

'Were you working on your business idea, señora?' she says.

'Yes my dove.'

'Tell me about it.'

'About my bookstore?'

'Yes.'

'Oh, I have much to tell you. First of all, do you remember the lothario from the court of Prussia who used to visit mother?'

'Si...'

'Well, you'll remember he used to bring mother the most wonderful books from Europe. We're still in contact. I've written to him, asking him to put me in touch with his dealer in Paris. Once I've established a relationship with the dealer, I can start shipping titles over here to stock my shelves. Naturally, I'll need contacts in the East – Cairo perhaps, or maybe Baghdad or even Isfahan. I'm sure there's a market for collectors here in Britain.'

Nothing of this is yet true, but it might so easily be.

'And where's your shop going to be?'

'Westminster, mi amor.'

'Why?'

'Because that's where the money is. If I set myself up in the heart of London, they'll gravitate right into my orbit. You see?'

Through her touch, I sense her excitement.

'When can I see it?'

'I haven't bought it yet. But I will. Soon. Then we'll go there together and we'll populate the shelves with all my new titles and I'll sell you my first book.'

I don't need to see her face to know she's smiling.

'Let me think. I would like a book on...'

'Italian crochet?'

'Yes!' She wriggles with delight. 'How did you know?'

'I know everything about you, my dove.' I hold her tight.

'It's like you can read my heart.'

I can, mi amor.

There's a certain irony in it, that I may open a bookstore. I remember how the *porteños* were treated under my father, the young romantics who brought their ideals back from Paris and set up their own salons – Echeverría and Alberdi, Mariquita and Mármol – and how my father watched with a vicious eye, waiting for them to take a step too far, and when they did they were driven from the city. They were the lucky ones. Their lives were spared, perhaps due to their profile. I too had my salon, but I was within my father's walled garden, under his protective wing. To us my father turned a blind eye, no matter what we read. The most unfortunate, perhaps, were the poor booksellers of the city, those who ended up impaled in the Plaza Mayor for their unwillingness to bend to my father's edicts. They kept peddling the ideas of the *beau monde*. They foresaw the renaissance of Argentina, its rebirth, but they did not foresee my father's wrath. Or perhaps they did. And for that, they're owed respect. They didn't deserve to die in such a way.

I was born in an orgy of blood and fury. My father thought I was shielded from it, but he was wrong. I am a child of suffering, of brutality. Such was my coming into this world. I am the pellucid omen of my time. How should I not reflect that into which I was born?

But what shall I sell in this new bookstore of mine? Shall I stock the shelves with books on the troubled story of my country, my continent? Shall I peddle tomes of ancient history, of the Greeks and the Romans? Perhaps. But what will attract them most is ideals. Virtue. I'll stock the shelves with books on 'Civilisation', and on the political and philosophical trickery that backs it up. For that's all it is, a word racket. Man, at heart, it's not civilised, but give him a book and he'll believe anything. A little Rousseau makes even a buffoon think he's wise. But maybe these British do not read the French? Yes, I have much to learn, but it won't take long to find out what it is that makes the Englishman feel himself superior, and when I do, that's what I shall sell him.

And then I'll get down to real business.

*

'Señora, you asked for George. He's downstairs.'

'Thank you, mi amor. You had him take off his shoes?'

'Of course, señora.'

'Good. Tell him I'll be down shortly.'

Mid-morning, the sun streams through the window. Sun! How long has it been since I've seen it? This country has many faults, but surely the greatest is its unwillingness to acknowledge the very mechanics of the seasons... do they know of spring? And what of summer? Does it appear on these shores? I'm curious to find out. Winter was a wet, miserable affair, but at least the smell was somewhat abated. Now with the months advancing and the cold retreating, the stink has returned. If we're graced with sunshine when 'summer' comes around, I can only imagine how we'll suffer. Still, my business will be underway by then. I've conceived a plan at last. It was Lord Palmerston who gave me the idea. It was a mistake to put off his meeting for so long. But now the seed has been planted and it won't be long taking root.

George is waiting in the drawing room. He stands when I enter, clutching his hat in hand. My eyes fall to his feet: socks torn, filthy toes poking from the holes. He squirms.

'Ma'am.'

'George. Thanks for coming.'

'Certainly, ma'am.'

'Sit down.'

We sit. My house is well decorated. There are fine upholsterers and drapers in this city, some of the best. Cloth from Paris I have in my windows, the finest chintz fabrics to decorate the furniture. Constancia, bless her, has put an antimacassar out for George. George is no dandy, but he's certainly no pig. He's loyal. And he does as I ask.

Constancia brings us tea.

'How've you been, George?'

'Very well, miss. Thank you.' *Fank you.*

'Did you secure new lodgings for you and your wife?'

'Yes miss. We has a nice little place just across the river. Very cosy.'

'Good. I'm pleased.' I sip my tea. 'I wonder, George, do you plan to continue working on the ships?'

'Well, m'lady, the missus has a bun in the oven, so to speak, so I would prefer as not to, but, things being, I may have to. Man's gotta earn a living, miss.'

'George, I might have an employment opportunity for you. I'm planning a business venture. It will require some work yet, but should it come about as I hope, there may be steady work in it, right here in the city. Would that be agreeable to you?'

He sits forward in his chair. 'Oh yes, it wouldn'half. But what nature of work would it be, m'lady?'

'We'll come to that, George. There's another matter. Do you remember the fellow who escorted us over here on the boat, an Irish gentleman by the name of Ryan?'

He nods. 'I do, miss.'

'I need you to find him for me. I believe I have work for him too.'

'Sure, miss. But London's a big place, if he's still here at all.'

'Go down to Limehouse. Search the Chinese places. I have a feeling you'll find him there.'

'Limehouse?' His face scrunches up. 'But how does you know, miss?'

'Call it a hunch, George. I'm certain if you have a good look around, you'll stumble across him.'

He's puzzled, but he nods. 'Alright miss.'

'I'll tell you what – you go down there when it's convenient to you, but in the next few days if you can, and when you find him, tell him to meet us at The Artichoke next Friday for lunch.'

'The Artichoke, m'lady?'

'It's a riverside establishment in Blackwall. Apparently they do nice lunches. Find Ryan, give him my message, and come back here on Friday at midday. We'll go together by ferry.'

'Very good, miss. And if I don't find him?'

'You will, George.' I smile.

He gives an awkward bow. 'Will that be all, miss?'

'Yes George. See you on Friday. And give my regards to your wife.'

'Thank you miss.'

He gets up and bows again. Constancia takes him to the door and returns. 'Is everything alright, señora?'

'Just fine,' I say. I stand up. 'It's time to get started on the antique book business. We need to support ourselves somehow.' I stroke her cheek.

She doesn't need to know the truth. My Constancia has a heart of innocence. I will not sully it. My own heart is of little concern to me. It's a fickle instrument, little use in guiding one through life's vicissitudes. It's an inconvenience, and I've trained to disregard it in favour of the gut.

The following Friday, George comes to the house and we leave together. Winters takes us to Waterloo Pier where we catch a steamer going upriver. I've come prepared. I wear a veil, scented in lavender. It goes some way to alleviating the stench. The good people of London seem used to it. I am not. But at least the day is dry.

George gives me the tour as we go: 'Temple Gardens, ma'am.'

'How interesting.'

I'll take Constancia on a trip upriver when the weather gets warmer. She'll like it. Our journey across the sea caused a deep itch in her for travel. I saw the change take hold on the crossing: spending more and more time on deck each day, taking in the ocean, and when we stopped at port in Rio and New York, the excitement was painted on the gay canvas of her face. How she longed to disembark in New York. Instead she got London. Perhaps she'll learn to love it when she sees it from the water, as I do now. Cities appear differently when viewed from a boat. They are more transitory and dreamlike. Yes, I'll take her upriver and give her the tour, perhaps I'll even remember some of George's information.

'London Bridge, ma'am. Built about fifteen year ago.'

'Marvellous, George.'

And a half hour later: 'Blackwall Stairs, ma'am.'

'We're here?'

'Yes ma'am.'

George helps me off the boat onto the bustling pier. We hop aboard a skiff and are ferried a couple of hundred metres downriver to the tavern.

'The Artichoke, ma'am.'

The pier leads directly into the establishment. The place is heaving, a marvellous aroma of fish in the air. I enjoy being amongst people again, the hustle of the crowd, the boisterousness, the gaiety. Wild chatter. Laughter and drunkenness. Yes, it's good to be amongst people. But only for a short time. They get tiresome so quickly.

Soon we're accosted by a frantic waiter. 'Table for two?'

'Three,' I say.

'Right this way.'

He leads us to a corner overlooking the river and we sit. I remove my hat and veil and order punch. The waiter runs off. George removes his cap. He seems nervous.

'I told him twelve, miss, I did.'

'Don't worry, George. He'll be here.'

And sure enough, just as I say it, he appears in the door, spotting us immediately. He approaches and takes off his cap. I get up to shake his hand.

'Mr. Ryan, thank you for coming.'

'Of course, miss. George here found me.' He throws an inquisitive glance at George.

We all sit.

'How've you been?' I ask.

'Very well, miss, thanks for askin.'

'I suppose you're wondering why you're here. Let's order some food then we'll talk business. Are you hungry?'

He clears his throat. 'This place might be a touch on the fancy side for me, miss.'

'Don't worry – I invited you. I've heard wonderful things about the fish here. Will we try?'

'Sure ma'am,' George says. Ryan nods.

'Good.' I raise a hand to catch the waiter. 'Business can't be discussed on empty stomachs.'

'Tremendous,' George says. He puts down his cutlery with more care than is necessary and looks around sheepishly. The tavern has a well-to-do clientele he's unfamiliar with. These people are above his social standing. Ryan doesn't seem to care. He's still picking at the fish.

I pour another glass of punch as the waiter whisks away the plates.

'Let's get to the reason I asked you here today, gentlemen. I have a business proposal, but I'll need help getting it off the ground. I've asked the both of you in particular for two reasons: number one, you're both familiar with the city. And number two, gentlemen, you're the only men I know here. That said, I'm convinced of your reliability. Ryan, you served me well on the journey here from Argentina, and George, you've been at my disposal since I arrived here six months ago. I trust you both, and that's why I'm asking you to help me in this endeavour.'

George clears his throat. 'As I told you, ma'am, I'd be very interested in a job that keeps me here in the city wiv' the missus. But I'm curious to know what is the nature of the business.'

'Aye, what kinda work is it?' Ryan says.

I lower my voice. 'It's my intention to open a gentlemen's club. You know, a place for men to... relax.'

'Is you sayin' what I think you's sayin?' George says.

'She means a brothel, Georgie,' Ryan says.

A few heads around us turn. 'Keep your voice down, Mr. Ryan.' I turn to George. 'Mr. Ryan's correct. However, it'll be a high-end establishment, George. Not for just any old loafer. I plan to cultivate a very select clientele.'

'And where would you be opening this club, ma'am?' Ryan says.

'Westminster.'

'Jesus.' Ryan laughs, George looks aghast.

'As I said, it'll be high-end. When I say I plan to draw in a select clientele, it should be clear to you exactly who I mean. We're going to be near parliament... not so close as to be conspicuous, but close enough to attract them.' I pause to let them digest it all. Ryan is less perturbed by this information than George. Perhaps George is a Christian man. Not to worry. Silver can be more persuasive than religion.

'Let me finish my proposal, George. Then make your mind up.' He nods. 'You two gentlemen will be front of house. I need a couple of men around in case any problems arise. You know the type of thing, I imagine. But there's another element to this venture I have to make you aware of – it's for this reason in particular you're here today, Mr. Ryan. You're familiar with certain Chinese *medicines* I believe. Yes?'

He pauses. 'Well... yes ma'am.'

'I also plan to make these available in my establishment. I expect your familiarity with the recreation will be of some use to me. We'll talk more on that later. But I need you to understand, gentlemen, that your discretion is of the utmost importance in this whole enterprise. Do you foresee that being a difficulty?'

Ryan shakes his head. 'No ma'am.'

'George?'

'Miss, are you sure I'm the right man for the job?'

'Please don't pretend you're innocent of such things, George. How long were you a sailor for?'

He scratches his head. 'Twelve years, ma'am.'

'And are you telling me you didn't set foot in a few ports and go looking straightaway for the nearest "house of ill repute"? And perhaps, when you got there, did more than simply admire what they had to offer?'

He blushes.

'Come now, George. I know you're a changed man, with a wife and a child on the way. Your employment with me will be perfunctory. You'll be there to ensure there's no mischief. To keep order. That's all.'

'Well, when you put it like that, miss...'

'Furthermore, I'll be paying you both thirty shillings a week to begin with. Now, tell me where you can find such a wage elsewhere in London?'

Both men are silent but their faces tell all.

'Lest I haven't been clear on it already, your discretion is key in this arrangement. Loose tongues will lead to immediate dismissal. I hope this is clear.'

They both nod. I pause to take a sip of punch, then look over my shoulder at the river. The Thames is the pumping artery of this city. The business I'm proposing would be impossible without it. Everything in the city flows in and out on its water. I turn back to the table.

'Gentlemen, before I do anything else, there's something we need to get to work on immediately. Obviously, I need an establishment, a place to do business. I need the two of you to find one for me. Can you both start work tomorrow?'

Ryan shrugs, then nods. George assents.

'I need a place in Westminster. Discreet. Two stories, perhaps with a shop front. Available for rent immediately. Start looking for me please.'

'Alright miss. And if we find something?' George says.

'Find two or three places you think might be suitable. When you've found them, come back to me and we'll go see them together. I'll choose the most suitable.'

'Yes ma'am.' Ryan looks at George. They nod.

'Perfect. Thank you for being so accommodating. I look forward to working with you both again.'

'Any time limit on this, miss?' Ryan says.

'How about this time next Friday you have some places ready?'

'Alright.'

'Wonderful. In that case, I'll be getting home. You'll see me home, George, will you?'

'Yes, ma'am.'

'Goodbye, Mr. Ryan. Thank you, and see you next week.' I hold out my hand. There is trepidation in his eyes. I intrigue him, and scare him too. He intuits what is sometimes spoken in dreams, what may come to a man while he sleeps. Perhaps he even suspects it's me who is the messenger. No harm. Better a man knows just enough but no more.

'Thank you miss.'

III

a myriad scattered souls

Constancia places the letter in my hand as we sit down to lunch. I know immediately who it's from.

'Aren't you going to open it? It might be important.'

'It isn't, mi amor. And it can wait.' Except that, in a way, it is important. I stir my soup, waiting for it to cool.

'It might be from Maximo.' Constancia smiles demurely.

'You know it's not from Maximo, because you read the return address.'

She throws me a stern look, upbraiding me for reading her mind. Then she softens. 'Why hasn't he written?'

I dismiss the question with a wave of the hand. 'Maximo is a nice boy, but still a boy. He'll come, in time.'

'Don't you want to get married?'

I sigh. 'Mi amor, why don't you worry about yourself. You – when are you going to find a man and settle down?'

She blushes. 'I'm afraid...'

'Of what?' *But I know what she's afraid of.*

She shakes her head.

'I'm going to find you a fine English gentleman with a cottage and a few fields, and maybe some cows. You can milk them every morning for your milky English tea.'

She bursts into laughter.

'Isn't that what you dream of, my dove? Pulling on wrinkly teets before breakfast?'

She is doubled over the table. To see her like this makes my heart swell.

My abuela grew up and lived her whole life in the country. She took care of every aspect of the farm. I saw her pull newborn calves, still wrapped in placenta, from the mother. She took care of every aspect of the farm. But she wasn't a sentimental woman. One day the Unitarians came to her door. The chief of police demanded she hand over all her horses for the cause. She refused because they'd be used to fight my father. But they persisted. They told her if she didn't concede, they'd break down the stable doors. When she didn't relent, they carried out their threat and forced their way inside. They found every horse and mule in the stables with their throats cut. Such a woman was my abuela. Much of what I am now, I owe to her.

'Don't let your soup go cold, mi amor.'

Opening letters after eating is less fraught with danger. I learned that from my mother. She received mail in the morning and waited until after dinner to open it. There's much I disagreed with my mother on, but not that. In that, she was wise.

Palmerston has sent an invitation. He's bought a new house and invites me to join him and his wife 'in celebration of good fortune'. I like parties. More importantly, I feel a tingling in my gut. These little alarm bells, I've learned to listen to. It's a kind of 'premonition'. I've no idea what it relates to, I only know the circumstances of the party may produce something pertinent to me, perhaps concerning my business affairs or my flight from Argentina. I'll follow this premonition. One learns to follow trails in life when one has become accustomed to spotting them. The right way never leads backwards. It may take a more or less circuitous route, but it always moves one ahead, one way or another, towards one's goal. One only need follow.

After lunch, since I've time, I go to my study. A fire still smoulders in the hearth. I take the book from the shelf and lay it on the desk. The *caapi* too. When I'm calm, I drink. It isn't long before I'm back in the deeper realms of consciousness.

The jungle of the psyche is the collective locus of existence and the graveyard of all our dreams. This is where we come to reside at the end of it all – the open sea of the dark mind, in which most of us drown. There are ways to sail over it. But there are places not even I have seen, and I have been far. Further than most. This is why the great hinterlands of the world – Amazonia, the Congo, the vast Atlantic – represent for Western man the greatest of terrors. They are the living metaphor of the unknown soul, the vast spectre of all horror, and what is horror but the silent intuition of one's own gods and demons?

As the *caapi* takes hold, breathing becomes a calculus, a sublime mathematical form, perfect in its mechanic simplicity. Breathing is key: master breathing and you command the self. My breathing subdued and my emotions restrained, I find myself once again in my shadow kingdom. I look over my shoulder into the vast darkness, there where even my light does not shine. Someday I shall have to venture in. He lurks in there, the *One Who Knows Darkness*. He is not afraid. Even the old man has never faced him. I turn away. Such thoughts are not for today. I pick my way through the jungle. Here and there, souls scurry. I see one such being crouch behind a tree as I appear from the clearing.

—You there, I say. Come here.

She peers out from behind the tree.

—Yes, you...

She steps out. Dressed in fine silk and carrying a parasol. How quaint. Her eyes are wide with fear.

—Who are you?

—Secilia is my name, she replies.

—How came you here?

—The priest brought me.

Ah yes. The fool in love. —And where is he now?

—I don't know, mistress.

—Do you know who I am?

—I have heard tell of you, she says.

Of course you have. —Run along.

She lifts her skirts and pelts through the jungle. How frivolous, the lost souls who drift within me. So many... some, I know not how they came here. A woman like me can never be lonely. I am a myriad of scattered souls and can summon them at will. Right now, I could call the priest if I so desired, but he doesn't interest me. I continue through the jungle towards the poor hut of the shaman. How ailing he has become. Such is the way when the powerful are subdued. I have yet to see what happens to the *karai* when his soul is destroyed. I have no love either way for the old man, but I do not desire his demise, at least not until he has served his purpose.

Outside, his fire is extinguished. I push open the door. He is on his mattress, a gourd of maize beer beside him.

—Get up, old man, before you drink yourself to death.

—Eh? Leave me, you foul witch! You are not welcome here.

—You're mistaken, *karai*. This is all my place, my inheritance. *You* only have a place here because I let you stay.

I sit on the floor and place the book on the table. —Come and sit with me.

—Get out! He leans forward, his face emerging from the shadow. —I don't serve your kind.

—Whom do you serve, then?

—I serve nothing. No one.

He sups from his gourd and falls back on the mattress. I get up and go to his altar. It has gone to ruin, like everything else in the hut. A single candle burns, behind it the skeletal remains of a priest of old. I light some *lumaka* from the small candle and let it burn. If anything, it will drive away the atmosphere of decay. I return to the table and sit.

—Come and join me, old man. I want to tell you a story.

He grunts. I could compel him to join me at the table, but I don't like to use magic on him. It only makes him more stubborn. So I wait, cajoling him, teasing, toying with him until he relents. He lifts the gourd to his lips, but it is empty.

—Come, and I'll fetch you more beer.

—You devil. Do you think you can buy me?

—A drunk can always be bought.

He sits up. His feet are caked with earth, his toenails long and ragged. He pulls up the hem of his tattered pants and propels himself forward onto two feet. Like that, he stumbles towards the table. He falls to the floor, propping himself upright.

—When was the last time you worked any magic, *karai*?

— Beer, he says.

Very well. I get up and go outside, where one of his captive souls has hung a gourd in the tree for him. I know they bring him things. It matters not. Their souls are his, and his soul is mine, therefore they too are mine. Part of the animistic hierarchy. I take the gourd from the tree.

Inside, the old man has fallen over. —Get up, you old fool.

He rights himself and I toss the gourd into his lap. He opens it and pours it into himself.

—A story then, old man...

I wait for him to cease sucking on the gourd and look me in the eye.

—There was a woman who lived in Pueblo Brugo who had three daughters: one negra, one blanca, one mulatta. The village people liked to talk, and everyone assumed she slept all around, and that her three children were from different fathers. They called her 'la puta del rios'. The wife of a fisherman, they said she took all comers from Santa Fe to Buenos Aires, and nights she would get in the husband's boat and sail downriver, and wherever the boat hit land, there she would open her legs and let any guy who happened along mount her...

The old *karai* is drunk, but he's listening.

—The woman was a pariah. They thought her dirt, and so the children were dirt too. The people treated the daughters like shit, spat at them as they walked the streets and called them 'hijas de puta'. But they were proud girls, and they kept their heads high. One day the father was killed. And some months later, the woman gave birth again, this time to an albino girl. *This puta has only just buried the esposo, and still she is whoring*, they said, and they laughed.

—But this woman was not doing like they said. Because her husband had a debt to Yaguareté, and so the wife was claimed by the god. At night, the husband would take up his mattress and sleep outside, and Yaguareté would come after dark when the village was asleep, and some nights he would come as a black jaguar, and some nights white... some nights he would wear his panther skin. This is how the woman gave birth to all colours, because they were the children of the Jaguar. And when the villagers saw the albino daughter and tried to burn the family from the house, calling her *bruja* and *demonia*, do you know what happened?

The old man sucks on his gourd. —I know the story, he says.

—Of course you do. I open the book on the table. —Do not continue to mock me, old man. There are things I need to know. Why did the Franciscan write in code?

I turn the book for him to see. He snorts. —You think too highly of yourself. You are no Yaguareté. And as long as I am captive here, you will get no help from me.

I sigh. —But you know, old man, that there's nowhere else for you to go.

Soon I may lose patience with him. Bitter old men are the most insufferable fools.

A heavy scent of musk comes to me from beyond the walls of the hut. Kurupi is near. I close the book.

—You and I will talk again soon.

—Bring more beer, he says.

Fool. I go out of the hut into the jungle. I know how to find the god – the scent leads the way. I go barefoot across the jungle floor. The vast mycelial network underfoot glows, sending news of my presence. He will know I'm here. Jungle fauna scatter. High up, a jacamar sings, calling to his mate.

The deeper I venture, the stronger the scent. In such dense, moist places does he lurk. Father of thousands, he is the living seed. But even gods can be bound.

There his abode, the rotten hut with a single, foul mattress. Maybe he slumbers within.

I hear movement from the trees and stop. Something stalks me. I can play these games, for there is no danger to me here. I walk towards the source of the noise.

—Come down from there, I say.

He slides down the tree and approaches.

—Are you hunting me? I ask.

His stench is overpowering. I reach out and stroke his ghastly face. He grins. His unearthly cock, wrapped thrice around him, uncoils from around his waist and slithers up my leg. The moist limb teases the inside of my thigh.

*

People reveal their true selves through the parts they play and the masks they wear. Seen through the right eyes, the public persona is a lens to one's innermost secrets. All you have to do is learn to read between the lines. I've always been a keen observer. A party is a stage, and for that reason, I've always liked them. While men and women perform and preen, I watch and gauge. Knowledge is my sustenance. I hoard it jealously.

Taking leave of the mirror, I close the door behind me. Constancia waits in the drawing room. My escort. I find her toying nervously with her hair in a state of agitation.

'Leave yourself alone, mi amor. Before you hurt yourself.'

She looks ready to cry. 'I can't, señora, I can't do it. I can't go.'

'Don't be silly, of course you can. Stop fretting and relax and everything will be fine. Here, let off playing with yourself.' I fix her hair and brush her cheek.

'I'll make a fool of myself,' she says.

'You won't. I think you'll find you enjoyed a better upbringing than most of the people you meet tonight. Don't look down on yourself. Stand up straight.' She rights herself. 'Push out your chest and pull back your shoulders.' She tries. 'God, where's your confidence? Stand tall.'

She lifts herself into some semblance of posture.

'Better. We're not out tonight to impress anyone, but if we do, then what's the harm? You look stunning in that dress,' I tell her. 'I told you it was a fine purchase.'

'Do I? I feel... lumpy.'

'I've no idea what you mean. Now let's go. Winters is waiting.'

'Promise you won't leave me alone tonight.'

'Constancia, I might have to. There may be business. And if I wander away, please know that I'll be back by your side in a matter of minutes. Don't fret. Now come.'

I take her arm and lead her out to the waiting carriage.

'Piccadilly is it tonight, ma'am?'

'Yes it is. We're being entertained. By no less than the Foreign Minister. What do you think of that?'

'I'm not paid to think, ma'am. But sounds like a fine evenin.'

'I'm sure it'll be very interesting. Do you like politicians, Winters?'

'I have no strong feeling for them either way. No doubt there's a few I'd like to slap.'

I smile. 'And there are many who would deserve it.' The driver lowers his head to hide a grin. I climb in. The carriage rocks as Winters hops up behind the horse. I look at Constancia and smile.

'You look stunning,' I tell her.

Only a short time later, we pull up on Piccadilly and onto the forecourt of number 94. Constancia and I peer through the window at the façade. Such a grand house. I feel Constancia's nerves overcome her. She reaches out to take my arm. I pat her hand.

'If conversation fails you, just smile and look pretty.'

Winters opens the door and we step down. 'Have a fine evening, m'lady,' he says.

'Come for us at ten please.'

He tips his cap. I lead Constancia up the steps; music drifts from within as a doorman greets us. I hand him my invite.

He looks at the card. 'Ms. Salome Azul?'

'Yes, that's me.'

And you are?' He looks at Constancia, who wavers.

'This is Her Ladyship, Constancia Isabella Santísima de la Concepción. Her name isn't on the card, but I can assure you Lord Palmerston is expecting her.'

'Well, I...er—'

'You can go inside and tell his Lordship that you left two ladies standing on the steps, or you can do your duty and let us in out of the cold.'

'Certainly, m'lady.' He opens the door and we sally in.

Constancia does her best to hide her horror. 'I told you I shouldn't be here,' she whispers.

'Of course you should. Just enjoy yourself.'

The house is resplendent. For a moment I'm back in our own home in Buenos Aires, under the chandeliers with the sound of violin and the excited chatter of the well-heeled, only the chatter here is in English and not Spanish, and in the streets beyond these walls no bloodthirsty men with knives roam. This is not that place, and I am no longer that woman, complicit in the murder and rape and torture sanctioned by my father. But tonight is not the time for such thoughts.

We're presented with a tray of champagne and we take a glass.

'Let's meander.'

'Que?'

'Let's walk.'

We step out, two émigrés in a foreign but familiar show. I lived all my life in high society. I know the ways, the mannerisms. I'm a foreigner here but I'm no alien. I've seen it before. I know them, but they do not know me. They take the measure of us as we pass; I smile quietly. Next to me, Constancia is tense. Her hand on my arm applies a touch too much pressure. I pat her hand softly.

'Where's the master of the house?' she whispers.

'Oh, he'll appear soon enough.'

'Is he handsome?'

'He's a politician, and a goat. And he's old.'

I turn to look at her. I see her catch the eye of a young soldier and look away demurely. She's blushing. I hope tonight holds no disappointment for her. I'd hate to see her crushed.

'I hear music,' she says. 'Will there be dancing?'

I turn to her. Her eyes are alight. 'Let's go see, shall we?'

We pass through the drawing room into a corridor, across which lies the grand hall. Through the doors comes the sound of a string quartet. We weave our way inside. Growing up as I did, even I'm impressed: neo-classical, gilt and damask, Versailles parquet and exquisite lighting, this is the loafing shed of a society animal. I look out over the floor. Palmerston is there.

I nudge Constancia. 'Right there, look – our host.'

'Dancing? And with him, that's his wife?'

'Yes. Aren't they a fine couple?'

'They are.'

Constancia is beholden. I feel bad momentarily. She misses our old life. I've dragged her from her home, her country, from a life to which she was accustomed and attached, and brought her here to this cold city where she knows no one, only me. She left everything she knew to follow me here. Cruel as Argentina was, we had a life there. Not one I could continue to live, but a life all the same. Constancia could have stayed. Instead I took her with me, a decision that has caused me much conflict since.

And if she'd stayed? But there are many 'ifs', and they amount to nothing. We are here now. A woman of purpose has no need of ifs.

The song ends and the dancers applaud, leaving the floor only for others to replace them. Palmerston catches sight of me, parting from his wife and making his way towards us.

'He's coming,' Constancia says.

'Yes...'

He nears and makes a polite bow. 'Ms. Azul? I wasn't sure you'd make it. Such a pleasure.'

'Thank you sir. I was much obliged for the invite. Your new home is splendid.'

'Kind of you, thank you.' He turns to Constancia. 'Your guest, m'lady?'

'Yes – this is Lady Constancia. A cousin.'

'A pleasure.' Palmerston takes her hand and kisses it. I glance at Constancia. She's not used to such deference, and shrinks.

Palmerston's wife appears next to him. He addresses her. 'My dear – you've met Ms. Azul. Do you remember?'

'Yes.' She smiles coldly, taking her husband by the arm. 'We're wanted over here, dear.'

'Yes, right. Don't leave before we speak again, Ms. Azul. There is something I absolutely must discuss with you.'

I nod.

She hurries him away.

'Yes, you're right. He's old,' Constancia says. 'A gentleman, though.'

'On the face of things.'

Across the room, Palmerston chats hurriedly to two young men. He gestures in our direction. I suppose he wants them to entertain us. Soon they make their way over.

'Do you feel like dancing?' I say to Constancia.

'Hmm?'

'I said, get ready to be asked to dance.'

'Oh no...'

The young men approach and bow. One, a fair-haired youth of about twenty-five, holds out his hand, asking me if he may have the pleasure. I turn to Constancia and smile. She looks panicked. I tell him he may, holding out my hand for him.

He leads me onto the floor and we join the waltz. Over his shoulder I see Constancia follow her partner onto the floor. She looks at me for reassurance and I wink. Poor girl. Too many years in my family's service, she never had the time to foster relationships. Now, almost thirty, she has no experience with the opposite sex. She does amuse me sometimes.

'You're foreign?' the young man says to me.

I gaze at him distractedly. 'No hablo Ingles, pero podemos hablar en Español si lo quieres.'

The colour drains from his face.

'No? Una pena.'

I suppress a smirk. *Quiet now, let us enjoy the moment.* As we move I gaze around, reading the room. Surely there's someone here I should be acquainted with...

The waltz ends and I part from the young man.

'Gracias,' I say.

I look over at Constancia whose attention is still taken. It appears they're lingering for a second dance. I have time to slip away. She'll be angry with me when she sees I'm gone, but she'll forgive me.

I leave the ballroom and prowl the ground floor of the house, stopping to take another glass of champagne for appearance's sake. It's an insipid drink. Alcohol has never been my vice. My mother was a staunch abstainer, never believed in its merits. But my mother was a woman who knew no joy nor pleasure. She had beliefs, though. She never stopped believing in my father, and was his greatest supporter until the day she died. I suppose that makes her a monster too. And I, their progeny – am I too a monster? Perhaps, but of a different sort. Their nature was contemporary, born of the time in which they lived. Mine is evolutionary, dare I say, *spiritual.* I'm not talking about any religious claptrap – spirit is not human. Spirit is animal. It's the sediment of our primaeval, original, selves. The self we've lost. Ironically, it's 'civilisation' that has alienated us from our true selves; evenings such as these only serve to reinforce the division of man from his nature. We were animals once, strong and fierce. When we sat around the fire, we knew no fear. Then we took a wrong turn. We planted our flag in the ground and built houses of stone, and manufactured sturdy beds and hung fine curtains in the windows. After, when we'd become attached to our new possessions, we built high fences to protect it all. The fear was in us. We were afraid to lose what we'd hoarded. We were lulled to sleep by music and wine, and lost touch with our base instincts. Politicians invented new paradigms, sold them to us at the point of a bayonet and we locked ourselves behind closed doors. Until now, that's where we remain, our true natures long estranged. It's still there, but buried far beneath. Such nature I encounter when I travel within, carried by the *caapi* into the far reaches of the seminal self: the hunter and the hunted, the butcher and carrier of meat; instinct, nerve, muscle and sinew, and the feet that carry one piston-like from one's hunters. The soul without a body, the body that needs no soul. The one that does not bleed. The archetype. The Jaguar.

That form is in my nature, unconquered. Still, here I am, one of the few 'animals' among the civilised. Perhaps the Goat is animal in his own right, but such men I eat. Among them now I prowl, watchful, my senses alert. Seeing. Hearing. Soon my instincts are triggered, a tightness in my stomach. Yes, I've learned to listen. A man who interests me catches my eye. He is speaking to a lady; their acquaintance is formal, their mannerisms tight and guarded. The conversation will be brief. He's not a politician – doesn't have the drama. He's practical. A businessman, I'd guess. Content only to make money and enjoy the trappings. No megalomania in him. Pretension, naturally. But I don't judge. Those concerned with appropriation cannot afford the luxury of judgement.

When his companion takes her leave, he makes a move towards the buffet and I follow. Hunting in the civilised world is easy. I meet him there, next to the *vol au vents*. I take up a plate.

'Good evening,' I say.

He glances at me and smiles. 'Evening, madam.'

'Nice party. Beautiful home.'

'Indeed. Are you here alone?'

'Oh, no. I'm with a companion.'

He catches my accent. 'Not from here, are you?'

'No. Argentina. I'm newly arrived.'

He grins. 'Ah. Fleeing the dictator Rosas, I presume?'

I smile. *Such indiscretion.* 'Yes.'

'And what brings you here? Are you known to Lord Palmerston?'

I turn to look around the room. 'We have a passing acquaintance. He was sympathetic to my asylum here.'

'Ah.' He turns with me to survey the room. 'Quite the welcome party.'

'Yes, in a way.'

He takes a few bites of food before speaking. 'My name is Andrew Jardine, ma'am. And you are?'

Jardine. Something about that name...

'Jardine? As in, Jardine Matheson?'

He raises an eyebrow. 'That's right. You know of us, eh?'

It clicks. 'Hard not to,' I reply. 'Your company is the world's greatest supplier of opium, isn't it?'

He freezes.

I hold out my hand and smile. 'Ms. Salome Azul.'

IV

virtue rewarded

'I think this might be the one, Georgie.'

Her footfall, slow and calculating, rattles on the floorboards above. By the way she moves over the floor, I sense she's taken with the place. The feet shuffle. Pause. Move back a few steps. Pause again. She's picturing it in her head, how it'll look when she fixes it up: placin furniture, hangin curtains, maybe puttin a few plants about the place to give it a certain feel, a bit of mystery. A boudoir, exotic like... layin down with a pipe and a few accommodating women, and who wouldn't be into that for an hour, maybe two? Oh, yes sir. She'll draw them in, the fine gentlemen. Wonder what kinda whores she'll put in the place...

Georgie's clean wrecked.

'You alright there, big fella?' I say.

He's a big hefty guy, good for short heavy work, not a man for stamina.

He shrugs. Looks tired and bored. Put him in a room fulla whores he'll soon perk up. That's some work for a man. Never thought I'd end up workin in a whorehouse, but life does flip on ya sometimes. It's not the whores that worry me, though. It's the pipe. If she's gonna have chandoo about the place, and me fond of burnin the midnight oil, what's that gonna come to? *You're gonna have to learn how to control yourself, son. Get a grip. Hold it together. Not like you're addicted anyway. You could be off it anytime you wanted. You're no slave to the Chinese poison.*

A man just needs somethin to turn to every now and again, and if it's not porter, it's whores, and if it's not whores it's somethin else. Just a little somethin.

'Hey Georgie – you ever stop in Rio?'

He looks up, scratches his face. 'Yeah. Long time ago now, Paddy.'

'You ever roll around with them black women? Ever get dirty with one of em?'

He whistles. 'Now you's askin... I'd have to say, you know the score when you roll into port. Black, white, yellow, it don't matter none. I been wiv' the whole rainbow.'

'Wonder will she put a few darkies in here, what do ya think? Pure black women, or maybe a few half'uns...' I whistle. 'Wouldn't that be somethin.'

'You watch what you be doing wiv' the madam's business interests, Paddy.'

'Oh now, Georgie, I'm just talkin about lookin. You won't find me fiddlin, not with the woman herself upstair...'

My voice drops to a whisper. I jab my thumb towards the ceiling. Her footsteps come to a rest right over our heads. I peer up. Don't like her there, hoverin over me. I go over to the wall and perch myself on top of a broken table. She moves across the floor in the direction of the back stairs.

The landlord appears in the doorway. A small man, and shrewd. He holds his hat in his hands. 'So, is your patron satisfied as to the place?'

'She'll tell you herself when she comes down,' I say.

George wanders into the store out front.

'Books, is it?' the landlord says.

'Aye, books. She's a great woman for the books.'

'How curious,' he says. He fiddles with his hat. 'And the rest of the place?' He gestures around the room.

'Well, I expect she'll need a lot of storage. For books.'

'I see...'

We hear the madam on the steps.

'Here she comes now.'

Moments later, she appears. She's striking, I'll give her that. Elegant. A cut above. She has a curious smile on her face as she crosses the floor.

The landlord comes over all snively. 'Ms. Azul – is everything to your liking?'

'It might just do, Mr. Cole. I'm not sure the shop is suitable, however. May I take another look inside?'

He bows. 'Of course, madam.'

She goes in the door George disappeared through only moments before. The two of us follow. George is on the street smokin. The madam looks around and sighs. I know she's only playin him.

'I just don't see that it's fit for books,' she says. 'What was it before?'

'It was an apothecary, madam.' He changes tack. 'But perhaps I could get a man in to put up more shelves for you. I have a very good carpenter.'

'Do you, Mr. Cole? And could he fix up the place right away?'

'I could have him here tomorrow, ma'am, if you need.' He senses he's onto a winner.

'I see, Mr. Cole. But we still need to discuss the rent. Is there somewhere we can sit down?'

When we're done, we step out into Chadwick Street. The madam climbs into the carriage satisfied.

'Can I give you two gentlemen a ride somewhere?'

'No thank you,' I say.

Georgie shakes his head.

'Thank you both. You haven't let me down.'

I nod. George tips his cap.

'So, next week the work really starts, gentlemen. Are you ready?'

'Yes ma'am,' George says. 'Anything you say.'

'Good. Take a few days rest and I'll see you Monday.'

The carriage takes off down the street. We watch it until it turns onto Horseferry Road.

George sighs, takes out his watch. 'Come on, Paddy. The wife'll have tea on. We'll get a bite.'

'You sure?'

'Yeah.'

There's a light rain comin down. We head over Lambeth Bridge to the Southside. George lives in a terrace end on Old Paradise Street behind Hodge's. The crow's nest of the distillery rises high above the terrace, one lone lunatic in its heights, scanning the city. The stink of ethanol in the air.

'Christ, Georgie, you'd get pished just breathin round here,' I say.

He chuckles. 'The wife swears she wakes up tipsy.'

We arrive at the door. 'By the way, Paddy, no talk of whores or whorehouses or anything like that. The wife, she don't need to know. You get me?'

'Naturally, Georgie.'

We go in, hang our jackets and hats. There's a fine smell of cookin from the kitchen. We find Georgie's missus at the table. She gets up when she sees me.

'George... I didn't know you was bringing someone back.' She looks awkward of a sudden.

'Allo love.' He kisses her on the cheek. 'You don't mind, do you?'

'No, course not. Could've done with a warning is all.'

George puts an arm around his wife. She's a small woman. Two hands rest on her swollen stomach.

'Paddy, this is my wife, Lorna. Love, this is Paddy... gonna be working together, me and him.'

I hold out my hand. 'Sean,' I say.

We shake hands. 'Sean?' She looks up at George who shrugs.

'I call him Paddy, 'cause, you know...'

'Call me what you like,' I say.

'I'll call you by your Christian name, Sean. You are Christian, aren't you?'

I nod. 'Yes I am.'

'Let's not make the man uncomfortable, love. Let him relax.' George points to the table. 'Sit down.'

I sit, George sits. His wife goes to the stove where a pot is boilin. She opens it, takes a ladle, and stirs. Then she takes an extra bowl down from the shelf. We sit quietly.

'So, how'd you get on today?' she says.

'Oh, you know... busy,' he says.

She sets two steamin bowls in front of us. 'Busy?'

'Yeah. Busy.'

She fills one for herself and sits. 'He's very tight-lipped about this new work of his,' she says. 'Won't tell me nuffink. You'll be working there too?'

'I will. We'll be open in a week or two,' I tell her.

'Oh aye? And what is it you's doing then?'

I look at George. I'm in no man's land. 'Books,' I say.

'Books?' She turns to look at her husband.

'Yeah. Books.'

She's gawkin at George. 'You? Working in a bookstore?' She howls with laughter.

'Well, now—'

I step in. 'Not *in* the bookstore. We're more distribution. Delivery and the like.'

She drops a spoon into her bowl, puzzled. 'Delivering books? To where? To who?'

George gets in on it, adds a little colour. 'You know, to rich folk and the like. Them that likes to read.'

'Rick folk,' I say.

'Well, well. Aren't you moving up in the world.'

George slips a hand onto his wife's leg. 'Aren't you glad I'll be here at home wiv' you and the little one, and not sailing away god-knows-where on some boat?'

'I am.' She turns to me. 'When he told me he had some mysterious woman gonna pay him thirty shillings a week, I figured he was pulling my leg. I thought, he's up to summink. God knows what he's into... I'm glad it's all above board, I am. And I'm glad he'll be working with a good sensible chap like you.'

I grin. *She had you sweatin there, Georgie boy.* Now I see why he invited me over for dinner. I'm his story.

'You see, love? I wouldn't lie to you, sweetheart.' He blows her a little kiss, then we all get back to eatin.

When we're done, Lorna puts on the kettle. We sit at the table, bellyfull and content. Outside, the rain's comin down. I hear it clatter off the upturned washing tub out back. Don't need to see it; my ma kept the same in the yard, and the same auld sound rattled off it when it was chuckin it down. *Rat-at-tata-at-tat-tat...*

The sound takes me back. Calms me. I could sit and listen to it all night.

Lorna brings us all a cup of tea. We sit with our hands around the scaldin hot mugs.

'Where do you live then, Sean?' Lorna says to me.

'I been stayin with a friend in Limehouse. Now with the steady work, I'll look for a room closer to the city. Maybe around here, I dunno. I can't be ridin up and down the river every mornin.'

'He can find a room round here, can't he George?'

He nods. 'Course he can. Find a room round here for four shillings a week.'

'Yeah, you need a room,' she says. She leans back and rubs her belly.

'Once I start earnin, I'll find a place,' I say.

We all fall quiet. With the rain comin down outside, they're suddenly wonderin what to do with me; they can't rightly expect to run me out into the pishin wet streets. So they blissfully ignore the rain. I take comfort in its music.

While we sit there in quietude, I get to wonderin about settlin down – marriage, that is. These two seem content, not like the other pair up in Fore Street, them two tearin strips off each other in some mutually dependent yet destructive way, Lynn gettin gargantuan on each piece of Barney she devours. Feedin on him. Their relationship is... cannibalistic. She'll eat him whole, and Barney will acquiesce at every step.

But what do I know? George is a big animal but he's a tame one around the wife. Maybe he feeds her too, in his own way. Come back in twenty years and see him, what'd he be like? Emaciated like Barney, stripped to the bone? Who knows. Even these petite quiet women can be carnivores at heart.

And what about you, you muck-raker? Thirty years gone and still not settled. Isn't it time?

Aye. Maybe. Time yet for a bit of frolicking. No rush. Just be quiet and drink your tea, and when the time comes, you'll find a nice petite woman to eat you alive too. Until then, keep the head down.

I take a good gulp of the tea and stand up. 'I'll be off, then,' I tell em.

'You what? It's throwing it down out there,' George says. 'You'll be soaked through.'

'No harm, big fella,' I say.

'Oh no, don't be rushing out,' Lorna says.

'Thank you for supper, Lorna. but I've things to be doing.'

'Mercy,' she says. 'Well, come again.'

I head up the hall and take my coat. George follows me to the door.

'You sure, Paddy? It's raining buckets.'

'That ain't no rain to the Irish. Nothin but a light shower.' I throw on my cap and grin.

'You facking nutter. See you Monday, then.'

'Aye.' I open the door. 'See ya.'

I walk out into the rain, a man with a joyous heart. I'm off to introduce some poisons to my blood.

*

'What kinda gypsy ruckus'll be happ'nin on this fine couch?' I say, droppin into the divan.

'For you? Nuffink,' George says.

'Oh, come now Georgie – don't ya think we'll be getting a bit of side action while we're here?'

'I don't want a bit of side anything,' he says. 'I just wanna do my work and get back to the missus.'

'You're a good man, Georgie, yes you are.' I run my hands over the material under my ass. 'What is this anyway? Silk?'

'No facking clue. Too good for you, whatever it is.'

'I think you underestimate my levels of refinement, Georgie.'

'Come and give us a hand here.'

I get up. George and I take the two ends of a side cabinet and walk it to the wall.

'Do here, won't it?'

I shrug. 'Gotta wait til the madam gets here, don't we. She's the one with the say-so.'

'Well, we'll leave it here outta the way for the time being.'

A fella comes up the stairs holdin reams of cloth. Curtains, maybe, or bedding. I dunno.

'Where ya want this stuff, lads?'

'Put it under the window,' I tell him. 'The boss'll be along in a bit to see how things are comin.'

He drops it and wanders back downstairs.

'Hey,' I say. I nudge George in the ribs. 'Wanna go look in the whore's quarters?'

'Leave it, Paddy. You's gonna get us in the shit.'

'Come on, let's have a gander.' I wander down the corridor and the big ape follows me. We go in the first room. I let out a whistle. A fine little single bed sits by the wall and there's a vanity desk with a mirror.

'Ever seen a new bed before, Georgie? See that? I gotta get a sniff o'that before it gets all soiled up.'

I go over to the bed and bury my face in the pillow and inhale. I rise up, a headful of new sensations.

'You gotta try that, Georgie. That's somethin else. When you gonna get a chance at puttin your head on a fine white pillow like that in your life?'

'You's a facking nuisance, Paddy.' He turns around and walks out.

'Chance of a lifetime, Georgie,' I shout after him.

I pick up the pillow and push my face into it one last time, before followin him out the door. We meet a man on the stairs carryin an armchair.

'Over there,' George says.

The place is comin together nicely. Once the curtains are hung and the rugs are down it'll be in right shape. I have to hand it to her, she wasted no time putting it together. She works fast and does what she puts her mind too. I wish I had her willpower.

I sit down on the divan and take out a smoke. Lifting the match to my face, I get a sudden flash: the candle flame, the pipe, the flame sucked into the bowl... the burn of it in my lungs... washin over me... *the gentle caress, everything a man needs...*

I suck deeply on the cigarette and fill my lungs, lettin it out in one long, meditative exhale. *Strange where life takes you,* I think. *Strange indeed.*

'There's one more bed downstairs, Paddy. Gonna help me hoik it up the stairs?'

'Aye.' I look up at the smoke rollin over the ceiling.

The madam arrives an hour later. We're in the bookstore. A dozen boxes have appeared overnight, fulla books, no doubt, but no shelves yet to put em on. We're sittin with our feet up when the carriage appears outside. We make ourselves busy sharpish.

She comes in the front, the bell above the door tinklin.

'Afternoon, ma'am,' I say. Georgie tips his cap.

'Hello gentlemen.' She gives us that enigmatic smile. 'How is everything?'

'Well, ma'am,' Georgie says.

She looks around. 'No bookshelves yet?'

I shake my head.

'Talk to Mr. Cole, George. Tell him I want them in by tomorrow evening.'

'Yes miss.'

'Shall we take a look upstairs?'

'It's lookin good, ma'am,' I say. I lead us up. She looks around, sees the couches and the paintings and the silk. She nods. Then she takes off her hat and lays it on the side cabinet.

'Alright then. Roll up your sleeves, gentlemen. It's time to get busy.'

And do we get busy. For the next three hours we set the place accordin to her whims, all to her bidding. A good deal of sweat and toil later, the place looks the part. I mean, real classy like.

When we're done, we sit around a small table in the corner and take in the room. I see the look of satisfaction on the madam's face.

'Well, what do you think, gentlemen? Would you pay for a woman here?'

George coughs nervously. I fumble an answer.

'I might do, ma'am. If I had the kinda money it'll take to put one of your girls on her back.'

'Taking girls isn't the only thing that'll be done here, Mr. Ryan. We'll have other pursuits too. Will you fetch that chest over please?'

She points at a wooden chest under the side cabinet. I get up and pull it out, and place it on the table.

'Open it, Mr. Ryan.'

I open the chest and take out the first thing my eyes alight on: a long bamboo pipe of the kind that has come to enchant me. I turn it over in my hands. My heart begins to race.

'I see you're familiar with the tool.'

I clear my throat. 'Yes I am.' She watches me carefully.

'What do you think... will it entice the kind of clientele I intend to attract?'

'I think between it and the women, it just might,' I say.

'And which do you prefer? Women or the pipe?'

I meet her eyes. She looks amused. 'Tough question, ma'am.' She waits. 'I prefer not to get too deep into either.'

'Quite a merry dance around the question, Mr. Ryan.' She smirks, then turns to George. 'Are you familiar with the pipe, George?'

'Never touched it miss,' he says.

'Probably best.'

Georgie throws a look in my direction, a warning type of glare.

She takes the pipe from me and turns it over in her hands, runnin it through her fingers. I never looked at her hands before, but now I see em, they're a touch on the rough side. Not a lady's hands by any means. Cut up, like as if she'd been in the field her younger years. Doesn't strike me as the type that grew up on a farm, though.

'I never tried it either,' she muses. 'I wonder, what would I experience if I did?' She looks at me.

'It's like smokin joy, ma'am,' I tell her. 'Like fallin into a deep slumber and wakin up in a field of dreams.'

'You make it sound enticing. Perhaps one day…' Her voice trails off. She places it on the table. 'There's something else I want to discuss with you gentlemen. On the subject of women. I've procured a couple of Latina ladies to come and work here, but I need more. Whores, that is. Are either of you familiar with any working girls?'

George coughs. 'Well, ah, no miss…'

'No, of course not, George. I expected nothing less.' She turns to me. 'Mr. Ryan?'

'I, eh, know one or two, aye.'

'Are they pretty? Well-mannered?'

Lizzy… well-mannered? 'I wouldn't say well-mannered, no… but put them in satin and it might cover up the – how can I put it? The *imperfections.*'

She nods. 'I may as well meet them. Why don't you invite them here? Thursday at two. They can have a look around and see if it's the kind of place they might want to work. Tell them it's a safe space. They'll be protected. And they'll be free to come and go as they please outside working hours.'

'Sure, miss.'

'Good.'

'You say you already have some ladies?' I ask.

'Yes.'

'From Argentina?'

'From Brazil. Does that please you, Mr. Ryan?'

'Not my place to say, miss. I was merely curious.'

'I've no doubt you two men will act professionally. I don't think I need to explain the bounds of your employment here.'

'No ma'am,' George says.

I shake my head. 'Of course not, miss.'

'Which reminds me. I want you both looking as professional as possible. Next week I'm going to have you fitted for suits. There's a street in the city renowned for its tailors – Saville Row. Are you familiar with it?'

'Yes ma'am.' George looks at me wide-eyed.

'I'll make appointments for you both, and let you know the time and the place. I want you looking first class, gentlemen.'

Georgie grins. I wink at him.

'Good. That's all for today, then. Tell Mr. Cole, George, that I expect my shelves up by tomorrow. I'll be back to check.' She stands up.

'I'll make sure of it, miss.'

'See you out, ma'am?' I say.

'No need, Mr. Ryan. Thank you for your assistance. And both of you, by the way, will be paid for a week's work on Friday.'

'Thank you.'

'Good day, ma'am.'

She takes leave, disappearin down the stairs.

I turn to George, who breaks out into a ferocious grin. 'Saville Row, Georgie...'

He gets up, puts on his cap and does a little spring, clickin his heels together.

I laugh. 'Easy, son – don't hurt yourself.'

'I'm gonna go find Cole, then I'm outta here,' he says.

'See ya, Georgie boy.'

Off he goes. It's just me now, alone in a whorehouse with no whores, above a bookshop with no books. I go sit on the divan and slip outta my shoes. Take the laudanum from my pocket and drain the bottle. Subtle tonics for evening sonnets. I lay down on the divan, rest my head on a pillow, imagine it's the lap of a big Brazilian girl, fresh off the boat, still smellin like manioc and papaya… maybe with a name like Rosa. Aye, big Rosa from Rio, fresh in, limbs like jungle vine and tits like continental grapefruits, can't ya see her now, if you only close your eyes…

Big Rosa, earthy dryad, swarthy inamorata, my heart for a suck at your teets. Bleed me dry, a man enslaved vine-like between your thighs, gone with delight. I'll lie down in the lap of Big Rosa and never wake up, because dreams spill from betwixt her thighs like the juicy seeds of the cocoa. I sigh. *Aye, I'm waitin for ya, Rosa. Right here waitin.*

I get up, put on my shoes and go downstairs into the bookstore. Peer out the window. Not dark yet, but soon enough. Next time I'm in here I expect there'll be books on the walls, books fulla things a man like me never knew nor ever will, books that someday I might have head enough to read.

I lock up and leave. Evenin, time for rest. Dream time. I wander up to Victoria Street where I nip into an apothecary and buy a bottle. Out the door, I take a sip and slip it into the pocket. It'll carry me to Joon Sing's, but before I do that I'll go see Lizzy. Tell her the madam's offer. Put a nice dress on the girl and fix her hair up, and put some silk stockings on her legs, and Lizzy'll clean right up. Maybe she'll give me a free hour for the news. Then I'll go dream at Joon's for the night.

The darkness is comin on and a light rain fallin when I hit Waterloo Pier. I pay the man and hop on. I take out the bottle and sip gently. There's no hurryin the river.

Wake up next to Lizzy. I slide the hand between her legs, find the nest damp. Girl wakes up wet. Ya gotta know the trick, though. Ya gotta play with her a bit before she comes round. Otherwise she wakes up pissed. Explain that one. So I slip in a finger, tease it a little, give her an auld flick. She stirs in the bed. 'Mmm,' she goes. That auld wetness between her thighs has the prick on me hard. The boyo knows what he wants. The finger's in, workin its magic, teasin the quim on her. 'Ooh,' she goes. Easy as that. Don't ya love a woman wakes up wet? She grips the prick on me, guides it to the holy darkness. 'Oh aye,' I go. Nice and easy, early mornin. Don't wake the neighbours. Just a paddle in the shallows before breakfast. She slips the boy in. 'Ooh fuck,' she goes.

After, I go out and get us a bit of fish and we eat. She's already packed. All her belongings in one trunk, sat by the door. There's a ruckus kickin off other side of the wall.

'You'll not miss that, will ya?'

'Who's gonna wake me in the morning?' she says.

'I'll come by and wake ya.' I rap the underside of the table with my knuckles and wink.

'You know she's not gonna stand for you stickin it in me while I'm workin there, don't ya?'

'Not even a quickie on a Sunday?'

'Nuffink. It stops today. You need to find somewhere else to dip it.'

'You're breakin ma heart, Lizzy.'

'Piss off.'

She's a good girl. We have fun together. True enough, I'll need to find another bed to curl up at night. Can't be crossin the madam.

I lift the plates and take them to the basin. 'What you doing with this stuff?'

'Leave it. Ailsa'll be by later to pick it up.'

'She keepin it for ya?'

'Yeah.'

'We'll be off then. I'll go get a cart for your trunk.'

Outside's dry as luck would have it. Down the pier I find a boy with a cart and take him back to Lizzy's. We load up her things and follow the lad down to the Hole pier and get on a steamer, Lizzy, me and her worldly belongings. Me, I've only the coat on my back and the boots on me to worry about. A traveller, I learned to go light. Never had cause for possessions. Only slow ya down. Never had money to buy em with neither.

We sail downriver on a cold, dry mornin. Lizzy's pensive. Dunno if it's the upheaval or bein on the water makes her so. Some people just get pensive on the water. Lose their grounding like, float away. Lizzy's afloat, somewhere. Don't wanna break her thinkings, so I stay quiet. I

take out the tobacco and roll a cigarette. I light it and hand it to Lizzy.
She takes it without word. Then I roll myself another. We sit smokin,
two drifters, adrift.

Comes back to me now as they all do, the auld tunes, song-spun
eddies on cool currents, they come, they go, in and out of my head like
sly minnow.

De colores, de colores son los pajaritos que vienen de afuera...

One I learned from a whore in Santa Rosa. Heard her singin it and
had her teach me the words. Aye, she knew how to use that beautiful
mouth. I shoulda stayed, married one of them big girls, all thigh and
rump. Never wake up cold a day in your life.

We sail on down, sail on down. Quiet the two of us, puffin
and dreamin, feet up on Lizzy's trunk, the sum of her worldly
appurtenances.

The cigarettes burn out and we light another, and like that we rattle
on downriver.

When we hit Waterloo Pier I find a young lad to cart her trunk
over to Chadwick Street. The bell above the shop door announces our
arrival. We drag the cart in.

'A bookshop?' she says. Looks proper mystified she does.

The shelves are up and some of em even populated. Little piles
decorate the floor here and there. Odorous, the must of the paper.

'Whores read, don't they?' I say.

'You takin the piss?' she says.

'Here's one...' I pick a book off the floor. '*Virtue Rewarded*... Not
about whores then.'

She chuckles.

I snatch up another. 'Or this: *Me-ta-morph-o-ses*. Good readin
there for the whorehouse.'

'So where is she?' Lizzy says.

'The madam? We're early. Let's get you upstairs.' I take hold of the trunk. 'How about we christen your new bed while we wait?'

She lifts her skirts to step over a small mountain of books. 'No one fucks for free in a whorehouse fulla books.'

It's gone about five when we hear the carriage pull up outside. Lizzy's been joined by Carla and Mary, two acquaintances from Limehouse, two more gonna whore it out for the madam. We're sittin in the lounge upstairs, me at the table the three of em on the sofa. They look nervous. Out of place. I dunno how three whores in a whorehouse look outta place, but there ya go. Maybe I fed a little too much about the madam into Lizzy's ear and she's spooked the girls.

'How should I call her?' Lizzy says.

'I dunno. Just call her "ma'am".'

'She French, is she?' Carla says.

'From Argentina,' I say.

'Where's that then?'

'Ya know Brazil?' I say.

'No,' she says.

'Round abouts there.'

'Oh.'

The footsteps on the floor downstairs are unmistakable. Others follow. She's not alone. At the sound of her boots on the stairs, we all stand. She appears, leadin two other women, two dark whores, big and lusty. *Big Rosa...*

'Mr. Ryan. Ladies...'

The girls give a little curtsy. Whores with manners, all of a sudden.

'Thank you for coming,' she says. She turns to me. 'Perhaps you should introduce us, Mr. Ryan.'

'Sure,' I say. 'Ma'am, this is Lizzy. That's Carla and Mary.'

'Pleased to meet you all. This,' she says, turnin to the others, 'is Camila and Luara. They're from Brazil. They know a little English.'

The girls nod shyly to each other.

Five of em. Enough for a bordello so long as the place is low-key, but I guess she'll bring more in.

'Come with me, girls. We'll look at the rooms. Mr. Ryan, can you amuse yourself for a time?'

I nod. 'Aye ma'am.'

The girls disappear with the madam towards the bedrooms. I sit down. My hand drifts to the box on the table and I lift the lid. Without lookin, I reach in and fondle the bamboo shaft, the metal mount. I take it out. Fine instrument. I put my nose to the bowl. Never smoked. Turnin it over in my hands, I think about them auld heads in Macau, Singapore... the prints on Joon Sing's wall of wizened old devotees of the pipe, old Chandoo Fu, lodged on a pillow, unmoved for centuries, eyes two dream-discs fulla golden light, a whisper of a smile on his lips. I should sail out to Hong Kong, find old Fu and sit with him, and tell him about Sroanderrig and the Salmon of Knowledge, and Big Rosa from Rio and maybe Lizzy, and maybe give him the secret of gettin a girl goin in the mornin, pokin her before she wakes, but then what does old Chandoo Fu care about such things, he's married to the pipe. Maybe he had a wife back in the day, maybe six or even six hundred, but old Fu knew the score eventually, found the path to true happiness, blue bliss on a foul pillow unwashed for centuries... yes, old Fu has a thing or two to teach us about bliss.

I place the pipe back in the box and close it, then take the bottle from my pocket and take a dose. Medicine, self-administered. That's the thing about growin up on an island, you learn to take care of yourself. What do I or old Fu need with doctors when we know the medicines? We got no need of the physician. Gimme a shilling and I'll make myself right.

I hear laughin from the rooms. The whores are getting comfortable, maybe testin the beds. Doing a bit of dry ridin, puttin the mattresses through the paces. Who knows what whores get up to when they're not buckin. But I appreciate the sound of laughter. It bodes well for the place. What else will they be comin here for if not for a slice of happiness, a little of Chandoo Fu's blue bliss? Aye, fine sound, a woman's laughter. It's a wise man that can keep em happy.

The madam appears in the corridor.

'Everything alright, ma'am, with the rooms n' that?'

'Everything's fine, Mr. Ryan. I have something else we need to do this evening. I need you and George to accompany me to the East India Docks. Can you do that? Around seven?'

'East India Docks, ma'am? Bit out of your way, isn't it?'

'We have something to collect. I'll be carrying a considerable sum of money and need an escort.'

I nod. 'I'll find George and meet you back here at six.'

'Thank you, Mr. Ryan.' She spends a moment or two readin my face. 'What do you think of our girls?'

'Fine girls, miss. They'll make the punters very happy, I'm sure.'

'Well, they'll need a little cleaning up, but they'll do nicely. I trust you'll be a gentleman when you're on the premises, Mr. Ryan?'

'Oh I will absolutely.'

'Good. See you at six.'

At seven, we're at the gatehouse on East India Dock Road. The masts of the Indiamen rise from the quays. A heavy smell of pepper. She hasn't said as much yet, but we're here to buy opium. There's a box of silver on the seat next to me. George knows nothin and is nervous.

The gatekeeper comes over to the carriage.

'Help you folks?'

The madam puts her head out the window. 'We're here to see Lieutenant Cornish.'

'One moment, please.'

He disappears.

'So this is it, ma'am?' I say. 'We get this and we're ready to open?'

'We'll open in three days,' she says. 'The only thing left to do then will be to spread the word, so to speak.'

'And how will you do that? I'd say the men comin in for books are not the same as the fellas comin for the other.'

'What we'll do, Mr. Ryan, is find a member of parliament with a big mouth and lure him. That should take care of getting word out. We want to start slow, until we have a feel for the business. I've never been involved in this kind of enterprise before. I don't want to rush things. But I do need an income. We may as well jump in with both feet.'

The gatekeeper returns and opens up for us.

'Mr. Cornish is waitin on the quay. Straight ahead, past the warehouses. Dock eight.'

Winters drives us inside, takes us past the warehouses towards the dock. The smell of pepper stronger now, and other things too, things a man like me barely knows, things that catch in the nose and make the head spin. George sneezes.

'That's it there, miss,' George says.

There's a fellow on the dock waitin. Behind him, the Bengal, a clipper of the East India Company. The fella approaches the carriage.

'Evening,' he says.

'Mr. Cornish?'

'That's right. You must be Ms. Azul?'

'Mr. Jardine sends his regards.'

The fellow nods. He opens the door for the madam and she steps down. We follow her out.

Cornish beckons. 'Come with me.'

A few dockmen are scattered about the yard. The sight of the madam has them lookin our way.

Cornish leads us into a shed. It smells of tar. Down the back, tucked away in the corner, he lifts a length of hessian to reveal two cases of Patna opium. I can't help it, I let out a whistle.

'Jardine said this is what you're looking for,' Cornish says. 'Lot of black here. You sure you need all this?'

'I wouldn't be here if I didn't, Mr. Cornish,' the madam says.

'Well, if your plan's to get all London wrecked on the black, then you've come to the right place.' He taps the crate. 'Forty cakes in here, 140 pounds.'

The madam turns to me. 'This is your area, Mr. Ryan. Is this what we need?'

I give a long, slow nod. 'Best there is, ma'am.' The side of the crate has the East India insignia inscribed on it: PATNA OPIUM. 'No doubt about it.'

'Good. Well, all that remains is to discuss the price. Tell me, Mr. Cornish, what do you want for one?'

'Five hundred and fifty, miss. Silver.'

'Mr. Jardine led me to understand the price was five hundred.'

Cornish shrugs. 'Five hundred if you're buying in Hong Kong, miss, or Macau. I have to take into account the cost of bringing it over here at considerable personal investment. I can do both crates for a thousand, though, if you like.'

'Alright, Mr. Cornish – I'll give you six hundred now, and you keep the second crate for me. The remaining four hundred will be delivered upon collection.'

'And when might that be, miss?'

'When I need it, Mr. Cornish.'

The madam is mercenary. There's man in her, more than some men.

Cornish scratches his head, then goes to spit in his hand before he catches himself. He holds out his hand and they shake.

She turns to me. 'Can you bring the box from the carriage?'

'Yes ma'am.'

Me and George go outside and carry the crate in and set in on a pallet. Cornish opens it, we peer in. Silver, a mountain of it.

'You can count it, Mr. Cornish. We have time.'

'Six hundred?' he says.

'It's all there.'

He closes it. 'No need. I trust any acquaintance of Mr. Jardine.' He whistles and an associate comes over and silently lifts the box. 'A pleasure doing business, miss.'

'Gentlemen,' she says, pointin at the crate. 'Can you?'

George and me haul the crate outside.

'You ever seen that much silver?' George says when we're out of earshot.

'I haven't, Georgie boy. That's a first.'

'What's she gonna do with all this, then?' he says.

We throw the crate on the back of the carriage.

'She's gonna get the government of England high.'

V

it's as if the shadows follow

Lizzy tries on her new gown and gives us a spin. Her face is beaming. She might've been wearing that dirty blue dress of hers since she was a child. The other girls clap. Luara whistles, the shyness all gone. Rio whores are brash and unapologetic. Now we see their true natures. My girls are loosening up.

'Come here Lizzy,' I say.

She comes over. I push up her breasts so they protrude from the dress.

'Si, mama,' Luara says and winks.

'I feel like a tart,' she says, then falls around laughing.

'Do you like, it?'

'I love it.'

'Then we'll get that one for you. We'll need it taken up. Come here.'

I tell the shop girl to bring me some pins and she returns with a pin cushion. I proceed to take up the hem of Lizzy's dress.

'I think we need a little more leg, don't you?'

She grins coyly. 'Don't matter when it's off.'

'When it's off, your money's been made. The trick is getting them into the bedroom.'

'I never had much difficulty with that, miss,' she says.

'Well, picking up dockworkers is one thing, Lizzy. At my place, you'll be entertaining lords. They have rather a different eye.'

'I'm sure they like having their willy pulled same as any dockworker, miss.' She giggles.

'Of course. When the pants come off, it's all the same. But up to that point, we want you to be a lady. After, you may be as whorish as you wish.'

The last pin, I take from my mouth and jab it into her shin. She yelps.

'Did I prick you? I'm sorry…' I call the shop girl back. 'Help her out of her dress please and have it sent to the seamstress. We'll start the next one.'

When she turns away I put my finger in my mouth, tasting the warm tang of her blood. I feel the triggers in my cortex, synapses lighting up. New delineations. Entire histories are contained in a single drop of blood, an archive of the whole being in a single cell. Soon she'll be known to me. I will know them all. I am a collector, after all.

'Camila, come over here,' I say.

Nunca sabrás lo que es pena hasta que juntes tu sangre con la ajena.

I was ten when I first tasted blood. My brother Juan fell in the garden and split his head on the ground. I held him while I waited for help. He bled into my hands and all over my dress. The colour of my mother's face when she saw us… she thought he was dead. I must have looked like I'd been at the slaughterhouse. I sucked a blood-soaked finger as the maid walked me back to the house. The sweet taste made my head swim.

No matter, all we are and everything we do becomes part of the great river of mythology anyway. Dreams, stories, myths… these things are what we become in the end: whispers in time, hinted half-forgotten memories and tales. Before we're even in the grave we're mythologising our own lives. Some start young, and myths overtake their reality before they're out of young adulthood. My father was such a man. He was a writer of his own story. He penned the tale of his life and still does. But no one paints beautiful pictures quite like a woman can. If she is of the right substance, she can create legends in the minds of all around her.

'Yes, Camila. Perfect. Have a look...'

Camila glances in the mirror with delight. Now she's equipped to tell the tales I need her to tell.

How a nice dress and a bit of rouge can change a woman. It doesn't take much to turn a street whore into a lady. Ephemeral, tactile, we can change face in the blink of an eye. Carla, Lizzy, Lady Palmerston, Salome Azul... one and all, we are façade and subterfuge. Try to find the real 'her' and you become lost in a carnival of masks, a Russian doll of seemingly endless surprises. Some say the mask is the real. I say not. Like a chameleon, we are moulded to our environment, each transition an evolutionary contortion, self-preservation the goal. Where is the true self, then? There is none. The philosophers say it exists, but it does not. When one has stripped away all guise, one finds nothing but a primordial vacuum; the chasm of the soul is devoid of all essence, desolate but for the whispers of life's mishap peregrination. Even the gods do not exist there. People live through their masks. Without them, they are nothing. And what are gods without a people to conceive of them?

Our power lies in this: Our true nature is that we are transitory and insubstantial. A gaping hole, a lack. When one realises this, one can become all things.

***

Georgie's nervous. Big fella like that, nervous. He's a fish outta water, here in the madam's bookshop–whorehouse. He is neither a man for the books nor a man for the whores. Fortunately, I'm both. Well, not so much a man for the books, as readin never was much in my blood. But I'm not afraid of the books; I'll pick one up now and again. Might not put much stead by it, since I ken the type that writes em. They'll fill your head with all kinds of harangues and rot, when it's better for a man to just have his mind *empty*. Thinkin is a luxury most can ill-afford. Who's got time for philosophy and theosophy, and politics and enlightenment? Not the likes of me. Though I like it when the auld night poetics hit me. That's it for me though – you can take your philosophy and stick it up Plato's shitter.

'Look lively, Paddy,' Georgie says.

He stands up from his chair at the sound of a carriage rattlin down Chadwick Street. We're sitting in the bookstore by the light of a single lamp, not even light to read by. Nice though, with the newly stocked shelves of the madam's store bathed in low light. Vast tomes of reading sit undisturbed on the shelves. Who knows if they'll ever be opened – who's gonna be readin when there's women upstairs openin their legs for a piece of silver?

The carriage passes right past the front of the shop. I can't swear to it, but I think I see someone peer out the curtain as it rattles by. Georgie turns to look at me.

'What's his problem, then?'

I shrug. 'Don't worry, Georgie boy. He'll be back. These gentlemen get spooked easy, you get me? They need time to get at ease with their sins. Men like you and me, we sin easy and with little frettin.'

'Speak for yourself, Paddy. I's a married man.'

'Come now, Georgie, don't be coy with me. We been in the same ports, me boy.'

'You's a scoundrel, Paddy. I's a god-fearin man.'

'Sure you are, Georgie. Sure you are.'

I get up and go to the window, and look out into the dark street. There's a few curious eyes been passin since the madam opened the store. Folks round here are like me, not really the readin type. Workin folks, mostly. On the poor side. Not much put by in this world, livin from day to day, meal to meal. Just wait til the carriages are linin up outside. Then the eyes'll be poppin. 'Sure who'd be buyin books at one in the mornin?' is what they'll be sayin. It'll come out eventually, what's happenin above the shop, I'm sure. With the madam's well-cut whores comin and goin, it'll not be long before people start to whisper. Speaking of well-cut whores...

'Hey Georgie, you get a look at Lizzy in them new skirts of hers?'

'I ain't been looking at no skirts, Paddy.'

'Some woman, isn't she? Put a quare kick into her step did that new finery of hers. And as much as she was thrilled to be in em, I could see she was just dyin to lift em too.' I whistle. 'She got me goin, she did.'

'Careful, Paddy. Caref—'

'Hold up now, Georgie boy.' Right on cue, the carriage sounds on the cobbles again. I crane my neck to look down the street. 'Here we go, big fella. I think we're in business.'

This time it slows. Aye, we've just got our first customer. I turn and wink at George. So's I don't put the fellow off, I turn from the window to peer at the bookshelves. The carriage sits idle.

'Aye, Georgie,' I say quietly. 'See what I mean? These gentlemen are skittish.'

Moments later out, of the side of my eye, I see the carriage door open. A man steps out. He says somethin to the cabbie then approaches the shop. I watch him come in. Ain't openin the door for him though. She ain't payin me to open doors for no rich pricks.

The bell above the door tinkles. The man steps inside, takin off his hat. Closes the door and clears his throat. He glances at me, then George. Then he turns to the bookshelves on the opposite side of the store.

All very awkward, this.

I look at Georgie who appears panicked. I guess it's up to me then. I step toward the gentleman and cough lightly.

'Good evening, sir,' I say. Professional like. 'Is there something I can help you with?'

He looks around, still unsure. 'Is this...?'

'Perhaps you're looking for something else, sir? Other than books?'

He clears his throat nervously. 'I heard there was a certain... establishment...'

'Ah, yes sir.' I glance at Georgie and grin. Then I turn back to the gentleman. 'If you'll just follow me.' I wink at Georgie as we walk past him into the back.

'Is this The Nightingale, my good fellow?' he says as I lead him up the stairs.

'It is, sir,' I say. 'You're in exactly the right place.'

At the top of the stairs, we're met by some kind of oriental fragrance, incense or the like. Intoxicating.

Before I take him inside, I stop at the door and turn to him. 'Whatever it is you desire, sir, I promise, inside you'll find it.' I smile. 'Come.'

We go in. Lizzy's up off her chair as she hears us enter. The rest of the whores are suddenly alert. Five of em, all ready to lay him down and suck the soul outta him.

'Evening, sir,' Lizzy says, her face all alight for the gentleman. I almost get a twinge of jealousy. She does look the part. Ain't no street whore no more. She's a lady now, only a lady who fucks for money.

'Thank you, Mr. Ryan,' she says to me, and gives a little curtsy. *Ha! You cheeky little cat...* Then she takes the gentleman by the arm. 'Why don't you come sit with us, sir, and we'll get you a drink?'

She leads him to the divan. With a single look over her shoulder, she grins at me and winks.

'Welcome to the Nightingale,' I mutter. I'm turnin to go out the door when Carla catches me by the arm.

'Not so fast,' says. 'The madam's looking for you.'

'Oh aye?'

She tilts her head towards the back of the establishment. I nod and go down past the rooms to the back, where herself has set up a bit of an office at the top of the back stairs. The stairs are dark; I knock on her door and wait for the reply. When she calls, I go in.

'Evening miss.'

'Come in, Mr. Ryan,' she says. 'And close the door.'

The office is simply done up. A large desk, which Georgie and I carried up the stairs, Georgie near bustin a lung. The walls are bare save for a pair of curtains that hang in the middle of the room, which is strange because it's a dry wall. Never saw them put up. She sees me staring at them.

'Like the colour?' she says.

I scratch my head. 'That is mighty confusin, miss...'

'Don't worry. Come and sit down.'

I shake my head and sit. On her desk is a single ledger, a pen and a lamp. Behind her a cabinet. Inside will be the chandoo. Perhaps that's where she'll keep her coin. I shift nervously in my seat and turn back to her.

'How's Lord Sotheby?' she says.

I raise an eyebrow. '*Lord*, is it?'

'He is indeed a lord.'

I grin. 'And how is it you'd be findin lords to come to this obscure little bookshop in St. Matthew's?'

She lifts her head a touch. 'What do you do when you have a little money, Mr. Ryan?'

I give a low whistle. 'Well now, I'd have to say—'

'Don't dance around the question. You can be direct.'

'I'm not sure I'd like to say, miss. You know, it's a personal kind of thing.'

She bats her eyelids very slow, the way a mother might admonish a child. 'Are you gonna make me say it for you?'

I breathe deep and exhale. 'I like to smoke a little, miss.'

'And?'

'And...'

'A whore now and again, yes?'

I grin and shake my head. 'Well—'

'It's not difficult to read you. Do you know why?'

'I'm sure you're going to tell me, miss.'

She smiles and nods, then shakes her head all slow like. 'It's because there's no difference between you and the next fellow. That lord out there getting ready to step out of his trousers and climb on a woman he's never met before... between him and you, there's no difference, Mr. Ryan. Nothing. He might have a little more money and live in a nice house, with a wife and a few children at home, but when you peel back the layers of a man, underneath, the fundamentals are the same.'

I smile. 'Are you sayin I could be a lord, miss?'

'I could make you one, Mr. Ryan, if that's what you wanted. And

I could also take Lord Sotheby out there and turn him into a beggar. Do you know how?'

'Because we're all the same?'

She smiles and sits back. 'Do you drink?'

'I'm not a great man for it, no. But I wouldn't turn one down if you're offerin.'

She opens a drawer in her desk and takes out a bottle and two glasses. The glasses hit the desk with a clink. When she has poured, she pushes the glass towards me. I pick it up and tilt it. She holds my gaze intently.

'*Salud,*' she says.

'*Sláinte,*' I reply.

We take a drink. I nod, lookin at the glass in my hand. 'I'm not all that familiar with the stuff, but I'd say that's a nice bottle.'

She tilts her head imperceptibly, her eyes closing slowly, like a cat's. 'I'm not a drinker either. I bought it simply to be hospitable. And I know it's not one of your vices. It's one of the reasons I found you when I was looking for capable men.'

'And the other thing – you're not worried?'

She sees my eye go to the cabinet. 'No. I know you won't touch it.'

'How do you know?' I look down at the glass in my hand and see that it's empty. I wasn't even aware I'd finished it. She opens the bottle and tilts it my way. I hold out the glass.

'Do you know how I was able to locate you, Mr. Ryan? I mean, I hadn't seen you since we arrived in London and you escorted Constancia and me to our hotel, yet I was able to send George with instructions where you might be found. How is that?'

My mouth becomes dry. I take a drink and put the glass down. 'I can't say I know, miss. It's a strange thing alright.'

'Can you guess?'

I reach nervously for the glass again, before pullin my hand away. 'Are you watching me, miss?'

'How would I be watching you?'

'I dunno, miss. Sometimes I feel I'm being watched.'

Her eyes are somehow murky and diamond-bright all at once. She doesn't take her gaze from mine, not for a second. She still hasn't touched her drink.

'Are you in my head, miss?' I tap a finger on my temple. 'Somehow, it feels like... do you get in a man's head like?'

She picks up the glass and sips, and puts it back on the table with poise.

'Perhaps you think too much of yourself, Mr Ryan. Why should I be concerned with what's going on in your head?'

When I don't answer, she turns to the bottle. Released from her gaze feels like my intestines are freed from an iron grip. She picks up the bottle and pours me another. Without a second's pause, I drink.

'Relax,' she says. 'Maybe you think too much. Maybe the poison you like to put in your body is putting you on edge. Have you considered that?'

'Maybe, miss.'

Then, in a split second, she changes. All business like as she pours me a final swally. 'So, our friend downstairs has an exceptionally loud mouth. Today, he's alone. Tomorrow, half a dozen of his friends will be here. I'm going to need you and George to split hours – at any hour of the day, I'd like one of you to be here. I was thinking since George is a family man he might do six to six – the day shift, so to speak. That would leave you here evenings. Would that cause you any trouble?'

I sit forward as if to answer, then pause.

'I know you keep strange hours, Mr. Ryan. I wouldn't want to interfere with your social life.'

'No, no...' *Are you man enough to tell her?* 'No, not at all, miss. I was thinkin about makin some changes to my social life anyway.'

'Are you sure?'

'Yes. That's fine.'

'Good then. That takes a significant weight off my shoulders.' She smiles.

I gub the drink and put down the glass, and twist awkwardly in the chair. I need reprieve.

'Thank you Mr. Ryan. Why don't you tell George to come up and see me and I'll talk to him about the new arrangements.'

'Sure.'

She nods. I get up, rightin the chair before goin to the door.

'And keep an eye on the girls for me, Mr. Ryan, if you would. Make sure they're not drinking too much. We can't let our own vices get in the way of business.'

I stop to look at her before I go out the door. Her eyes have lost their edge. The diamond sharpness is gone.

'Will do.'

When I go out, I feel like some little bit of me has stayed in the room with her. Like a part of me is missin.

***

After Ryan leaves, there are noises from just beyond the wall. I get up, go and part the curtains and look inside. Incredible, that I can see them and they cannot see me. Carla even comes to check herself in the mirror as the man takes off his jacket. My heart almost stops as she squints, seemingly at me, I peering back like an unseen reflection. For a second, a very brief moment, that's exactly how I feel. When I am certain she has no idea I'm gazing back, I even raise a hand to my face to mock her movements. We are sisters across a divide, separated only by glass yet far divorced by the oceans of chance and circumstance. Why shouldn't it be me on the other side of the mirror? In another life, another timeline, it almost certainly is. With the help of the *caapi*, I have glimpsed other worlds. They are multitude. They fold together like the strands of hair my maid used to plait together for me when I was a child. Or like the embroidery I used to sit and watch my mother's thin fingers weave. Yes, that is a more apt metaphor. Picture it: a hundred different threads, each a different hue yet of the same origin, all coming together to form a complex tapestry, an unfathomable whole. For that's the life of a human: we're not one but legion, and we are not temporal but eternal. I've seen my former lives: I was a saint, a seamstress, a soldier – yes, male too, for we're not constrained only to one sex – a fishwife and a farmer, a physician and a poet. A knave, a princess, a seer. A wandering mendicant on the shores of Mansarovar. I sat under a tree and meditated for twelve hours a day. Even then I collected souls – I had thousands. I amassed them like the black pearls of a necklace that spans worlds and aeons.

I was not always as I am now. There were times I was on my knees like a beggar, with nothing but the rags I was clothed in and the cup I held in front of me. A soul must climb from the gutter like the first writhing primal organism that crawled from the aggregate swamp of life. We all begin somewhere, and our beginnings are not pretty. At first we are base creatures with no depth or dignity. But, as we grow and devour and shed our skins, we evolve into that which all souls must in the end reflect: the singular essence at the core of each of us, that contained in every particle which makes up each form we assume as living beings. Some beings are mice and some are gods. Some are merely men. Evolution is not kind or cruel, it is merely logical. It is an intelligence perfect in its precision. Once you see that, there is nothing to fear or fret for.

Carla and Lord Sotheby: two mere plots on a map, two birds that pass in the night, two stars whose course was plotted long before, unwavering and persistent, knowledge of which they never had and never will, but which determines their every decision and action. Carla was a whore before she was even born. She may have been many things other, but the whore was always her destiny. Lord Sotheby too had no such license. Born into a certain station, this station long decreed. Yet he has been a knave and will be again.

Carla pouts. I catch her lips tighten with distaste as she looks over her shoulder in the mirror to see the Lord ready himself. Whores do what whores must. We all do. Even I who have knowledge of our complexities and our constraints.

But what of free will?

Aha! Therein is the question – the only question.

Here is my reply: What choice has the peasant but to plough the field? Should he starve, let his children starve? And what of the whore who must open her legs or face a life in the gutter? Or the lord – should he forfeit wealth and privilege that others may thrive in his foolhardy sacrifice?

We each do what we are called to in this short life, nothing more. The calling is in our birth, in our blood. And there is nothing we can do to change it.

We are that we are.

When I return to the house, late at night, Constancia is still awake. She's waiting in the living room for me, and she's in a state of anxiety.

'Señora! Where have you been? Oh God, they have found us, they are here…'

When I've calmed her, she tells me a man has been watching the house all evening from right across the street.

'Right outside?'

'Right across the street – go, look. See…'

I nod, but make no move to the window. I soothe her, whisper all the little things that put her at ease. Tonight it is not working. I call the maid and tell her to make a tonic, and give her something to slip into it, something that will put Constancia to sleep. When it's ready, I make her drink it.

'It will help, I promise,' I say. 'Come, let's get you to bed.'

When I've gotten her upstairs, I go to my study which has a view over the street. Discreetly, surreptitiously, I peer through the curtains. The street is quiet, no one afoot. As is usual this time of night. Doors closed and curtains pulled – there's no one so private as the British.

Still, my dove's unease has upset me. I feel something is amiss. I'm sure she's not mistaken.

We are being watched.

In the morning, she's still subdued. The disquiet is in her. I got up early and surveyed the street to see if I could catch any sign of our spy, but still there is nothing.

'You believe me, señora, don't you?'

'Of course, mi amor. I don't doubt you at all. But do you believe me when I tell you I'll do everything it takes to keep us safe?'

Reluctantly, she nods. 'But *what* will you do?'

I'm quiet for a moment. 'I'll contact Lord Palmerston and tell him there may be a foreign agent on British soil. They'll have to arrest him.'

'So you think it is? Someone from Buenos Aires?'

I shake my head. 'I don't know. I really don't. But we can't take any chances, can we?'

When she next speaks, my heart nearly breaks.

'We can be happy here, can't we? We can have a life here, tell me we can...'

I take her hands in mine and look her in the eye. 'We can. And we will.'

I do my best to reassure her. I will allow nothing to come between her, I, and our right to a new life. I kiss her on the cheek and embrace her.

By the time I leave the house, I have murder in my heart.

When I arrive at the shop, no one's there. No George, no Ryan. Only an empty shop. Given that my business is in fact whores, this isn't a tremendous inconvenience, but it doesn't look good.

'Why is there no one in the shop?' I ask Carla when I get upstairs.

'Cause we sent George out for breakfast, miss,' Carla tells me.

'Carla,' I say, 'I have men about the place in case something catastrophic happens—'

'Like a fire, miss?'

'Like a fire, Carla, yes. Or maybe someone tries to rob us. Now, what do you suppose would happen if either of those things happened and there wasn't someone here to stop it?'

'Like stop a robbery, miss?'

'Like stop a robbery, Carla.'

'Well, we could do something.'

'You? And what would half a dozen whores do in the case of a robbery?'

'We'd fight em off, of course. And stop em.'

'Would you indeed?' I sigh. 'Carla, George and Ryan are not here to run errands for you. Next time you want breakfast, put on your shoes and go and get it yourself, do you hear?'

'Aw, miss...'

'If any of the girls are not yet up, then get them up.' I turn to go. 'And when George gets back, send him to see me.'

'Yes miss.'

In the office, I sit at the desk and open the newspaper delivered to the house this morning. My homeland is on the front page – Las Malvinas and the blockade, what else. Palmerston, up to his usual tricks. It seems a very British thing that history may be rewritten merely to suit the occupier:

'The rights of Her Majesty to the Falkland Islands are of ancient standing and have never been relinquished. The British Government, at one time, thought it inexpedient to maintain any garrison in those Islands; Ten or twelve years ago, however, the Falkland Islands, having been unoccupied for some time, were taken possession of by Great Britain, and a settlement has ever since been maintained there. But Her Majesty is not accountable to any foreign Power for the reasons which may guide her in making such arrangements with respect to territories belonging to the British Crown... Great Britain had always disputed and denied the claim of Spain to the Falkland Islands, and she was not therefore willing to yield to Buenos Ayres what had been refused to Spain.'

The words of a snake. Very convenient, to be able to reshape the world with a few choice, snaky words. The eels of truth are slippery indeed. The more I hear from him, the more I come to dislike the goat. He is only a product of his class, after all; like others of his ilk, merely the by-product of a certain strand of evolutionary dispensation. *How lucky for you, Lord Palmerston.*

There's a knock on the door.

'Come in...'

George enters, taking off his cap. 'Ma'am.'

'Good afternoon, George. How is everything?'

'Very well, ma'am. Is there anything you need?'

'You could bring me some water, George. I would like to have tea.'

'Certainly, ma'am.'

He leaves. In several minutes he returns with a pot of hot water. I take out my maté and my cup, and prepare the tea. George is watching.

'Would you like some maté, George?'

He shakes his head. 'Never did get a taste for it, ma'am.'

'Una pena.'

He scratches his head.

'How was everything when you came in this morning – there was no problem with Mr. Ryan, I take it?'

'No, none at all. Mr. Ryan put the takings in the box, like you instructed.'

'I have no doubt. Thank you. One more thing…' He raises an eyebrow. 'Don't let the girls take advantage of you, George. Next time they want breakfast, or lunch, or dinner, or anything at all, you tell them to go out and get it themselves. They're big girls, and well enough capable of looking after themselves.'

His face turns a plump shade of pink. I smile and pick up my tea.

By late afternoon, the gaudy sound of whore's chatter and revelry can be heard beyond the door. Several customers are in. They're getting drunk and frisky while my girls are doing what such girls are born to. Overnight, we've become a 'living' brothel. From here on in, men will teem through these doors, and not just any men. Here we'll cultivate only those we have use for: the business elite, the politicians, and lest we forget, the bankers. Nothing happens in politics without the say-so of money. The two are an unholy cabal that determines the thrust of change. What of the vote? The ballot box means nothing. It's business makes the calls and politics pulls the levers. Power is not, and was never, held by the people. The people are mere cattle. Not that those in the halls of parliament have any real power either – those men merely pull the chains they're instructed to. The illusion of power is what keeps the whole charade standing.

George knocks on the door and I call him in. When he casts his eye towards the cabinet, I understand what he wants.

'One of our guests would like something to smoke?'

'Yes, ma'am. I need a pipe and some of the black stuff.'

'Come then.'

I go to the cupboard. I take out the key and open it, and George lifts out the chest and puts it on the desk. I open the lid and we both look inside.

'How much does one need?' I say.

'No idea, ma'am. Never was my thing.'

'Well, can you guess?' I take a knife and hand it to him.

'Oh bugger...'

I watch as George clumsily takes the knife and proceeds to lop off a small wedge of the ball-sized lump of opium.

'Are you sure that won't kill him?' I say. His face turns white. I shrug, taking the ball from him and placing it back in the chest. 'I'm sure he'll be fine. When Mr. Ryan gets here, bring him here. We'll have him instruct us on the proper preparation of the stuff.'

He goes out, taking the tar-like substance and a pipe with him.

It isn't long before I discern the first sickening traces of smoke in the air. I'm curious about its effects, of course, but I'm beholden to my own 'medicine'. Nothing could ever replace the *caapi* for me. It's my only master. Others find comfort in medicines, but comfort is not what I seek. I seek power. And power only comes with sacrifice. Let those who seek comfort find it, and let those who seek power embrace sacrifice. This is the way of the *karai*.

I pass through the bookstore on my way out. Ryan's there alone, his feet on the desk and a book in his hand. He lifts his feet from the desk in a hurry and begins to stand up. I raise a hand.

'Don't get up on my account, Mr. Ryan.' He sits, closing the book. 'What are you reading?'

'Uh... Voltaire, miss.'

This elicits a smile from me. 'You're reading Voltaire? Why don't

you read me a passage from Voltaire,' I say as I take my gloves and put
them on.

'You want me to read to you?'

'Go on. Pick a passage at random. I'm sure you've got a very nice
reading voice.'

'Alright, miss.' He opens the book at the page where his thumb
is jammed between the pages. He clears his throat. 'There is an
infinite distance between God and man, but if, in the system of the
ancients, the human soul was regarded as a finite portion of the infinite
intelligence, sinking back into the great whole without adding to it; if
it be supposed that God dwelt in the soul of Marcus Aurelius, since
his soul was superior to others in virtue during life, why may we not
suppose that it is still superior when it is separated from its mortal
body?'

I raise an eyebrow. 'What do you make of it then, what you've just
read? Do you suppose your soul is part of a greater whole?'

'I would have no idea about that miss.' He puts down the book.
'Never spent much time thinkin on God and souls.'

'And yet you've experienced your soul leaving your body, yes?'

He's about to answer when George comes in. 'Your carriage is
outside ma'am.'

I nod.

'There's something else,' George says.

'Yes?'

'There's a man at the bottom of the street. He appears to be scoping
us out. Watching the shop.'

'How long has he been there?'

'All afternoon, I guess.'

'Really.' My instincts are suddenly taut. 'Give me a second please,
George.' I go back upstairs.

***

After goin back up the stairs, the madam doesn't reappear. It's dark
out now and her carriage is still sittin outside. And Georgie's away.

Lizzy comes through the door behind me, doesn't even look at me as she walks to the front of the shop.

'Where you goin?' I say.

She holds up a hand. Shuts me up with a gesture. She goes and looks out the window, down the street where the man Georgie saw is parked out. She opens the door and goes out.

'Lizzy!' I shout, but she's away out in the street. I put the book down and get up, and follow her. Her dresses all out awry around her like a quiet storm. I watch from the door as she approaches the man clingin to the shadows. Lizzy slips into the shadow and whispers in the man's ear. When she steps out again, it's as if the shadows follow. She leads the man into the alley.

Seconds later, when she emerges, her blue dress is stained black with blood.

The Sage Darkness

I am the seed and the sky, I am the song of the spring river bursting with spawn. I am the sun-spilled crest of light that catches at dawn the tip of the eucalyptus. I am the thunder of the night and the moon-eye; I call to no one and terrify. I am the sage darkness. I am the harpy's claw. I am the anaconda's heart and the tapir's tongue; my words you hear and fathom not. I am the fell shadow that burns the soil in winter; I am the season that obeys no earthly law. When man comes afoot into my domain, he is prey and I am predator. When woman comes under my eye, her first-born shall be as my own. I am the cusp of the earth and the forestalled descent of heaven; my night is everlasting. In my howl is the voice of all beasts. I am beast and god, and I am the soul that contains all souls.

The jaguar sky silences all. Night comes and the jungle falls hush. Even the souls are still. Among them, one wanders. A daughter of Wahari. Barefoot she steals across the ivy weave of the jungle floor. Her jungle. Her territory. But her territory ends where mine begins, and at the boundary, the edge of her domain, she crouches and peers into the dark. She does not see me.

The flesh is white but her soul is dark. The black triangle of her cunt shews between her thighs. With such she may enslave men, even some amongst the gods. Beasts will be beasts and there is power in congress, but true power is attained by devouring one's prey. This she knows, yet has not the heart to hunt true prey. She crouches by the guaimbé, her hand clasping the rough hew of the trunk, still without the eyes to see what she seeks. She is young; to be *karai* is not for the young. I am the Ancient. I have devoured young and old. Where there is darkness it is under mine eye, and where there is light, is it I that have shown the way. I am the one who sees and remains unseen.

Before man, there was Yaguareté.

One day, on the scent of a woman, Yaguareté stood up on two legs and was transformed, and became Yaguareté-aba. Yaguareté-aba made the woman his consort, and taking up at her hearth and her bed, one night lay down to sleep. While he dreamt, the soul of Yaguareté left him and went back to the jungle. Now he was only Aba. Aba was incensed. Aba resented the desertion of his eye-soul, so taking up his spear he ventured into the jungle in search of Yaguareté. To this day he has been hunting his descendant and kin. Yaguareté was the soul of man, and that soul abandoned him. Now man seeks to kill.

Women too are killers. When their husbands left and went into the jungle in search of Yaguareté, woman became angry. Instead of killing the husband, she too seeks to kill Jaguar, for in killing Jaguar she takes back her power. It is easy to kill a man, but to kill a jaguar one must look death in the eye and live.

I am the soul that contains all souls. I am Yaguareté. I am Jaguar. The trees do not contain me. The jungle does not contain me. The sky is above all yet sees me not.

I descend silently to the jungle below. The ground does not hear me yet I set foot on its soil. I am the crepuscular eddy of the earth's night, a ripple in the vast dark. Silent is the jungle, yet quieter still it falls as I pass. Tonight the woman encroaches. My domain is unassailable and I must mark my territory. Woman is hunter but I am a killer. I have her scent. She has neither eyes nor nose for Yaguareté. No soul roams where I stalk.

Woman, you will die here.

I pause. Creep closer. I am earth and I am vine. I am the ivy that catches at your feet. I am the darkness that makes you tremble. Her limbs are taut. Her eyes strain. Her toes claw at the earth. Perhaps there is still trace of Jaguar in her blood. Now she senses me.

I leap, teeth bared.

Part Two

up from the wastes of the mind

Hands on my neck, on my face, pulling the hair from my eyes. Fingers trembling on my skin. A suffocating smoke. A scream.

I open my eyes; the maid douses my desk with water. Constancia's face, drawn with terror.

'Señora... que pasa?'

'What?'

'What happened...?'

'I... I don't know...' I sit up. The air chokes me.

'Come, let's get you out of here, come...'

Constancia puts an around me and raises me to my feet. I forget her strength sometimes. She draws me towards the door.

'Wait... my book...'

'Your books are okay, señora. Let Charlotte take care of it.'

'No—'

'Come. Now.'

I am too weak. I let her carry me out of the study and into the bedroom. She lays me down on the bed.

'Stay right here. Don't move.'

I feel it like a knife in the gut: I am helpless. Nothing but a wounded animal, without even the strength to defend itself. My hands slide into my hair and pull, feeling the scalding tug of the hair at the roots. I want to scream. *Gods, I want to scream...*

In minutes, Constancia is back with a basin of water. Concern in her eyes as she watches me. She places the basin next to the bed then dips a cloth in the water and puts it against my forehead. The water is cool. I close my eyes. For a brief moment I'm on the recliner in Abuela's sitting room. I am eight years old. It's still morning, I think; I'm not sure, because only a short time before I was kicked by a mule. I'm disoriented and feel ill. Vincente, one of Abuela's farmhands, found me lying unconscious outside the mule pen. He carried me inside and lay me on the recliner, and Abuela, like Constancia now, fetched a basin of water, came and sat next to me and cleaned my face and my arms. The memory is jarring; I try to push Constancia's hand away but she is firm.

'What on earth were you doing, señora?'

'Mi amor, please, don't trouble me...'

'You nearly set the house on fire... what were you thinking? What were you burning this time of night, we could have lost everything.'

'Please – I was simply reading. I had the lamp next to me on the desk for light. I must have dozed off and knocked it over. It was a silly mistake. It won't happen again.'

'No, it will not. You must stop whatever foolishness you've been doing in the evenings.'

'Don't trouble me. I've heard enough for one night. I only need to rest.'

'Si?'

'Please.'

She squeezes out the cloth and places it next to the basin. Then she turns to me. 'Is there something you're not telling me? Some nights you go into that study, and when you come out...'

'What?'

'...when you come out... it's like you are not... *you*.'

'Mi amor, I don't know what you're talking about. At night I spend a few hours studying. When I finish, I'm preoccupied with the things that consume my mind. That's all. It's hard for me to switch off, you understand?'

She shakes her head. 'Santa Maria,' she whispers. She gets up and takes the basin. Stopping at the foot of the bed, she watches me for a long moment. Her look is full of unknowing. Worry, too. And love.

'I should stay here with you tonight,' she says.

'No. That isn't necessary. I'll be fine.'

She shakes her head once more before lowering her eyes and going out the door. I turn to the window. The curtains are not drawn. It's dark out and the street is quiet. From down the hall, I get the scent of smoke. What have I done? I hope I haven't destroyed the book. Never have I suffered such a blow. These are hard lessons. Sometimes when one thinks they've attained all the knowledge there is to attain, these hard knocks come along with savage unpredictability. I was caught off guard. I, the one who hunts, became the hunted. I haven't learned what I need. Still I am no *karai*. Mere human only. Weak.

'How are you, señora?'

'I'm well, mi amor.'

'You gave me a fright last night.'

'I'm sure. But don't worry. I feel fine. Here – come and help me into this dress.'

When I'm dressed Constancia goes downstairs to ready breakfast. I go to the study where I examine the aftermath of last night's mishap. I see with horror that the pages of the book have been charred by the oil which spilled from the lamp. Not only that, but the pages are sodden where the maid tossed water over the desk. I should have her whipped, but I know it wouldn't make me feel better. The book will dry, but how much has been lost by the damage?

'Puta madre.' Once again I want to scream.

I leave the book on the sill and crack open the window that the pages may dry.

After lunch, I tell Constancia to call the driver.

'But señora, you need to rest! Where must you go that is so important?'

'I have to go to the bookstore, mi amor. There are things that require my attention.'

'God forbid, no... in that case, I'm coming with you.'

I give her a hard look. 'Constancia, not today. I really don't have time.'

'But when? You promised to take me since opening, and you keep putting it off. Why? What is it I'm not allowed to see?'

I sigh. 'Fine. I'll take you tomorrow, alright? And I promise, you can even take away a few books for yourself. But please, mi amor, not today.'

She looks forlorn. I sit down next to her, put a hand on hers and kiss her on the temple. 'We'll go there tomorrow, together. Si?'

'Si.'

I squeeze her hand. There is great warmth in it. 'I really have to get going. I'll see you in the evening. And please, don't worry – I'm fine.'

Ryan is in the shop when I arrive. Several people are in the store browsing.

'Morning miss.'

'Morning, Mr. Ryan. You look bored. Would you rather be upstairs?'

'Oh no. Far too much excitement for me up there. I'm fine right here.'

'What are you reading today?'

'*The Life and Opinions of Tristram Shandy, Gentleman.*'

'I'm sure it's fascinating.'

The small bell on the wall behind the desk rings. I had it installed so the girls could call for help if they need. It means one of two things – there's trouble, or someone wants opium. Ryan puts down the book and gets up.

'I'll see to it, miss.'

I nod. 'I'll be in the office.'

He leaves, and I go up by the back stairs so I don't have to walk through the salon.

In the office, I take off my overcoat. Goat noises come through the wall. It makes me angry. I know how foolish it is, to get angry at the sounds of fucking in a brothel, but I can't help it. Passing the desk, I pick up the letter opener that sits there. It's of silver, Chinese origin, a thing of beauty. I go to the 'window' and part the curtain. Beyond the glass, I see the sight of a man, a 'gentleman', on top of Camila. He is fat and he is gross. A pig. My hand tightens around the jade handle of the letter opener. I place my thumb against the point and press. Filled with a sudden fury, I realise with little surprise it's the pig on the other side of the glass I want to plunge the silver blade into. Gut him. Slice him open.

Yet this is not the way. There are better ways to take possession of men.

*

The morning sun through the window warms the dining-room table. Constancia is taking tea, reading the paper. Her hair shines golden in the light. When her forehead is not creased with worry, she still looks young, even pretty. The lines of her face are aristocratic; were she not a servant she should certainly be a lady. The wife of a duke, perhaps. All I know is her father died on the crossing to Buenos Aires. Her mother, thrown upon hard times, was forced to put Constancia to work. Thus she came to me, as lady-in-waiting. But seeing her now as she sits so gracefully at the table, the arch of her back and the slope of her neck, I wonder... our positions could very easily be reversed. Does she intuit another self?

What strange conundrums life thrusts upon us. Did I want the life I was cast into? No. I always felt my true calling was elsewhere. I was not made for the court; such encumbrances were endured by necessity. Not all born into privilege are made for it. This is why I'm a disciple of the *caapi*, and why, night after night, I seek the wisdom that ayahuasca opens the doors to. I am a seeker and a seer. Women such as myself are few and far between, but we're born to it. It's in our blood. My *abuela* was one such woman; it's to her I owe my nature. And what is in our nature can never be denied.

Constancia turns to see me watching her. She blushes. 'Señora?'

I shake my head. 'Nada, mi amor. Nada.'

The sun fades. Like so much else in this country it is fickle. The golden hue of my dove's hair returns to its chestnut sheen. Her face loses its sharp aristocratic edges. Once again, she is my lady-in-waiting, and I her lady.

'Shall we take tea out this morning, by the river?'

She turns to me, her mouth in a grimace. 'English tea?'

I laugh. 'Oh mi amor, of course English tea – what else do they drink here?'

She shakes her head, her face disgusted.

'What should we drink then? Champagne?'

She scowls.

'Alright, fine. I'll take you to the shop.' Finally, a smile. I can put her off no longer. Once her curiosity has been satisfied, she'll lose all interest in the place anyway. 'When you're finished, get ready. We'll leave in an hour.'

We arrive shortly before lunch. Constancia is unimpressed with the area. She throws me a look of despair.

'Don't worry. It's only the street. The shop is just lovely. You'll see.'

Inside we find George, looking entirely out of place as the attendant of a bookshop. It may be that I have to hire someone else, a man dedicated to running the store. But that could lead to a whole new host of problems. I hadn't anticipated it would be a thriving business in itself. Even now there are a few men perusing the shelves – not just those passing through to the brothel.

'Hello George.'

He stands up awkwardly, clutching the two lapels of his jacket, looking from me to Constancia. 'Good afternoon, miss. A very good day to you.'

'Thank you, George. Is everything well here?'

'Very well, miss. Very well.' He has a great smile on his face as he turns the ledger to show me the day's takings.

'Oh... oh, very nice indeed.' I smile. Of course, it's a pittance compared to the money we're taking upstairs, but it's a joy to see.

George is positively proud. 'Well done George.'

'Thank you miss.'

'George, you know Constancia, of course.'

He bows. Constancia nods and smiles. Then she drifts away to browse the shelves. I give him a glance; he looks over his shoulder at the door. He understands. The girls know not to come down during working hours, but it would only take one mishap.

'What time will Mr. Ryan be here later?' I ask.

'Around six, miss,' George says. 'He's usually punctual.'

'Good.'

I drift over to Constancia and slip a hand through her arm. 'Anything take your eye?'

She shrugs. But I can see her eyes alight on the books with curiosity. She's enchanted. Something else from her former life. Had she the life she was born into, no doubt she'd be well-read and equipped with her own library. My dove is filled with a curiosity about the world that life in my service has kept her from. Maybe a few books will go a good way to satiating those unfulfilled needs.

The bell above the door rings and I turn. I know immediately from the countenance of the man that he's here for the brothel. I look at George, who has a panicked look on his face. The man approaches George, coughing nervously. George is looking at me. I step over.

'George... this is Mr...?'

The man coughs again. 'Mr. Ingleston.'

'Mr. Ingleston.' I take him by the arm and propel him toward George. 'Mr. Ingleston is the gentleman who ordered the set of encyclopedias a week ago. Why don't you take him in the back and see if you can find them.'

'Yes miss. Right away, miss.'

George goes out through the door; our 'guest' follows him inside. I turn to see that Constancia has been watching. She frowns.

I brush it away with a wave of the hand. 'Sometimes we don't have what they want on the shelves. Some men are harder to please than others.'

She's holding a book in her hand. I walk over and take it from her.

'I want this,' she says. *A History of Silk.*

'It's a relief to me, mi amor, that you are *extremely* easy to please.' I smile and take her by the arm. 'Come on then. Let's go for lunch.'

***

I scope the mad-lookin contraption standin in front on me. Never saw such a thing. Ain't it fine what the thinkers of this world come up with?

'So what is it?' I ask her.

She looks at me with a knowin kind of smile. The kind of smile makes a man shudder.

'It's a daguerreotype, Mr. Ryan.'

'A what?'

'A camera. It's going to take pictures.'

'Of...'

'Yes.'

'Aha. And what'd the pictures be for, miss?'

'That's not something you need to concern yourself with.'

Shit. A right messy business this. The kind of thing could get a man locked up for the rest of his known days. Possibly hangin on the end of a rope.

'Miss... I'm not going to end up in the gaol, am I?'

'Mr. Ryan, what I rely on here is discretion. The men that come here expect it too. And that's what I'll give them. This device here, and the pictures it will produce, are a form of—'

'Blackmail?'

'*Currency*. They'll be for my eyes only. The things you see here, and hear, I expect you to forget. It'll be as if they never happened. And if a time comes that one of these photos needs to be used, or put into circulation, then I assure you, you will not be privy to the consequences.'

'Am I to use this thing?' I point at the machine.

'You'll be here late in the evenings, when many of the most

influential clients will be visiting. I'm going to give you a list of names. If any of these men come to The Nightingale, then you'll have the job of taking pictures of them while they, you know, *frolic*.'

'As they make the beast with two backs.'

'The girls will be instructed. They'll be shown how to make it so the men are caught in compromising positions and with their faces on show. We'll develop a set of signals between you and the girls to make this happen without a hitch, and in a way the men are motionless long enough that we get clear pictures. This will be done rigorously, night after night. It'll be up to you to make sure we have a record of everything that happens here.'

I inhale and blow the air out in a slow whistle. 'Incredible, what can be done nowadays. So go on, show me how this thing works.'

That evening, I camp myself in the madam's office to test it out. I'd sat down with Lizzy to work out a way of signalling the picture was ready to be taken. Lizzy would lie crosswise on the bed, either on her back or on her front, facing the mirror. On the other side of it, I'd be sittin at the ready. She'd get him to stand still for a minute by havin the fella rub his mickey on her snatch, and while he was at that, I'd be settin the daguerreotype to take a picture of his grinning mug. Oh, it was devious. And what would happen after? That wasn't for the likes of me to know. I didn't want to, truth be told. Once the picture was taken, I never wanted to see it again.

Lizzy's outside with Lord Foley. He's havin a sup of brandy, but soon as that auld liquor hits him and starts the spark in his loins, Lizzy'll take him to the room. I know nothin about Lord Foley other than he has too much money and holds some place in the British government, but that's all I need to know. And if a man like that's playin around in a whorehouse and is likely to get in trouble for it, well that doesn't cause me no hardship at all.

I slip the bottle of laudanum from my pocket and take a sip. Can't help it, the nerves are on me.

When they come through the door on the other side of the glass, the shirt on him is half-unbuttoned and he's got the hunger in his eye.

I'm watchin, ya mongrel ye, I'm watchin...

Lordy Lord, with the wife at home, lady of the manor, and here he is suppin brandy and stickin his mickey into Limehouse whores. Makes you wonder – maybe the wife's got a face like a pony's hole. Maybe she's an auld bitch, never leavin off at him. Maybe with the manor house and the liveried servants and all the gowns and the jewellery, she's still not content with her lot in life. Aye, that'll be it. And the lord here, goin home to look at her with the face on her like a slapped haddock, he's thinkin, *Fuck this, who'd come home to this with a smile on his face? I'm goin to find my smiles elsewhere. I'm off down The Nightingale for a thruppenny whore and a sup, and maybe an old toke; only then will I go home and look at the miserable bitch.*

And fair play til him, I say. Life's too short. Take your pleasure where you may. Even if it's between the legs of a Limehouse lush.

Barely are they in the door and the lord has his hands all over my Lizzy. What can I say? Girl's gotta earn her keep. She ain't 'my Lizzy' but when I'm puttin silver in her palm. When it comes to coin, she's anyone's Lizzy.

She's rubbin his tired old tool, gettin him fired up. The jacket's off now. He's gruntin like a hog. Trousers open, the belly on him near hung down over his balls, the poor sod. What girl could look at that and still wanna put him inside her?

'Better close your eyes, sweetheart, if you're gonna let him climb up on ye,' I whisper. I pop myself under the black hood like the madam showed me to check the camera's all lined up proper.

Lizzy sits on the bed. Parts her thighs. Shows the lord the holy quim. He reaches out to grab it but she takes hold of his arm and says, 'Kiss me from here to here,' points from her toe to her snatch. *Oh yes, he's thinkin, I'll have me some of that...*

That's when Lizzy tilts her head back and blows me a kiss. Not the signal we'd agreed upon, but hey ho. I take the cap off the lens as Lizzy clamps her suitor's face between her two feet, him lickin and kissin and rubbin his peter over the back of her stockings.

114

'Jesus, Lizzy...'

God knows what the madam'll be wantin with such a picture. I know what I'd be doin if there was pictures of me like that doin the rounds, I'd be throwin myself into the Thames. But who gives a shit about a fella like me?

I'm there with the lens cap in hand, waitin for the lord to break free. Soon as he moves, the cap goes back on. There. Best I can do.

'God bless ya, Lizzy. You're a saint.'

I take the plate from the machine and put it in the box like the madam instructed. While I'm doin it, the noises from next door are getting heated.

'Oh, sir!'

'Oh sir' indeed. I'll give you 'oh sir'.

When the plate has sat in the box long enough, I take it out and dowse it in the salt solution, then rinse it off.

'Oh sir, a gentleman would *never*...'

Lizzy, puttin on the airs and graces. Ha! Not the woman I know, but the women know how to turn it on when it suits em.

Finally, I heat the plate to seal the image. When it's done, I hold it to the light. A touch blurry, but he's there alright, belly and balls all. Top hat on his head too. Can the face on him be made out? Not sure. I'll see what the madam says. Still, only my first time. It'll get better with each go. Soon there'll be a whole cupboard full of little picture plates – all those fat parliament pigs will be captured and filed away.

I hear the bell ring and I put down the plate. When I go out, Camila's there.

'I need black,' she says.

'Sure,' I tell her. 'Wait here.'

Chandoo, whores and brandy. Everything a man could wish for.

Gone five in the morning and the gentlemen have all cleared out and the whores are in recline, and I'm sitting with Lizzy and Camila in the lounge. We treat ourselves to a sup of brandy. As you do at five in the mornin. The girls are spent and I've a gentle buzz on, and the only thing missin from the evenin is a pillow and a pipe and an Oriental boy to light it. Maybe I'll saunter over to Joon Sing's after breakfast where they'll hearken the call, and feed the need of one who desires commune with the oriental liniments. But for now, we sit draped over the madam's fine upholstered recliner passin a cigarette between us. Camila's got one leg rested on my knee, her fine dark thigh only inches from my hand, the dark thigh of the Amazonian whore, the madness of many a sailor. The reason most of em put to sea was to shore up between two dark thighs such as these, and to wade in the gentle lap of continental rivers. Life therein. Many's the man who put sail down them rivers and never returned. Some were never seen again. I know one fella went into a whorehouse in Porto Alegre and never came out. We did have the lark about that: 'He got a sniff of a Rio quiff and never woke from it', or 'He was clean knocked out by a coconut', or 'They say he's still crawlin around up there'. Aye, we had banter. Probably dead, poor lad. Tried to take on too many at once and they ate him alive. One's all you need. Any more than that and you're askin for trouble. One pair of dark tremblin thighs is all you need, and when they open...

I turn to look at Lizzy. She's had it for the night, I can tell. Even if I was daft enough to do somethin under the madam's roof, tonight's not the night. Still, with the girls close, and the heat and the scents, and the brandy causin a stir, who can blame a man for the mind wanderin?

'Tell us a story, will ya?' Lizzy says. Her eyes are sleepy. She's ready for the kip.

'A story? The only stories I know are of boats and whores. What kind of story is it you wanna hear?'

'Have ye not any old Irish yarns ye can spin?' She raises the glass to her lips, but it's empty. With one hand, she seeks out the bottle on the floor.

'Irish yarns, is it?' I lift the bottle and pour her a drink, and top up Camila while I'm at it. 'Aye, why not. A quick one then.' I rattle around in the head for an auld story. One drifts up from the wastes of the mind. 'Right then, I'll tell you the story of Mish. Are you listenin, Camila?'

'Si.'

'So, Mish was the daughter of one of the ancient kings of Tara, Daire Dunn. One year, when Mish was not far into young womanhood, her father rode out to take on a foe in battle. Mish went along to witness her father's victory, but things did not turn out the way she expected. Instead, she watched in horror as her father was slain on the battlefield and beheaded—'

'Paddy, this is not—'

'Hush now, Lizzy, and lemme tell the story. So traumatised by the sight was Mish that she walked out into the midst of the battle and picked up her father's head and drank the blood that poured from it—'

'Aw, Paddy, fuck sake—'

'Quiet now, Lizzy, I told ya – you asked for a story and I'm givin you the story. Now, after drinkin her father's blood, Mish went mad, and she fled into the mountains above Tralee. They said she became a *nGealt*, a madwoman, and took on the appearance of a kind of beast, hairy all over and even growin wings so she could fly from tree to tree. She lived in the mountains and ate of the earth, and they say she even made congress with the beasts. There was many a terrible tale told about her in them parts.

'So pervasive was her presence in the mountains, and so frightening, that the people became terrified to venture in. Them that did regretted it, for they were attacked and driven from her territory, which soon became known as Sliebh Mish, or the "Mountains of Mish". Well, the king of them parts grew fed up and sent in his soldiers time and time again to hunt her down and execute her. But all his sallies failed. The soldiers were unable to rout Mish, and many men were lost in the attempt. You see, what he failed to realise is that, when you're fightin an enemy whose mind is that of a beast's and who has the power and the cunning of a beast, sometimes it's not enough to hunt it like for sport. Sometimes, it takes a whole new smarts to win over it.'

'And so?' Lizzy says. 'What did they do?'

I yawn. 'You know what, Lizzy, I think I've proper forgotten how the story finishes.'

I take a punch to the arm, a punch with far more power than a drunk and exhausted whore should wield.

'Fuck you, Paddy.'

unto myself the holy sacrament

In my study, I stand over the chest. It lies open. In it, the ingredients of my *caapi*. Other things, too – hashish given me by a visitor from Morocco. I tried it once. It was pleasant, but didn't have the depth that *caapi* does. If I medicate, I want to encounter myself: even the fear, horror and madness. What's the purpose of this life if one isn't forced to examine the true meaning of one's existence? What's a life lived for pleasure alone? Most people go a lifetime and never consider who or what they are. This is a life wasted. I want to know all, even if it means embracing the most profound terrors. I have the heart.

Or do I? I haven't touched the *caapi* since last time. Last time I encountered Yaguareté and was defeated. He's the last. All other gods of the heart and soul I have conquered, only the Jaguar stands in my way. How to defeat him? He must be faced in the dark jungles of the mind; there, where he is king. I have not yet the fortitude. I am not the woman I need to be. I need the knowledge of the *karai*, the one I killed, whose soul now resides within me amongst all the others, all those I have subsumed. Only Yaguareté remains.

I reach into the chest and take out a knife. It's a beautiful piece, a long thin blade and the handle jade and silver. I can scarce remember where it came from; maybe it was gifted to my mother by one of her many admirers, or maybe it was in my family generations further back. No matter. I was always drawn to it. Before I left my father's house, I made sure I took it. Some possessions speak to you, and those which do must be cherished. Those which do not may be discarded. All the things I care for in this life, I brought here in a couple of chests. Apart from Constancia, but she is not a possession. Some things you must not take ownership of.

I put the tip of the blade to my finger, and apply pressure until a prick of blood forms on the skin. I taste it. It's warm and metallic. *Sanguineous.* Can one take oneself as 'communion'? Am I unto myself the holy sacrament, body and blood? One may consume someone else with a mere taste of their blood or flesh. If only it were as easy with oneself. Why should it be so? Isn't some part of our soul contained in each atom? How then can we not consume and know ourselves?

I drop the knife on the desk. I grow tired of myself so easily these days.

Downstairs in the drawing room, Constancia is reading.

'Can I sit with you, mi amor?'

'Si, señora.' She closes the book and looks at me, eyes blank.

'What's wrong? Are you reading about silk?'

'Yes...' She looks at the book and shakes her head.

'What have you learned? Tell me...'

'I can scarce repeat it...'

'Go on. I think I can take it.'

She shakes her head again and opens the book. 'I... ah, señora, it's horrific.'

'Well now you have to tell me. I'm intrigued.'

'There's this story about the emperor Zhengde in China. He was a filthy man and had hundreds of concubines in his court. But even this wasn't enough...' She stops.

'Go on,' I urge her.

'He got bored of his concubines and started dressing up as a commoner and going outside the palace, roaming the streets and visiting brothels the poor folk used. Then one day he became obsessed with eternal life. He started kidnapping girls from the street, thousands of them, and kept them prisoner in his palace, feeding them only mulberries and dew to keep them pure.'

'But why?'

'So he could drink their... monthly fluids.'

'Good god.'

'It's horrendous. Lots of them died from starvation. Then some girls grew tired. They decided to kill him. One night, while his was with his favourite consort, the concubine withdrew and fifteen girls snuck into his chamber. They tried to strangle him with silk threads from their hair, and when that didn't work, they throttled him with a silk curtain cord.'

'Did he die?'

'No. He was too fat. One of the concubines panicked and told the empress, and she had all the girls killed by cutting them up a little piece at a time.'

'Oh my.'

We sit in silence as she looks at me, incredulous that such evil exists in this world.

You are pure, mi amor, and you will always be pure. Let not this world sully you.

Late the next evening I'm in The Nightingale, in the office with George. The daguerreotype is trained on the window. Behind it, Mary and one of our clients. George can barely watch. His modesty is disarming.

'Miss, I ain't sure this sits right wi' me. This is a queer business, I has to say. Now, I don't care what a man does in his private hours, god knows I done enough messing meself, but I think he should be able to do it in private, if you get my meaning, miss.'

'George...' I sigh. 'I know you feel bad about this, but I need you to understand, that these are not good men—'

'These is ministers, miss...'

'Exactly. Now listen, I want you to understand something. Believe it or not, I grew up around men like these, and I can assure you, they don't give a damn about you or your wife or your unborn child. The only thing your son will ever be to them is a boy stupid enough to take a rifle in his hand and go off and get killed so these men can make more money off the back of dead soldiers. Because that's what you and every other man in this country are to those who run it. Don't you see? They don't give a damn about you. They don't care if you live or die. These are the men that run this country...' I point through the window. 'See for yourself, how they conduct themselves in private, when they think no one's watching. See how they treat these girls? Do you think these men are worthy of respect?'

George is silent. But I can see his little brain ticking away. Fortunately for me, right at this minute there's a man on the other side of the mirror acting like a beast: pulling Luara's hair and tearing at her stockings. George is watching. George is disgusted. I drive it home.

'That could be your *wife*, George, or any other woman in this country. They do as they please, take what they want, and they don't give a damn what anyone thinks.'

'Bloody bastards,' he mutters.

'You're doing no wrong by doing as I ask. And these pictures will probably never see the light of day. All the same, they may come in useful in a sticky situation. I do it as much to protect my girls as anything else.'

'Alright miss.'

And that is all it takes.

She squirms under his fat frame as he slides back and forth over her. She makes all the noises a whore makes from necessity. Or boredom. How dull it all must get after the third or fourth time each day. After a while there can only be numbness. Whores need to be first-class actresses. It's not their body they're selling – their bodies are merely the means of exchange. They're selling a fantasy, a four-minute make-believe. Sometimes it's tragic and sometimes farcical. Sometimes, like now, it's quite disgusting. It's the least intriguing of all our human instincts, and when one sees it too much, it is outright repulsive.

I myself never took great pleasure in it. When I did it, more often than not I had some ulterior motive. Not to say I don't take any joy in it, but it's something that requires a lot of things to go right, when so many things are of the tendency to go wrong. On one level, it's a complex mechanical act with extremely sophisticated machinery, and all things must work in harmony if there's to be any 'success'. On another level, of course, it's a base copulation, a mere carnal spasm. If only people understood the true intentions of the act, they wouldn't go to it with such gross abandon.

'Oh, *sir...*'

The same refrains, day after day, night after night. A whorehouse caterwauling. A bawdy chorus repeated nightly in a musical that never ends.

As the man spends himself Lizzy pulls his hair and jerks, raising his head to the mirror. She holds him like that as I take off the lens cap. He's pinned, his face a mask of grotesque ecstasy. Certainly there'll be no mistaking such a face, even if the picture does come out blurred. Far from the image of him that no doubt hangs over his fireplace. Far from the face his wife knows, or his fellow lords. In this instant, a man is truly exposed. His face will reveal his greatest fallacies and fears: the megalomaniac will wear a mask of triumph, the romantic a face of sorrow, the misogynist a face of disgust. It's written in every screaming line of his visage.

Lizzy lets his head drop and I replace the lens cap. Time to process the plate.

When it's all finished, I take the box from the cupboard and place it on the desk. Inside is the collection we've made thus far. Some of them will be reused – the images are simply too vague and ill-defined to be of any use. Others are not. Others show in sinister detail men in their 'primal nakedness', men who, day to day, sit at the helm of state. But these too, for all their influence, are still only men. Men naked are each the same as the next. Class does not matter, wealth has no bearing. Unclothed, we are all but beasts.

I've just put the box back in the cupboard when there's a knock at the door. Ryan comes in.

'Evening, miss...'

'I was just getting ready to go home, Mr. Ryan. What is it?'

'You know that fella you showed me the photo of, told me to let you know straight away if he ever came in?'

'Yes...'

'Well he's here.'

My heart quickens. 'Has he said what he wants?'

'He won't say, miss. He wants to talk to the madam.'

'He said that?'

'Yes.'

Why would he want to talk to the madam? My going out there is not an option.

'Mr. Ryan, I need you to go out and make excuses. Tell him the madam is not available, that she'll be here next time he visits. Ask him what his pleasure is, and how we can accommodate him.'

'Yes miss.'

'And Mr. Ryan – say nothing of me.'

*

'Lord Palmerston will see you now.'

'Thank you.'

I step into his office. He stands and greets me, and gestures to a seat. I sit down opposite as he orders tea.

'So good of you to come in to see me, Ms. Azul. I hope I haven't inconvenienced you.'

'Not at all. It's not every day one is summoned to see a foreign dignitary. You do me an honour.'

'An honour, I hope, which you will continue to indulge me in. I pray you won't take offence, but it seems your presence here in London may be more troublesome than we had originally envisioned.'

'Oh? How so?' More direct than last time. Perhaps he grows tired that I'm not the bargaining chip he hoped I'd be.

'I've had a visit from Señor Moreno. It appears that Buenos Aires has been made aware of your presence here on our shores. We don't think they know exactly where, or how, but they have received intel that we are sheltering you. And that, Ms. Azul, presents us with a problem.'

'Are they aware, Lord Palmerston, because you have made them aware?'

'No.'

'You haven't let slip through one of your emissaries, perhaps?'

'And what would be the benefit to me – to *us* – of that?'

His footman knocks and enters. When he has dispensed with the tea, he bows and leaves. Palmerston watches me throughout. I hold his gaze. Politicians cannot be trusted. When it comes to their word, they speak with forked tongues. In between their words, one may discern their true intent. It takes a diamond mind to see through the duplicitous weave of a statesman. Their entire posture is performative. In that, they are not so different from whores.

'Well, regardless of how our friends have found out about my refuge here in London, can I count on your discretion that there'll be no further cooperation between your government and the emissaries of Buenos Aires?'

Palmerston picks up the cup and saucer and drinks. Ignoring the way he speaks, or his dress, or the way he fixes his hair, one can always tell an Englishman by the way he takes his tea.

'You can,' he says.

'For that, I am thankful,' I say. If not entirely convinced.

'Ms. Azul...' He replaces the cup in the saucer and puts it on the table. '...may I ask, and I believe that up until this point I've been a model of discretion – what was your reason for coming here, and what is it you hope to do while a guest in this country?'

Such questions are the height of hypocrisy and make me indignant. But I don't show it. 'Are you afraid, sir, that I'll come to rely on the British state for support?'

'Not at all.' He dismisses me with a wave of the hand. 'I'm merely asking your purpose in being here.'

I sigh. 'I'm a woman of means, sir, and I've come here for asylum, that's all. I have no *purpose* here, as you say, only that of living a peaceful life, and to the extent that's possible, an enjoyable one.'

'So you have an income?'

'A sizeable one.'

He flexes his neck, raising his face to the ceiling. His affectations wear thin. Viscount. Statesman. Gentleman. Frequenter of brothels. *What are your vices, sir? What delinquencies enjoys a man such as yourself? Tell me and I'll provide.*

'Well...' He picks up his cup and sips. This time, his mouth twitches, as if he has tasted something that displeases him. He puts the tea down. '...all things considered, I'm not sure I'm in a position to help you more. If you were more forthcoming about your intentions here—'

'As I've already said, all I desire is a quiet life. And to that end, I ask you not to interfere with Buenos Aires in my affairs.'

The words offend him. There's a flash of consternation in his eyes which he quickly suppresses. Perhaps he's not accustomed to being spoken to in such a manner by a woman. A *foreign* woman.

He stands up. 'Ms. Azul, thank you very much for coming today. Please be reassured that I am not prying into your affairs, but I'm merely concerned that your time here is a fruitful one. I must put the wellbeing of my country at the fore. As you know, there are already many problems between London and Buenos Aires, and we cannot afford to create more. Rest assured, you have my discretion. But we cannot conceal your whereabouts indefinitely. Moreno, acting on your father's orders no doubt, is determined to make contact. And we can have no part in that parley. If you want my advice, you would be better to get ahead of the situation and reach out yourself.'

'Thank you, Lord Palmerston. Your frankness is always welcome. But you don't need to worry about me. I am a woman, but I'm not defenceless. I can hold my own when it comes to international relations. And when the time comes, I'll do my utmost to contribute to the better relations of our countries.'

I get up and extend a hand. We shake.

'Madam, we have no eternal allies, and we have no perpetual enemies. Our interests are eternal and perpetual, and those interests it is our duty to follow.'

Truly the words of a politician.

VIII

clocks stilled by the emptiness of night

There's nothing offends me so much as a cunt in fine clothing.

'And who are you?' he says. Ignorant fucker gives me a glare.

'I work for the madam. She sends her apologies. She's unavailable.'

'What's an Irishman doing in a fine establishment like this?'

'Would you rather talk to an Englishman?'

'I'd rather talk to the madam.'

I nod. 'As I say. She extends her apologies. She'll do her best to be here next time you visit. In the meantime, can I get you something? Will you take a brandy?'

'Go on then.' He look around, eyes alighting on a gentleman sitting on a divan with Luara and Camila.

I turn and walk away. Prick. They don't half make it clear, these arseholes, that they're above the rest of us. I'd like to take em all, to a man, out back and give em a whippin. Perhaps I'm not the man for workin at The Nightingale after all. Could be I'll get myself in trouble.

I go over to Mary and tell her to bring a drink to Palmerston. Then I go back to the madam.

'So?'

'He's back again, but he just wants a brandy. Doesn't seem too bothered about the girls.'

The madam shakes her head. 'No, that's not the problem. He's more careful than the rest. He needs to know who's running the place.

He needs to know that anything happening here will stay secret. He won't do a thing until he meets the madam.'

'Are you gonna go talk to him then?'

'Absolutely not. I'll need to hire someone else to do it. I should have done it sooner. A place like this needs a face, and it can't be me. We need a woman. A lady.'

'One of the girls not up to the job?' I gesture with a tilt of the head beyond the walls.

'No, Mr. Ryan. The girls are all too young. I need someone older. Someone who can carry herself. Someone tough.'

'Well, I can't help you with that, miss.'

'Don't worry. I'll find someone.'

'I've no doubt you will.'

A couple of days later, she does, and into The Nightingale appears Miss Emily. The madam explains who Miss Emily is, what she's gonna do around the place. Suddenly the girls are all alert, like they ain't got the run of the place no more. Miss Emily's older, got a touch of worldliness about her. God knows where the madam found her, but I guess if she wants to put the gentlemen at ease, then I can't see a better woman for the job. She makes Georgie all coy – maybe she reminds him of his mother. Big Georgie, the sailor returned in search of a bosom. Ain't no shortage of bosoms here. You're in a whorehouse, big fella.

'Miss Emily will be here from late afternoon to early morning,' the madam explains. 'That means she'll be here through most of your shift, Mr. Ryan, which will leave you free to take care of the door. And the opium, of course.'

The opium. Five weeks and I haven't hit the pipe, just been suppin at the laudanum, but that very night watchin the gentlemen toke I get the hunger for it. I finish my shift at six in the mornin and hop on a boat upriver and find myself back in Limehouse. Joon Sing's, always open to the weary traveller. And now wouldn't it be I've no shortage of silver in my pocket, a man of means, no more lumpin guano – shovellin shit in other words – now that I've a fine pair of shoes on me and a pocketful of coin. Doors are always open when you're flush.

The sun just up but the room's dark, the boy kickin out all the relics of the night's broken quintessence, men with the pockets and the hearts emptied and with the wind blowin through their souls like a warm sirocco, turfed out into the cold street where they'll struggle to find their feet and trip and traipse their way into next evenin, when perchance they may have coin for another slumber. But that is tomorrow and today is today, and I take my place on one of the empty dream-filled pillows, and I even take off my shoes because I'm here for the long-haul – 'Wake me before five' I tell the boy, but he just looks at me with them inky oriental eyes, doesn't know time, his days not marked by the ebb and flow of the tides or the rising and setting of the sun, all he knows is here, this room, and the smoky somnambulance of the chandoo charlies, the seekers and the sorrowful, and the horse-mad denizens of the parlour. 'Before five,' I say and roll my finger like the hand of a clock, as if the boy'll understand my foreign digitating, he speaks no tongue that I or anyone else can decipher, then I sound out five bongs like a clock, mad now, mad with the whiff of the smoke, the tetanus shudder creeping up my spine, alerting me to the fact that, moments from now, I'll be sailin sweet on smoky streams. The boy is lookin at me. Am I still wavin, gesticulating? I laugh and lie back on the pillow, the scent of the night on it, Brilliantine, saliva and sorrow and a thousand shore-cast dreams. Maybe I'm stoned already. Stoned on weeks of deprivation, weeks of dreamin, haunted by the ghosts of my desires and regrets. What virtue in denial? We are but our instincts, our vices our victories. Readin too much, my head swimmin with the cant reliquaries of wisdom, 'enlightenment' as they've christened it. I wonder, do any of these men who preach enlightenment imbibe of the pipe? Have they smoked the wisdom of the night on sweat-stained pillows? Do they have the reek of madness beneath the finery of their words?

The boy is back. He gazes at me, eyes unblinking and with the heaviness of men's dreams. Then we get down to business, silently and with the solemnity of old sages. Wizened in our way, torrid in our desires. The ken of timeless deserts in us. Ticking clocks and the blaze of burning suns nothin to men like us. Our senses have been scorched, our nerves cut raw – we have seen the palace of the diamond poets. This is why the boy is silent. The smoke fills my lungs. All at once, I am sage and my night is timeless. I know not where I go and remember not where I venture, but when I awake, I have but one picture in mind: the streets of London barren but for the low-hung fog and the silent stone halls smart with the dew, clocks stilled by the emptiness of night and devoid of all sound but the silent eddies of the river, and at the heart of the city, a ghost, an intruder, paws soft on the cobblestone of the city streets: a jaguar, the night's eye, come to grow vast on a multitude of souls.

*

Young the morning yet. Nigh on dawn and the last of the revellers are tetchy. The whores all drunk and salty and itchin for bed. Madam Emily has em drainin the pockets of the night's dishevelled. Cupshot, they dispense the last of their silver for a flagon of brandy or a grope of a tit. Luara and Camila are draped over a lardy banker, Mary sits fey with a gentleman of Her Majesty's government. Lizzy, alone on a recliner, eyes droopin. Miss Emily is in the office, cashin up. I sit down beside Lizzy, roll up a smoke, and hold it out to her. She pushes it away.

'I feel sick,' she says.

'Wanna get some fresh air?'

Without a word, she pushes herself to her feet.

I get up and slip a hand through the crook of her arm. We go past the office and out a door that takes us onto a small balcony overlookin a courtyard, where the buildings behind The Nightingale come together to form a grim little close that shelters coal bunkers and an outhouse, and a dumpin ground for every manner of London detritus. The stink of coal and piss rises up on the night air. The sky above clouded and wary; candlelight behind a curtain opposite where the shadows of a husband and wife coalesce beyond the window. Out to the west, the rooftops of St. Stephen and St. Peter, the city a gaunt array of slant and parapet. The night tarries in the city's grim solace. Lizzy throws her wrap around her shoulders and sits back against the wall. I sit beside her. Somewhere a cat shrieks.

'Hey Lizzy,' I say, then I light the cigarette and pass it to her. She takes it and sucks on it and passes it back. I make no attempt to continue my line of thought, and she doesn't ask, so we sit and smoke the cigarette down to the bone in earthly silence.

After a time the night weighs upon us. She says, 'I got this weird feelin, Paddy, like...'

'Aye?' I say.

'Like, I dunno, like someone's watchin me all the time. And it's not creepy like, it's comfortin almost, but it's just like very strange is all.'

'When did it start?'

'When I came to work 'ere.'

'Lizzy,' I start again, 'you wanna tell me what happened that night, you know...' and I peter off like I don't know how to tell it.

'What night?'

'You remember the fella out in the street outside? The one you put your hands on...'

'I put my hands on a lot of fellas, Paddy, but never choked someone's charly outside The Nightingale.'

'Lizzy – you killed a fella, for chrissake. Would you listen to me n—'

'Fuck is you on about?' she says.

I look at her. Look at her long and hard. It's clear – she has no idea what I'm talkin about. None.

'Lizzy... I dumped the body in the river. The madam had me do it. He had a knife in his throat. You stuck it in him.'

I stare at her good and long, then she bursts out laughin. A tired and wretched laughter that shakes her from head to toe.

'Has you been smokin the madam's tar, has ya?'

I laugh too. 'Aha! Ah Lizzy, what the fuck am I on about... it's late,

Jesus Christ, it's late. Get me to me bleedin bed...'

'Lay off the tar, Paddy. Your head's near away.' She puts a hand on my knee to get up.

'Hey Lizzy, before you go...'

She blows and puffs. 'What now?'

'Did the madam ever stick anything in ya, like her nail, or a pin or somethin?'

'A pin?' She looks away out at the sky for a second then back at me. 'A pin?'

I shake my head. 'Never mind.' I get up and take her hand and pull her to her feet. 'Come on, let's get you to bed.'

'Don't you be finkin you'll be crawlin in wiv' me, you mongrel.'

'The man's too tired for it, Lizzy. Too tired by far.'

Who can I tell? Lizzy's mind's cleaned of the deed. Can't tell George, he hasn't it in his heart to listen to dark confessions. The madam? Twas for her the deed was done, I'm sure of it. 'Do this for me, Mr. Ryan, and say nothing of it.' *Aye, dump a body for ya? Certainly, miss. Sure why wouldn't I? I'll take this fella with the throat on him cut and wrap him up and sail him out on a barge and dump him downriver. Why wouldn't I?*

Jesus fucking Christ... maybe I need my head tested. Maybe I need committing. Took too easy to it, I did. Wasn't the hard task at all, and I didn't wonder for a second who he was, or where he came from, or had he a wife and a child to go back to like Georgie. Maybe it was cause he wore a top hat. Easier when it's a rich fella, is it? I've no idea. Seen a fair few put in the ground before. Never troubled me too much.

Not the proper place for a body the river, mind. The sea, maybe, but not the river.

Right before dawn, George shows. I'm in the store below with a book and a lamp, the eyes on me threatenin to close. Upstairs, the sleep is on em. Soon it'll come for me.

'Mornin, Paddy.' George claps his hand and blows into them.

'Go on upstairs and get yourself a cup of tea. One of the girls left a taste of cheap whiskey here if you're needin something to warm ya.'

I open the drawer on the desk to show him the bottle and wink.

'Might be needin it, Paddy. Might do.' He pulls up a chair and sits across from me. The scarf tight around his neck. His head sits heavy and fat on his shoulders, like the tip of a butcher's sausage. His breath fogs the air. 'What be the news then? Any colour above last night?' He tilts his head ceilingward.

'Not much at all,' I say. 'One louse got swift on the gin and tried to ride Miss Emily.' I shake my head and whistle. 'Won't be doin that again in a hurry.'

'Ain't no soft woman that,' George says. 'Lord or lumper, that's a woman requires respect. What'd she do?'

I smile. 'She took him by the ear and led him to the door. Thought she was gonna bend him over her knee and give him a whippin.'

Georgie chuckles.

I lean across the table. 'Hey Georgie... did the madam ever stick a needle in ya?'

He raises an eyebrow. Then he turns to glance over his shoulder. 'A needle, you say?'

'Aye. Like, just the prick of a needle. You mightn't have even felt it.'

He shakes his head all slow like. 'Can't say as she has. Like, I fink I woulda felt it, ya know. Why?'

I wave a hand. 'Nothin, forget I asked. I think I'm just in need of kip. The night is heavy on me, know what I mean? You have an auld sip of brandy here and there, and before you know it, voices be talkin to ya, ain't that the way?'

'Voices... you be hearing voices now, do ya? Women sticking needles in ya, now you's hearing voices... go on. Go and get out of here. You's needing the sleep, bloody right you is.'

I snap the book shut. 'Sleep it is then, Georgie. Sleep it is.' I get up and put the book back on the shelf, and take my overcoat and throw it on. 'I'll be off then.'

'Cold out there, Paddy. Make sure and wrap up.'

'Aye. Colder than a witch's tit it is, fella. Get some of that whiskey in ya. I'll be seein ya later.'

He tips his cap as I take to the door. The bell sounds in the dark as the door shuts, and I'm off on scant feet into the night.

With the night dyin I tramp home. Joon Sing's is callin again, but I've half a bottle of laudanum in my pocket. Joon Sing's will still be callin tomorrow, and the night after. Tonight I'll reacquaint myself with the bed. And with a sup or two of the bottle, there'll be dreams too. What's a night without dreams? Nights a man can be too cold to dream, but with a little somethin to warm him, they come strong enough. This life ain't nothin without dreams. Times it's the only thing a man has to live for. I squeeze the bottle through the breast pocket of my coat, just to reassure myself. My breath fogs on the crisp air. Somewhere south a boat's horn bellows, a howl over a city that doesn't want to wake.

I turn onto Horseferry Road heading towards Regency Street. Passin an alley in front of the hospital, somethin smashes into me and I'm thrown into the road. A boot in my face. Kick into the stomach. I curl up and roll away, but the feet keep hoofin into me.

'Bastards!' I shout.

One of em grabs me by the lapel of the jacket and hauls me forward. A hand goes inside the pocket. I stick a finger in his eye and he screams. Then I feel the sharp hotness in my gut. There's two of em. I emit a choking moan and grip my side as the two of em rifle my pockets.

'You facking cunt, givus what ya got...'

'Fuck have you gone and done...' I whisper. He shuts me up with a belt to the face.

The pockets ransacked, one of em gets up and spits, and turns. 'Fack 'im.' The other follows.

'Fuck did ya do?' I moan, as the hot blood oozes through my fingers.

The Curse of Ka'akupe

Silent and alert, the two young boys followed the trail of blood over the tangled crawl underfoot. Their caked brown feet made obeisant communion with the earth, spears held apoke from their bodies, eyes alive to the thousand-shade green of the plaintive jungle. A rustle from the undergrowth gave them pause. They stopped. Listened. No word or glance was shared between them, yet by silent assent, they moved on. Only one moon afore, the infant son of Ka'akupe had been plucked from his bed in the dark assail of night. The villagers talked. Said he'd been transformed into animal and was now afoot in the jungle. They said there was killing in the air. And now the blood.

One of the young boys stopped and dipped his finger in the blood trail and put it to his lips, then he looked at his friend and shook his head. The boy, perturbed, flicked the hand, the spear now in an overhand grip, the weapon at head height, the point of it out before him poised to transfix. The other boy, spear aloft, stopped the younger with a touch on the upper arm, then moved out ahead of him similarly astance. A moan up ahead caused the two of them to bristle.

Taking crouch behind a bush, they peered across the morass. They scanned the ground, the trees too, for a good hunter knew the threat from above. Spears ready, they moved again, feet now braced against the earth.

The man lay at the foot of a jacaranda, hand gripping his side, blood oozing through his muddied fingers. He was conscious but fevered.

He did not hear the boys draw near, did not open his eyes. The boys saw him and knew, even if they prayed in their hearts it was not so. The man was without knife, without spear. Naked but for the red body paint that decorated his limbs, and the blood he was bathed in, his body had the appearance of one who was not long for this earth and destined to return to the ancestors. The boys drew close. One poked the man in the shoulder with his spear. The man's head rolled from one side to the other, and he mumbled, *'Tapeho Rahab rógape, penohe chupe ha ihentekuérape.'* The boys glanced at each other. The man's hand fell from his side. Seeing the gaping wound thereon, the younger turned to the elder, uttering a single word: *'Yaguareté.'*

They turned and fled.

When they had returned with some of the older men and had brought the injured man back to the village, he was placed in front of the hut of the *karai*. All the villagers came out to see the spectacle, and they gaped at the horrific gash in the man's side and whispered that it was indeed the work of Yaguareté, and when Ka'akupe came and saw what had happened, a great keening came over her and she was taken away by some of the older women who enclosed her in her hut and prayed to Teyú Yaguá that the woman be granted peace and the soul of her infant son may show mercy to the village and those who lived there.

When the *karai* returned he took the man inside his hut and built a fire, and treated the man's wounds and performed rituals, yet when all this came to naught, he summoned the grandmother of Ka'akupe.

'Eremína pe kue kuñakarai,' he said, and the villagers knew it was serious because the old man hated the old woman, and if he was calling for the old woman it was because the curse of the jaguar was beyond his power.

After a day and a night, the old woman emerged from the trees. She came alone and with the scent of the jungle on her, dressed in naught but the frightening markings of her slavery. Her skin like stretched leather and her paps like two dried wineskins, her appearance in the village filled them with trepidation. None spoke to her and she looked none in the eye. She disappeared into the hut of the *karai* as the villagers watched from a distance; the two boys who'd found the man still sat sentinel outside the hut of the *karai*.

The old man had left the village the night before. The old woman found the hut empty save for the body on the ground and the stench of sickness. The man was close to death. His soul was already departed on the journey even if his heart still beat with a grasping stubbornness. From a pouch that hung between her breasts, the woman took out her herbs and mixed them in a clay pot, spitting into it and burning it on the fire until it was a thick black paste. When it had dried, she applied it to the man's side and wrapped it, and laid a blanket over him. Still he had not stirred.

She waited til nightfall. When the moon was in the sky and the macaw had gone quiet and the capybara was setting out on his perambulations, the woman lit her fire and sang her dark song and clothed the man in the smoke of the black flame, and when the cries and the howls were rent from him the village snuffed out their candles and prayed, prayed that Yaguareté might release them. The man howled and village sent their prayers to the god, and when morning came, a garrotte quietude was the only evidence of the night's violence.

They did not see her leave. She departed without a word. And when the first of them left their huts to stoke their ailing fires, the death aura was off the village and they knew in their hearts that Yaguareté was a killer of men but that he had mercy in his heart too, and they prayed that their children might have the strength and the heart of the fiercest of gods.

IX

without raiment or perfume or position

Miss Emily glances up from the daguerreotype when I come in the door; there's a look of glee on her face. She likes the work. Takes great pleasure in it, in fact. She grins and turns back to the camera, and when I come up next to her, I see Carla on the other side of the glass with a client. She has his hands tied behind his back and he's bent over the bed, his mouth gagged. She holds a cane in her hand.

'What's she doing to him?'

Miss Emily doesn't take her eye off the scene on the other side of the mirror. 'Giving him just what he paid for,' she says.

'My my.' Perhaps I'm too naive for this job. I had no idea men's desires took such turns. 'If that's what he's paying for, then I guess we provide it. Carla seems to be enjoying herself.'

'You put a cane in a poor girl's hand, madam, and she will extract every ounce of suffering she has ever endured.' Miss Emily smiles. I appreciate the logic. It's not often one gets to take out one's frustrations on those above them. There's a kind of fury written on Carla's face that betrays her; in this moment, this fleeting moment, she is regent. She reaches forward and takes the man by the hair, and pulls back until his neck is taut. She holds him.

'There, right there...' Miss Emily takes the cap off the lens. 'What a beautiful sight. Look at his eyes...'

Is it a symptom of power, the impulse to debasement? Does every man of station have a deep yearning to be cast down, to have his true self shown to him? What does he see, this lord, as he gazes into the mirror and beholds the wretched creature staring back, and the whore standing over him, cane in hand? Perhaps this is the crux of his desires. Perhaps this is man stripped clean, without raiment or perfume or position. Man laid bare. Do they all yearn, in the very depths of their soul, to see themselves like this?

Carla beats him across the back and he grunts like a dog. I turn away as Miss Emily slips the cap back on the lens and proceeds to remove the plates from the camera. She puts it in the box where it is exposed to mercury and lets it sit.

'I haven't seen Mr. Ryan,' she says when she's closed the box. 'Ain't he 'ere tonight?'

'George is having trouble locating Mr. Ryan. He didn't come in at six as he should have. He'll turn up. Perhaps he's had some trouble we're not aware of.'

'Oh? Why do you say that?'

'Just a hunch. Mr. Ryan is very dependable. I've known him since I came here. In fact, he came over on the boat from Argentina with me. He was my porter. He hasn't let me down yet.'

'Well, let's 'ope he turns up soon.'

The sound of the cane on bare flesh resounds through the walls.

'How many men do we have in?' I ask.

'Just three. Last night after midnight we had eight at one point. It was busy. Maybe we need another girl or three, watcha think?'

I sit down at the desk and take out the ledger. 'Maybe we do. We can probably accommodate another two – there's a room at the back that'll convert. But any more and things will get crowded. This is a discreet establishment. We can't afford to have our business spilling out into the street. I want to keep it small, and exclusive. Let's make sure things don't get away from us.'

'You could always open another,' Miss Emily says. 'Or three, or four. Each could have a theme. One could be oriental like, with Chinese girls, and another with local girls, and so on. You get the picture. No reason why you shouldn't grow. Maybe even in different cities, eventually.'

I smile. 'I like the way you think. Let's sit down and talk more about this. I feel you have good ideas, Miss Emily.'

She takes the copper plate from the mercury and rinses it with sodium thiosulphate then with distilled water.

'I'll happily give you my ideas, madam. I'm not short of a few. Always wanted to be in business, like yourself. It just so 'appened I was never in a position to chase it. But I'm grateful to be here. I'm too old to be on the game, but I know how the business works and I run a tight ship. I know just how to 'andle the girls. The men too, as it 'appens.'

'I have faith in you.'

When she has rinsed the plate, she douses it in a gold chloride solution then holds it over the candle. She tilts it to see the image and smiles. 'Look...'

I nod. 'They're getting better every day. I can even tell who he is. Wonderful work.'

'Thank you.'

Having perused the accounts, I put the ledger back in the desk. Then I go to the cabinet by the wall and open the locked drawer and take out the money box. There is paper money. An entirely token form of exchange, but it's easily transferred to something more solid. But that's not all. There's silver. And there's gold. I roll up the notes and put them, along with the coins, in my purse. Takings are increasing day upon day. The girls are bringing in money, and so is the opium. I have not made a bad choice of business. Vice is worth its weight in gold.

There's a knock on the door and Lizzy enters.

'Miss, I need some of the black stuff.'

'Come in.'

I go to the cabinet and open it. On top of the chest is a smaller box. I take it out. Ryan has prepared one of the opium cakes into 'grains', each a single serving of the drug. I put one in Lizzy's hand. She nods and leaves. When she's gone, Miss Emily says, 'And that's another thing, madam – you need to separate the whores and the opium. If they come to smoke, they don't fuck. And if they fuck, they don't wanna smoke. Do you see what I mean?'

I nod thoughtfully. 'Yes, you're absolutely right. I need two establishments.'

'Or more. But you need to separate the one from the other. They don't mix. Men like to keep their pleasures separate, if you get me.'

'I do.'

She's right. I've tried to do too much with one place. At very least I need two different lounges. The ones that like opium don't touch the girls, but they like the attention. I could open an opium house staffed entirely by sultry and mysterious Chinese girls, whose only job is to serve men their fix. I'd need some that spoke English, mind you. Or maybe not. Maybe they only need administer the medicine the men come for.

'Would you say we could house the two in the same building?' I ask Miss Emily.

She shrugs. 'Sure. Maybe on different floors. I'd say it'd be better if they were in different places, know what I mean? Because they both should have a certain *je ne sais quoi*, if you get me. They need to feel different, to give each man what he desires. You know, like, the man that comes for whores wants a drink and some music, because he's nervous, and the brandy helps him relax. And the man comes to smoke wants a nice dark room and a bit of quiet, so he can dream lovely dreams. That's why t'would be better if they occupied different establishments, see.'

I smile and nod. 'I may have gotten more than I bargained for with you. Anytime you have a feeling about something, you just tell me. I think there's more in that head of yours than you let on.' Miss Emily smirks, a glint in her dark eye. 'A woman like you, I think I'll hold onto you. And I'll make it worth your while, I promise.'

'Thank you, madam. It's good to see a woman make a business for herself. I'm 'appy to be 'ere.'

I check the clock on the wall. 'Well, it's getting on. I better be going, before my household gets worried. I trust you have everything in hand.'

'Oh yes, madam. Don't you be worrying about me. I don't take no shit from no—'

George bursts in through the door, without even a knock.

'George? What the hell's going on?'

He takes off his hat, scrunches it nervously in his hands. 'I found him, ma'am – I found Ryan. He's in a bad way.'

George retrieves him from the hospital. They bring him to The Nightingale on a stretcher, carrying him upstairs to a back room where we lay him on a makeshift bed and try to make him comfortable. He has a stab wound in the belly and is bruised all over. He looks a mess.

'What do you suppose happened, George?'

'I suppose he was mugged on the way home. His pockets were emptied when they found him.'

'How did you know where to look?'

He shakes his head. 'Saw the blood, ma'am, on my way home. Right outside the hospital. And I got a bad feeling. So I went in and found him all patched up. They said he hasn't come round since he was taken in.'

'He hasn't woken?'

'Not once. But they said he'll live.'

'He's fair cut up,' Miss Emily says. 'But I seen worse.'

'What are we gonna do?' George says.

'Well, if he's gonna live, then we'll keep him here for a few days and let him rest. I have some herbal medicine at home that may speed his recovery. I'll bring it first thing tomorrow and we'll patch him up. We'll see if we can't bring him around.'

'Is you a nurse, ma'am?'

'No, George. I'm not. My grandmother was a healer.'

He nods, but he does not understand.

'I have to go, it's late already. I'll have one of the girls check on him and make sure he's warm and comfortable. You should go on – you've done enough for tonight. Your wife'll be worried.'

George nods and puts on his cap. Taking a last look at the man on the table, he turns and leaves. I turn to Miss Emily.

'Tell Lizzy to keep an eye on him. We don't want him getting feverish and coming around not knowing where he is. Better he knows he's looked after.'

'Sure. I'll look in myself now and again throughout the night.'

'Thank you.'

'A shame. He seems like a good enough fella. But London is not the pretty place on the best of nights.'

'No, it is not.' I put on my hat. 'Sometimes one must be an animal to stay alive.'

***

I moan and sit up. My hand goes to my side. Pain there, and burning. I try to stand up but the pain cuts through me. I lie back down.

'Fuck happened...?'

I lift my shirt, see the side of me bandaged up. I put a finger to it; stinging, and hot. Then it comes back to me – the faces red rotten, the stink of gin, the fist in my face, the blade...

'Aw, ya whore ya... away to fuck.' I groan dully.

I wanna lift the bandage, see what the cunts have done, but it's on tight. It'll need cut off. My head is still reelin, some kind of drowsiness still on me.

The door opens. Lizzy comes in, smiles and shakes her head.

'Facking state o'you,' she says.

'Aw, Liz. You're a sight for sore eyes, I tell ya. Come here and help me up.'

'You'd best be layin there til the madam gives the say-so. If you rips the dressing, she'll have your guts.'

'The madam?'

'Aye, the madam. Was her fixed you up and dressed the wound.
146

You'd probably be fightin death if it weren't for her.'

'I didn't know the madam was a nurse.'

'She ain't. And she fixed you up fair queer like, with some kinda herbs. But I 'as to say, it fair worked. You was sweatin and fevered and all kinds of blotchy. You's a changed man now – look at ya. It'll be no time before you's up tryin to poke me again, don't you worry.' She laughs. Her laughter is a tonic.

'I don't know about that, Liz my sweet. I feel like I've been dragged by a horse the length of London and back.'

'Here. I brought you this.' She takes out a bottle of laudanum and passes it to me.

'Jaysus, Liz, you're an angel.'

'Don't let the madam see.'

I take a nip and slip the bottle under the pillow. She lifts my shirt and sighs. 'Come on then. Let's get this changed.'

I pull the shirt up and lie back.

'I been changin the dressing twice a day on the madam's orders. Ain't you the lucky fella.'

'How long I been out for?'

'You been sleepin for two days now. George found you Sunday. It's Tuesday.'

I whistle. She takes a pair of scissors and cuts away the bandage, peelin it off where it sticks to the skin. I hear her inhale sharply.

'Well, would ya look at that…'

I lift my head from the pillow to see. The wound is packed with some kind of grass. It looks black. The skin around it is red and inflamed.

'What the fuck is that?' I say.

'I told ya, the madam fixed you up wi' summink strange…' Lizzy pulls at the crusted mess.

'Fucken leave it be, would ya…'

'Let me alone, I know what I'm doin. The madam herself showed me.' She scrapes away the crud. 'Well I'll be damned…'

'What is it, Liz?'

'You's almost healed right up…'

She takes a bottle from next to the bed, opens it. I get a whiff of gin. She douses it into a rag and starts cleanin my belly.

'Liz, if you're gonna waste good booze on an auld cut in my side, I'll kill ya meself.'

'Shut it. You's under orders. I'm just doin her bidding. Wouldn't be me wasting the stuff on ya, you ungrateful prick.'

When she's most of it washed away, sure enough, the wound is almost closed over.

'I never seen the like of it in my life…' Lizzy peers at it up close. She turns to me. 'Eh? Ain't that summink, Paddy. She's a right one, the madam, ain't she? Maybe she's a *witch*…'

'Aw now, Liz, don't be talkin like that about the madam. There's no call for that.'

But maybe she's right. I reach out to touch the wound but Lizzy slaps my hand. 'Don't even think about it. What you wanna go and do that for? Leave it be, you silly sod.'

Maybe she *is* a witch. This here, this is just one more thing in a line of strange happenings with that woman. I never saw a man healed from a stab wound in two days. Unheard of.

'Gimme that bottle, Liz,' I say.

She hands me the gin. 'You gonna take to the sauce now, is ya?'

I take a good tan of it and pass it back. 'Christ Almighty. I'd shoot a man for a bit of fish and a spud. Any chance of somethin to eat here?'

'You're lookin a bit perkier than the last time I saw ya,' George says.

'Last time you saw me Georgie, if I'm not mistaken, I was on my back with a big bloody slice in my belly,' I say.

'And look at you now…'

Just look at me now. Up and walkin about already.

'That is a miracle,' he says.

'Aye, Georgie. Miracles do happen in this world, after all. Ain't it somethin…'

Georgie puts out his arm for me. He leads me to the door. 'Where you wantin to go?'

'I'll go see the madam, Georgie, before she leaves for the night, if that's alright.'

'If you'd only wait a bit, the madam'll be along to see you herself.'

I shake my head as I reach for the door handle. 'Nah, I'm not havin that, big fella. I'm gonna walk down there on my two feet and march into that office and thank her myself. I'm not havin her come see me sprawled on that stinkin bed.'

We take the corridor down past the lounge. Through the door, I hear singin. The raised voices of a couple clients. The girls puttin on their graces and giggles. The waft of chandoo in the air.

'What've I missed then, big fella? Anything saucy?'

'Lizzy got proposed to by a Turk,' he says.

'You what? A Turk? She kept that quiet. I heard them Turks only went for the rosy-cheeked young fellas. What is it he wanted with a nice fine English lass?'

'Is you jealous, Paddy?'

'Ah fuck off, would ya.'

We get to the door. Georgie raps it and the madam calls us in. He leads me inside as the madam gets up from her desk.

'Mr. Ryan... shouldn't you be lying down? I'm not sure it's time to play the hero. You risk tearing open your wound.'

I stand there in front of her, leaning on Georgie. 'From what I saw, miss, the wound is pretty well closed up already.'

'That may be, but it doesn't mean you can't undo the healing. Here – if you're going to leave the sick bed, then sit down.'

Georgie puts me in a chair. 'He insisted, ma'am. Wouldn't take no for an answer. Pig-headed, these Irish be.'

I pat him on the arm. 'I'll forgive you the slur, big fella. You're alright for an English prick.'

The madam pours a glass of water and hands it to me. She sits down at the desk and sighs.

'So, Mr. Ryan, do you know what happened? I mean, clearly you were stabbed, but have you any idea why, or by whom?'

'Agh...' I wave a hand. 'A couple of thickoes, miss, lit on gin and lookin for a quick take. Wasn't nothin else to it. I let my wits get away with me and they took advantage.'

'That's it? It wasn't anything to do with here, or one of our clients?'

'Nah, miss, nothin like that. Like I say, just a couple of sossed-up chancers.'

'Alright. Well, at least you're on the mend. We can be thankful for that.'

I shake my head. 'Well that's it, miss, I can't get my head around it. And the others been sayin too, what a canny thing it is my wound just closed up like that. Don't get me wrong, I'm not ungrateful...'

'But you want to ask what I did?' She raises an eyebrow.

'Well yes, miss. It's sure a strange thing. I guess I'm curious as to the medicines you used.'

This time, it's her dismisses me with a wave of the hand. 'Something my grandmother taught me, Mr. Ryan. An old woman's cure, nothing more. And all natural. Or maybe you think I did some kind of magic on you, is that it?'

'Aha!' My laughter is more nervous than I anticipate. I shake my head vigorously and hold out a hand. 'I'm a man raised by women – my own grandmother had more than her fair share of cures. Say no more. I know better than to question a wise woman about her ways.' I glance at George. He looks away and starts scratchin his ear. When I turn back to the madam, there's that queer smile of hers on her lips.

'A wise woman? I have not a pinch of the wisdom my grandmother had. If only it were so...' She turns away, her thoughts suddenly elsewhere. There's a dead silence for a moment or two, which I see fit to break.

'Well, I do thank ya, miss, for bringin me back to health. If it wasn't for you, I might be dead already.'

She picks up a letter on the desk and begins to peruse it. 'Well,' she says, not lookin at me, 'take a few days to get yourself fit. We'll be here waiting for you.'

I raise my arm and George takes it. 'I'll be back in the mornin, miss, don't you worry.'

Engrossed in the letter, she says nothin.

'Come on then, big fella – let's get outta here.' At the door, I stop and turn. 'Thank you again, miss, for all you've done.'

'Hmm?' She looks up. 'Ah yes, thank you gentlemen. Close the door on your way out.'

'What do you think, Georgie,' I whisper when he's closed the door, 'do you think she's some kinda, you know, witch?'

Georgie makes the sign of the cross on his chest.

***

Lizzy pokes her head in the door. 'There's a man here, miss. Asking to see the madam.'

'Who is he? Have you seen him before?'

She shakes her head. 'No I ain't. He don't look like no lord, neither.'

I gesture to Miss Emily, who follows Lizzy out. When guests ask for the madam, it generally means one of two things: They want to be assured of our discretion, or they're about to ask for some speciality or other, like they want to hurt a girl, or have her urinate on them, or some other disgusting thing. Some of it scarcely warrants thinking about. I almost feel sorry for the wives. Imagine having your husband come home after... but no, I don't feel sorry for them at all. They have the life they want. And in return, their husbands do as they please. There are no victims here. Only flagrant and unapologetic excess.

When Miss Emily returns from the lounge, she's wearing a look of faint mirth. I ask her what's wrong.

'Man outside, he's asking for boys.'

'Boys?' For a moment, I don't understand.

'Boys. That's what he likes – I showed him the girls, but he wasn't having it. Wants to know if he "may get acquainted with a young schoolboy", is how he put it.'

'You told him we don't do that here, didn't you?'

'Naturally, I did. But if I may say, miss, there's a club right here in London, and gentlemen pay two guineas a time to play with such boys.

There's money in it, if that's what you're in the game for.'

'*Two guineas?*'

'Oh yes. And the boys that work there make good tips n'all. These men have money to throw about, lemme tell ya.'

'Who is this man?' I get up and make for the door.

'Sitting outside, wearing a purple necktie.'

I go out. From behind a curtain, I spy into the lounge. He's sitting drinking with another of our guests. Lizzy was right – he doesn't look like one of our regulars. In fact, he looks like a teacher. I can't say I've ever set eyes on a sodomite before, though there were rumours about some of the gentlemen in Buenos Aires. My father had them all castrated. This fellow, he looks out of place. But I have an inkling there's some other connection here, something I can't put my finger on.

I go back to the office.

'Miss Emily, what do you think? Should we accommodate him?'

She lights a cigarette. 'Well, you know, I'll be perfectly frank with you – this is also the kind of thing t'would be better suited to its own establishment, like the opium, but if it's a matter of keepin your clientele and having em spend their money with you, then it can do no 'arm gettin a boy or two in just to catch the clients. Later, you can let it be known you're openin a new place, you know, that specialises in sodomy, or opium, or any damned thing you please.'

'Miss Emily... do the English have no shame?'

'None, miss. So long as it's behind closed doors.'

I take a deep breath and sigh. I look down to see I'm drumming my fingers on the desk restlessly. I recall with interest this was a habit of my father's and cease immediately. I turn back to Miss Emily, who has taken out her pipe and is filling it with tobacco. She watches me as she works.

'So where would we find a couple of schoolboys then?'

*

When the cab pulls up outside the house, I feel a sense of foreboding. Looking out the window of the carriage, all seems normal. But something is off. Winters opens the door for me and helps me down.

'Thank you.'

'Ma'am.'

I hurry up the steps. Constancia is in the hall, I see her through the door. She's heard the cab. Even her posture is off. My heart pounding now, I hurry inside. Her face is white, fraught.

'Mi amor, que pasa?'

She raises her hands in a futile gesture, then he appears from the door behind her.

'Maximo?'

'Mi amor... que tal? Donde has estado?'

He rushes forward and takes my hand, and kisses it. The gesture leaves me cold and I snatch my hand away. He looks at me in incomprehension. When I turn back to Constancia, her face is beset with confusion. Normally she'd be happy to see us together, but now she's worried. For other reasons.

'What are you doing here?' I demand.

'Mi amor... vengo por ti.' He looks at me with such a lost and pleading look. I too might have been happy to see him, if his coming was not so inopportune. As it is, his being here only triggers me.

I take off my hat and my shawl and place it on the stand. 'I need a tea. Constancia...'

She nods and hurries to the kitchen. I look at Maximo. He looks tired, and gaunt. Not at all like the fresh-faced and energetic boy who showered me with affection back in Buenos Aires.

'Come inside,' I say.

We go into the living room and sit at the table. He reaches out to take my hand but I withdraw it.

'Mi amor, you look as beautiful as ever,' he says, but his affectation is grasping.

'How did you get here?' I ask, curtly and without care. He pauses, searching my face before answering.

'I followed you by boat, like we agreed I would...'

'We agreed you would wait until I summoned you. And what I'm asking is, how did you find me? Not even Moreno knows where I am.'

'Si, I know... I have been trying to send letters to you for six months now. They go to Moreno and I get nothing back, and when I ask, he says he has no idea of your whereabouts. Why the secrecy, tell me...?'

'Por dios, answer my question – how did you find us?' I ask it with such violence that he looks stunned.

'Mi amor... your father told me.'

'My father?' *It can't be... how is it he knows where we are, and hasn't sent someone already? No...*

'Tell me the truth,' I demand. I stand up. 'Tell me, or god help me...'

He holds up his hands. 'I would never lie to you...'

'Sangre de dios...'

Constancia appears in the door with a tray. I beckon her in and slide back into my seat. She puts down the maté gourd and a pot of hot water. Maximo looks at it and smirks.

'What is this? Didn't you leave this behind when you came here from Buenos Aires? This is a peasant's drink.'

I glare at him. 'We don't all sell off our heritage so easily.' I don't realise the vehemence with which I've said it until I catch Constancia's eye. She looks away, her face hot. I see too that Maximo is uncomfortable.

I shake my head. 'Look, it's late, and I'm tired. You have caught me unawares, coming here without warning.'

'Yes, Constancia says you are working – you have a bookshop?' He sneers. 'It is not befitting a woman of your station. If you would onl—'

My hand strikes the table. Maximo jumps, Constancia too. I get up and walk to the window, fury rising inside me. Then I turn to face him.

'How dare you come in here and tell me what's befitting me. That is for me to decide and me alone, no one else... certainly not you, who until today have been on the other side of the world. Who do you think you are? What makes you think you can walk in here and tell me what to do with my life, you who've no idea who I am?'

His face is white. He's trembling. I realise my hands are clasped behind my back, the nails of my fingers digging into my palms. And I know if he opens his mouth again, I'm going to reach out and claw his face.

I look at Constancia, who is frozen by the door. 'Constancia, see Señor Terrero out please. Tell him we'll call on him when we wish to see him.' I say this while looking him in the eye.

He rises to his feet and opens his mouth as if to speak, but the words catch in his throat. Constancia comes up beside him and puts a hand on his arm. He looks at her hand, startled. Then he turns back to me. But I'm already looking out the window.

'Vamonos,' Constancia says gently. I feel both their eyes on me but neither says a word more. A short time later, I hear the front door open, and the mutterings of their brief exchange.

When Constancia returns, she stops in the door. She stares at my back for a long time.

We lie in silence on the recliner. The glow of the fire lights the room, the warm glare of the streetlights filter through the curtains. I have an arm around her waist. I feel the quick of her breathing as her chest swells, her back pushing against my breasts. I lift a hand to brush her hair from her neck. Her body is tense, but my dove is always tense. I let a finger graze her neck and feel her shudder.

'He knows,' she says eventually.

'Yes. He knows.'

She greets this with a long and thoughtful silence. Her hand toys with the locket around her neck, a locket containing a picture of her mother and father.

'Why hasn't he sent someone?'

I squeeze her shoulder lovingly. 'I don't know. Maybe he's afraid.'

'Afraid? Your father is afraid of nothing.'

'He's afraid of one thing.' I toy with a lock of her hair. 'He is afraid I no longer love him. He lost my mother. I'm the only one who remains. If he loses me, he has lost everything.'

'Then why doesn't he send someone here to make you return by force?'

'Then he would surely lose me.'

Her hand rises to her neck. I take it lightly, let her fingers find comfort in mine. Her breathing has quickened. Mine too. My breasts heave against her body. My mouth is dry.

'I don't understand...' she begins, and stops.

'Don't understand what, mi amor?' I ask.

'Why... you behaved such a way with Maximo. I thought... I thought you loved him.'

'I have never loved Maximo. He's a nice boy, and loyal, and it's useful in life to marry someone loyal.'

'But...'

She doesn't finish her sentence. I pull her tighter. Her body intimates confusion. I feel the heat from her, her cheek is flushed red. Through the fabric of our gowns, our bodies speak one to the other. And tremble. I have never... I am not...

'Constancia?' I whisper.

'Si?'

'Te amo.'

Her silence is pregnant with longing and terror.

baring more of our souls than we wish

First I don't get what he's sayin. I have to ask a second time.

'*Boys?*'

Georgie nods. 'Young lads, like. For the dirty old bastards. Facking nonces. We had one come in last week, asking 'bout schoolboys.'

'And the madam agreed?'

'Aye.'

I whistle. 'There are some right queer ones about, ain't there Georgie.'

'There is, Paddy. There sure is.' He tilts a head. 'Come on, I'll introduce ya.'

'Right queer ones,' I mutter.

He takes me upstairs to the back room where I made my recuperation. 'Things is a little different in here now, Paddy,' he says. He opens the door.

Aye, things are different alright. The room has been fitted out as a boudoir. And sittin on the bed, chattin all hush and saucy like, two little Mary-Anns. Even got make-up on em.

'Alright, boys,' Georgie says. Comes over a bit embarrassed Georgie does. 'This here's Mr. Ryan. Mr. Ryan's on evenings, and if anything 'appens or you need anything, you come see him, you 'ear?'

The boys nod.

'Lads,' I say, and nod. Don't know what else to say.

I glance round the room. There's a large mirror on the wall one side of the bed. I'd guess the madam has one of her spying stations set up beyond.

'Can we get a drink?' one of em says, brazen.

I look at Georgie, then back at the fairy. 'A drink? Like, booze?'

He nods.

'Are you lads old enough to drink?' Georgie says.

'If we's old enough to pull the yardsticks of old misters,' he says, 'we's old enough to take a drink.'

I smile, look at Georgie. 'Come on then, lads, we'll get yis a drink. Can't have yis pullin on charlies without a stiff whiskey in ya.'

'I'll be off, Paddy,' Georgie says, puttin on his hat. 'The madam's still in the office. Maybe catch her before she goes.'

'Aye, Georgie, I'll do that.'

'See ya, Paddy.'

Off he goes. I take the two Mary-Anns and we go out to the lounge. There's a couple of gentlemen sittin with Luara and Camila. The atmosphere changes. The gentlemen get shifty. The Brazilian girls turn and gaze in wonder at the pair.

'Don't worry, fellas, they'll soon get used to ya.'

Lizzy comes over. She smiles. 'I see you met our new girls,' she says and laughs.

'Aye.' I scratch my head. 'You two got names?'

The one nancy-boy goes on to tell me his name is Ben but he goes by 'Masie' when he needs, and his friend is David but can be 'Angie' when the job requires.

'I see...' I pick up the whiskey and pour em a couple of drinks, and take a shot myself. Help get things straight in my head.

'Lizzy, can you entertain the, eh, lads here while I go see the madam.'

'Sure I can, love...' She takes the boys by the arm and leads em to a recliner. 'Just you come and sit with Auntie Lizzy now...'

The gentlemen are bein pawed over by the girls, but now one of em is throwin glances at the nancy-boys. Mary's singin a sweet tune. Ain't it all heaven up here in The Nightingale...

I knock the door of the office before goin in. The madam's alone in there, at her desk. No Miss Emily.

'Good evening, Mr. Ryan. How are you feeling?'

'Much better, miss.' I touch my side. 'The wound is closed over. Still sensitive, like, but I can't say I'm in too bad a way. Hard to believe.'

'The old ways are still the best ways, don't you think?'

'Well, I can't say I ever saw my own grandmother fix up a knife wound, but I guess she had a few tricks up her sleeve, if you had the shingles like, or a stye in your eye.'

'We're too often ready to give up the old ways at the hint of something modern, or at the latest discoveries in medicine or science. This is a mistake. The old ways should be preserved. The wise men and women of our respective cultures have much to teach us, if we would only listen.'

'If I'd listened to my own grandmother a little more, I'd still be stuck on Rathery,' I say.

'Where?' She points to the seat. 'Sit down.'

I take a seat. 'Rathery. Little place I was born. Not much to it, to be fair. A rock, by any other name. Water on four sides. And water from above, too, day and night,' I add as an afterthought.

'You were born on an island?'

I nod. 'Aye, for my sins.'

'That explains much,' she says.

'Aye? Like what?'

She takes off the bracelet she's wearing and places it on the desk in front of her, and regards it for a few moments before answering. 'You recall our trip here from Buenos Aires?'

I nod. 'I do.'

'Well, I had occasion to watch you from time to time on the journey over, however long we were on that boat – three, four, five weeks, I don't remember. But I saw you often on the deck. I saw how you looked at the sea.' She smiles wistfully.

'And how was that, miss?'

'Like a man who has found the object of his desire but knows it will kill him.'

I say nothin.

'One day, you will drown, Mr. Ryan. And on that day, you'll find great peace. It's a shame, isn't it, that the thing we love the most is often the thing that kills us.'

I clear my throat and shake my head. 'That sure is a lot for a man to hear, miss. You'll take it kindly if I don't know quite how to answer.'

'I don't expect you to.' She lifts the bracelet and turns it with her fingers, like she's sayin rosary. 'Did you meet our new girls?'

'Aha...' I raise my eyebrows. 'I did, miss. Maybe it's not my place to say, but are you sure it's a good idea? You know the law don't look kindly on buggery, if you get what I mean.'

'Don't worry – I've made enquiries. The law has a poor tendency of looking the other way when the offender has money or station, haven't you noticed?'

I nod. 'I have, miss. It does seem to be the way of things. In that case, I'll say no more about it. I'm not the man to be tellin you how to run your business.'

'Good. On the subject, though, I'd ask you to talk to the boys. They'll need to know what we do here, how we operate. More so than with other gentlemen, any clients who make use of the boys will need to be monitored. Make it clear that I want as much information on the gentlemen as possible – names, positions, associations, memberships... all these things need to be recorded. And you'll need to instruct them on the procedure for getting pictures. Can you do all that for me, Mr. Ryan?'

I get up from the chair. 'I can, miss. Just leave it to me. I'll see to it they're well prepared.'

She nods and gets up. 'I'm leaving for the evening. Miss Emily will be here shortly. I leave the place in your capable hands.'

'Right you be.'

She gives me a look of appraisal. 'Do you have any misgivings about working here?'

I shake my head. 'None at all. I'm very happy here, miss.'

'You and George are different fish.'

'George is more of a family man, if you get my meanin. Good Christian morals on him.'

'And you? You're not Christian?'

I tug on the lapels of my jacket. 'Well, brought up one, in a manner. Then life gave me other ideas.'

'Religion is a silly superstition, Mr. Ryan. Don't let anyone tell you different.'

'You don't believe in god, miss?'

'The gods are a different matter.'

'Gods?'

She takes up her handbag. 'It's late, and I must be getting on. We'll talk on it some other time.'

'Evenin miss.'

By way of departure she nods, then like a whisper on the air, she's gone.

From a discreet corner of the room, I watch the whores at work. The haze of cigar smoke and the hum of drunken tunes imbue their mannerisms with an air of the occult; I feel like I'm watchin a primeval lore, an act of ancient Dionysian comedy: spilled glasses and hoary looks, the fair knee of a courtesan and the swollen nose of a souse; a maiden glimpsed through the fronds of some exotic plant, an oriental fan aloft in her hand with which she keeps the smoke from her face; by candlelight two whores kiss to the uproarious cheers of drunken sots, while a fey lady-boy crosses the floor on tiptoe, afeared he may be waylaid by the ribald revellers; one man, off from the rest, the look of awe about him, the opium frieze of his countenance imparting his inner flight. A man gets onto his knees and crawls to the foot of a whore to take her stocking between his teeth... she kicks him and he rolls over in drunken mirth; a girl extracts a tit and squeezes a nipple, and a little spurt of milk shoots from it toward the open maw of her companion; 'let's see what the Mary-Ann has between her legs!' one fellow shouts, and gets up and chases the boy around the room; caught, he's dragged towards the group; he fights, playfully, holdin tight his breeches. I turn to see Lizzy eyein me with a queer distant stare. I give her a slow blink, as if to say, 'all is well under the saturnalian sky, and no ill will a-bodes'. She has a glint in her eye, a look like she's just awoke in the bed when I've had the mickey up against her thigh and she stirs with the wetness on her. I turn away... *Not under the madam's roof.* I try to focus on the raucous tumble of em on the couch across the room, but now the lad on me's stirrin. Once it's on ya...

I turn to look at Lizzy again. She throws another glance my way. *Fuck.* Then she gets up and crosses the floor, passes me headin to the back and I turn and follow her. She opens a door to one of the vacant rooms and pulls me in.

'Jesus, Lizzy, there ain't no good gonna come of it, I'm tellin ya...' But she's already pullin at me, so I lift her skirts and slide a hand between her legs. 'Christ, you're wet as hell...'

She tears the pants open and takes me in hand. 'Up against the wall, Paddy, just like this... rough like, don't put your lips on me, just stick it in...'

I stick it in alright. Slide right in and hammer her there for a whole minute against the wall before I spend and stumble back pantin, sittin on the bed with the trousers round my ankles. She fixes herself up, shakes her hair, and goes for the door.

'Wait a minute,' I say. 'What was that for?'

She blows out a hard breath and pushes up her corset. 'Sometimes I'm just dyin for a real dickin, ya know?'

Then she goes out. The door closes behind her. Head in hands, I mutter a silent 'fuck' then slap myself twice in the face. 'Fucken eejit,' I mutter. I get up and pull up the trousers. Then I take out a cigarette.

I'm still cursin myself when I go outside. Miss Emily's in the lounge. I try to dart to the staircase to make it downstairs, but she waves. I go over, she takes me by the arm.

'We have a gentleman. I've led him to the back room already. Take the boys. He's waiting.'

'Both of em?'

'Yes.'

The boys are with Camila and a drunk. I tap em on the shoulder and give a flick of the head. They get up.

The drunk protests. 'Just hold on a minute, now...'

'Sorry sir,' I say. 'But their company is required elsewhere.'

'Jolly rotten form...' he's goin as we walk away. I ignore him and lead the boys to the back room. Outside, I pause.

'Now, remember like I told you... find out all you can about him, you hear? I'm gonna ask you after. Alright?'

They nod and grin.

'Go on then.'

I glance in the door as they nip inside. The gentleman is standin by the bed, nervously toyin with his hat. I wink and close the door.

***

'Do we know who is he?'

Miss Emily and I are behind the mirror, peering into the room. Ryan put up a dry-wall enclosing a space in the corridor outside; it's inside that we now stand. It's small and does not have the space my office does, but for what we require of it, it's sufficient.

'He goes by the name Vallans, but his real name's Vaughan. He's headmaster at a very prestigious boy's school here in London.'

'Why does that not surprise me.'

'He was here last night. Spent two hours with the boys.'

'Now he's back again.'

Miss Emily nods slowly. 'When you got a man like that, it's like a compulsion. Like someone who can't get enough of the gin, or the opium. He's an addict.'

On the other side of the glass, one of the boys is sitting on the man's face. The other lies on the bed and watches.

'He's asked for a cane, miss. Should I give him one?'

'He wants to beat them?' I ask.

'Perhaps. But I more suspect it's so's they can thrash him, if you get me. I think he wants to be humiliated.'

I sigh. 'Put one in the room. We can allow the boys to take a bit of a caning, but not on their faces or upper body. If it happens, put a stop to it at once.'

'Yes ma'am.'

We stand and watch in silence for a time. The mechanics of it are curious, the act fascinating.

'Is this common here?'

'Oh yes,' Miss Emily says. 'All behind closed doors, of course, but there's plenty of appetite for boys, 'specially amongst well-to-do gents. Go to parks in the city at night, they's full of gentlemen hidin out in the shadows all toyin with each other's pricks. Like I say, miss, it's a compulsion.'

I shake my head. 'What about women? I mean, women and women... does it happen too?'

Miss Emily gets animated. A lifetime in the trade, I suspect she's seen it all. 'Toms? Oh yes. You can find it all in London. There are clubs here just for women too. All underground of course, on the quiet. You go to jail for these things. Maybe that's what makes it fun...' She trails off, like she's said too much.

'Have you ever...?' I say.

She grins, turns back to the mirror. 'I couldn't say, miss.'

I smile and nod, then shake my head. How sheltered a life I've lived.

The enjoyment of sex always seemed periphery to the deed. A side effect. Maybe I've missed something. That said, women aren't supposed to derive enjoyment from it. Having children is our purpose: to provide sons and heirs, or daughters who'll become good wives. Female sex is procreation. Men, it seems, have found a multitude of holes they can stick their bayonet in and not have to worry if it results in a baby. The scales are imbalanced. Why should a woman not enjoy it? Is her body meant solely for the benefit of her husband's line, or should she not do as she pleases with it?

A memory comes back, from deep in the past. I was eight or nine, playing in the garden with my brother. Mention of our childhood nanny brought the talk around to nakedness; suddenly we agreed to expose ourselves to each other. I would show him my '*cosita*' if he would show me his '*pico*'. We did. That was my first glimpse of the male anatomy. Juan shook it like a little chorizo and asked me if I wanted to touch it. I squeezed it like I was milking grandma's cow, then he touched me and said it felt like a plum. After, I was filled with shame, terrified Juan would tell our father. Why does the memory come back to me now, twenty years later?

Perhaps the *caapi* will also reveal the secrets of my sex. It has been too long since I've partaken. I've been afraid of the medicine since my last encounter. It's time to go back and face it again; gods must be challenged. They must be stalked and hunted, and confronted. With fear or fearlessness one must look them in the eye and instill submission.

The gods are in us, and desire only control. They must, therefore, be enchained.

I find Ryan in the small room adjacent to my office. He's preparing the opium. He looks up when I come in but turns back to the pot immediately. He has the air of a silent alchemist. I close the door and approach, and watch silently over his shoulder as he balances the copper pot over the flame. He's engrossed in the task. I take a seat and drag it to the small table, and sit down. He catches my eye and nods.

'It's a funny thing, miss, the black stuff...'

'How so?'

'Well, we got so much trouble and strife in this world, and yet here's this stuff, this little piece of black tar, that makes all trouble disappear. It's like, when you smoke it, you find contentment. And it feels natural, god-given.'

I shake my head. 'Why should things be so easy? Don't you think we have trouble and strife in this life for a reason?'

He shrugs. 'Oh, I dunno. I can't say things would be so much different if it weren't so. People wouldn't be up to high dough all the time.'

'Up to what? Sometimes I don't understand you, Mr. Ryan.'

He smiles. 'So wound up. So antsy. So growlin.'

'Ah.' I watch as he pours the solution into a copper tray to cool. Then he adds some of the solids to the copper pot and begins again. 'So you think the answer is just to smoke and be happy, is that it?'

'Sure seems like a better life to me.'

'Do you consider yourself an addict, Mr. Ryan?' The sickening tang of the tar is thick in the dim room. There are no windows, a single candle on the table the only light.

'Are you asking if I could stop and never smoke again, if I wanted to?'

'Yes.'

He thinks for some time. 'I could stop,' he says. 'I could get on a boat back to Ireland tomorrow, and if I never saw it again, it wouldn't kill me.'

'But you'd dream about it, yes?'

'Yes.' He rotates the pot. 'Once it's in you, it's in you.' After a second, he adds, 'But I've never touched your stuff, miss. You know that, don't you?'

I nod. 'Yes, I know you wouldn't.' His eyes betray something else. I let it pass, and turn my attention to the pot. 'I haven't taken much of an interest in what you do here, but perhaps I should. It would be wise for me to be familiar with everything that happens under this roof, don't you think?'

He gestures with a flick of the head. 'Of course. If I'd been killed thon night when I had a blade shoved in my belly, who'd there be to prepare the chandoo?'

'That's not all you're good for, Mr. Ryan. But yes. I should be better prepared. Now tell me, what've you done to the raw opium since you took it from the chest?' I point at the mess in the bowl.

'I dissolved it in water, miss. Left it overnight. Then I strained it and let it dry for an hour or two. Now I'm boiling it in the pot, twice.

That'll turn it into the nice tarry grain smokers are familiar with.'

'And how do you measure it?'

'One of these balls of Patna is about three Chinese cattys. One catty is sixteen tahil, and one tahil is ten chee. A chee is about a grain, what one man who's familiar with the stuff will smoke in a sitting.'

'Very interesting. I've much to learn.'

When he's done with the pot, he empties the contents into another copper bowl, and returns the first 'batch' to the pot. He begins to cook it again. I pick up one of the small grain-sized pellets he has already prepared and roll it between my thumb and forefinger.

'You never tried it, miss?'

'No. Nor have I any desire to.'

'Aye. You don't seem like a woman who needs much contentment.'

I raise an eyebrow. 'What does that mean?'

'Well, you're just like, very self-contained is all. If you get me.'

'I think that's a compliment. I'll take it as one.'

He glances up from the pot and smirks. 'It is, and do.' Then his face turns dark.

I sense his intention. 'Go on. What is it you want to ask?'

He hesitates as he takes the pot from the flame and puts it down. He looks me in the eye, then shakes his head.

'Nah, it's nothin, miss. You'd think me a fool.'

'Go ahead and say it.'

'Somethin about you, miss, doesn't sit quite right with me. It's...' I frown, waiting for him to continue. '...it's like, ever since we came back on that boat, I've felt like, *you're in me*. Does that sound mad? Cause it feels like it. And I don't know how else to explain it, it's wild, it's impossible, but that's how it seems. And how you were able to find me, and then how I fixed up so quick after I was stabbed, then that thing with Lizzy...'

'What's Lizzy got to do with it?' The conversation should be galling me, but I find it thrilling. He's like a fish on a hook.

'Well, that's the thing, miss. You asked me to get rid of the evidence, and I did, and I had no qualms about doin it. But Lizzy, she doesn't even remember killin the fella. It's like it wasn't even her done it.'

I sigh, and smile. 'So let me see if I understand... you think I might be in you, and now you're saying I might be in Lizzy too, and had her kill a man, for...?'

He shakes his head and laughs. Then he picks up a pinch of the tar and rolls it into a pea-sized ball. He puts it with the others. 'Forget it. Forget I said anything. You know my head's been all messed-up of late, I'm not thinkin straight. Forgive me for speakin out of line, miss.'

'Not at all. I find it intriguing.' I pick up one of the grains and smell it. 'You're not the first Irishman I've known, Mr. Ryan.'

'Oh aye?' He stops rolling the grains. 'The other one gone in the head too, was he?'

I smile. 'He was a priest. He had a... vivid imagination.'

'Most priests do. Kinda goes with the job, doesn't it? You know, big man in the sky and all that.'

I stand up. 'I don't know how you haven't a headache already, with the smell in here.'

'I'm used to it, you could say.'

'Well, don't get too used to it. "Be not a slave lest the angels are set upon to free you".'

He looks up. 'Is that scripture, miss?'

'That's wisdom, Mr. Ryan.'

'Ah so.'

'I'm going home for the evening. Keep an eye on things for me please.' I stop at the door. 'Mr. Ryan, you keep an eye out for the girls, don't you?'

He lifts his head but doesn't look over his shoulder. 'Aye, miss.'

'Good. I care about their wellbeing.'

With a heavy silence lingering in the air, I go out.

***

By the time she's gone, I'm all hot under the collar. Sweatin like. I grain up the rest of the chandoo and put it in the case, and when it's done I take it back to the office. The madam is gone but Miss Emily is in there. I put the case on top of the chest of raw opium in the cabinet.

'For the lovers,' I say.

Miss Emily smiles. 'How are ya?'

I nod. 'Not half bad.'

'That wound all closed up, is it?'

'It is. Proper strange, but it is.'

'Can I see it?' She blows a puff of smoke and sits back in the chair.

'Sure.' I lift up my shirt to show her. She looks at it right n'long and takes another drag on her pipe. She exhales, blowing smoke over the wound. 'What about that, eh?' I put down my shirt.

She shakes her head. 'Funny thing, ain't it.' The pipe in hand, she points at me and says, 'I was married, once upon a time. A right bastard he was, used to beat me black and blue. Me boy, too. One day I broke. He cornered me in the kitchen and laid into me, so I grabbed the nearest thing at hand, which was a meat fork, and I jammed it in his stomach.' She pauses. 'You know what, he didn't even cry out. He stared at it for a good 'alf a minute, then he looked at me like, *What's that for?*

'You kill him?' I say.

She shakes her head. 'Nah. Next bit's the mad bit. He just pulls the fork out his belly and drops it on the floor. Then he goes to the fire, takes out the poker and sticks it right in the 'ole.'

I wince. 'And he didn't scream?'

'Oh, he facking screamed alright. He screamed. Then he pulled it out and fainted. Fell to the floor and cracked his head on the hearth. That's what killed him.'

'Think I'd rather get healed the madam's way, to be fair. I'm not the man to go stickin pokers in myself.'

Miss Emily raises an eyebrow. 'That is a canny thing, innit... how she 'ealed you up like that.' She takes a long puff on the pipe, her gaze on me. When she exhales, she shakes her head and says, 'She's not a regular woman, you know. The madam. Not a regular woman at all.'

I cough. Turn to the door.

'But if she was, you might be dead.'

'I'll be thankful, then, she knows a secret or two.'

Miss Emily smirks. 'Aye, she's got a few secrets alright. But folk like you and me know better'n to ask.'

I put my hand on the door handle. 'I'll check on things out front, see how they are.'

She nods, winks. 'Aye. Have a gander in on the boys too, see what they're up to. Has the madam got her 'ands on a second camera?'

'Not yet. Comin though, if I believe right.'

'Alright then.'

I go out and close the door.

I exhale long and take a deep breath. Jesus Christ. It's not the men in this life you gotta watch out for. It's the women. Fucken mental, all of em. If it's not the knives they're threatenin you with, it's the cunt on em that'll have you against the wall. Now, I never raised a hand to a woman in my life, wasn't raised that way. I wouldn't dare. But sure as shit stinks if I was baytin on a woman regular, I'd expect to wake up with a knife in me. Probably deserve it too. It's the quiet ones you gotta watch the most, though, cause you just can't read em. Turn your back and they'd have you fucked six ways from Sunday. There isn't a man alive could contend with the best of em.

The lounge is quiet. All the girls must be fuckin. Sure enough, gruntin from the nearest room. So I don't have to listen to it, I go back to the boys' room. Occupied too. Satisfied everything is just fine, I go downstairs.

The bookstore is dark. I light a candle and sit at the desk, pick up the nearest book and put the feet up. Can't be dealin with whores and tricks all the time. A man needs a break.

I'm just settlin in for a bit of readin when the doorbell tinkles. I look up. You know, you just know, when a man's here for the salon. This fellow ain't. He might even be here for books.

'I'm sorry sir. We're closed.' It's gone after eight. He's got no business out shoppin for books at this hour.

'Oh, I'm sorry. I was just passing, and I thought the shop looked most intriguing.'

'Well, maybe come back tomorrow?' I say.

'I'm not from this side of town. Would it be a trouble if I had a look around now?'

I sigh. 'Go on then.' I wave a hand. 'Knock yourself out. Is it somethin particular you're lookin for, pal?'

He looks at me queer like, sighs, and turns to the shelves. When he turns back, even in the dim light I can see a tear in his eye.

'I, I can't say...'

I open my book. 'Maybe you just tell me if you need some help, alright?'

He takes a step towards the shelves, then stops and turns around. 'Maybe you have a light?'

I regard him for a moment before going into the desk and taking out another candle. I light it from the one on the desk and hand it to him.

'That do?'

'T'will. Thank you.'

He takes it. I get a good look at his face as he dips to take the candle from my hand. The tip of his nose is missing, like it's been sliced off. One of his eyes is white through, the cornea clouded. The other is pointin the other way, skew-eyed. Hard to tell if he's lookin at me at all. I nod as he takes the candle from my hand then turn back to the book.

Because, even with your kind of savvy, you can't avoid having them buzz around you. So let them rave whenever they lose their temper, and close your ears to the 'whore, pig, slut', which they'll utter in a single breath; and although they try to crush the world with the words they drown in spittle, spattering the face of anyone nearby, nothing more will come of it.

I pause and look up at the gentleman by the shelves. He has a book in hand, face raised to the ceiling as if in prayer.

'Sir, you alright?'

'Hmm?' He turns around.

'You alright?'

Before he can answer, shadows darken the front door. It's thrown open and two soldiers enter, drunk and boisterous. The man at the bookshelves looks from the soldiers to me. I nod as the men pass me on their way upstairs. Hearing them recede, the man watches me, waiting for an explanation.

'Renting rooms upstairs, they are,' I say. I pick up my book.

...their anger is like an overcast sky in July: despite the thunder and lightning, after twenty-five drops have fallen, out comes the sun again. So your patience will make you rich.

Through the ceiling I hear boots on the floor. Like someone's kickin out a quick-step. The soldiers could get outta hand. I'm fixin to go upstairs when the one-eyed man approaches the desk. He's clutchin a book to his chest. He regards me for a moment, then pulls up a stool and sits down.

'You want that, do ya?' I say, indicating the book. He doesn't answer, just looks at me before reachin out across the desk with the candle. I take hold of it but he doesn't let go, and for a moment we're like two ghosts of the night caught across the rudiment of the naked flame, scalded reflections perhaps baring more of our souls than we wish. He relents and lets go of the candle. I snuff it out and slip it back in the desk. A single candle flickering outside our periphery lights the store. Above, again, the sound of boots. He looks to the ceiling.

'I was in her majesty's forces upon a time,' he says, his wayward eye still fixed on the ceiling when he turns his face back to me. 'I was posted in Ceylon as part of the fifth regiment. Have you been to Ceylon, sir? Seems you have the air of travel about you.'

'I have not, sir.'

'Tea country. Do you take a sip?'

'I do not.'

'Well, maybe you'll join me in a drop of this...'

He takes a bottle of laudanum from his pocket and holds it out. When I take it from his hand, he nods in approval.

'It's the only thing eases the pain.' He pulls the lapel of his overcoat down from his neck to show a scar that disappears into his shirt. 'Ever hunted?'

I shake my head.

'Never had an appetite for it myself. But out in Ceylon, there were many in the service did. Officers, you understand. Now and again, if we were in favour, we'd be invited along on the hunt. The officers, see, liked to have a few boys around to say "hurrah", and "jolly good", if you know what I mean. It wasn't enough for them to shoot something, they needed to be seen to shoot it. Wasn't a real prize unless there was someone there to talk about it, see. One time we were in the jungle. The native boys go out ahead to chase out the tigers, swinging sticks and shouting. This time, they missed one. Maybe it was nursing young, they said – the reason it might've stayed put. Anyway, I stepped right into its lair and disturbed the thing. It went for me, bit me right in the neck. They had to shoot it in the head before they could prise the thing off me. I felt its teeth in my throat. Was this close to death. Still wake up in the night with the pain.'

'Hurts?' I say.

He turns his head a quarter turn. 'Can't but turn my head only that.' Then he points at his nose. 'I dunno, but they say his claw took off the tip of my nose. All I know is it was gone when I woke up in the army hospital.'

I point at his eye. 'What about that?'

'Oh that... that's another story.'

We stay silent for a moment. Above us the soldiers are kickin up a fuss.

'Wanna know the strange thing about it?' he says.

I shake my head.

'They say it left a piece of its tooth in my shoulder. Broke on my shoulder bone.'

'Unlikely,' I say.

He nods. ''Tis, but it's true. I've a bit of tiger in me.'

'You ever feel like eatin anyone?'

'You joke, but I'll tell you this, sir, and this is the god's honest truth... I woke up one night back in the jungle – not even a dream – I awoke in bed with this bird sitting on my chest, this golden-red jungle bird. The thing whispered something to me. Told me things.'

'What'd the bird tell you?' I say.

'Don't joke with me, sir. I tell you true.' He sighs and stands up, turns towards the door.

'I'm not joking with you – what did the bird tell you?'

'Terrible things...' He turns back to me. 'I wish I could tell you, but it was in no tongue a man would understand.' His white eye is lookin at me with vague intensity. He lifts a finger to his forehead to bid me goodnight.

'Hey... the book.'

'Ah.' He returns to the desk, hand digging in the pocket of his coat. He fishes out a couple of coins and drops them on the desk.

'The nights don't treat me so good,' he says, then he turns to go. 'Be well.'

'Aye. Take her easy.'

The bell announces his retreat. When he's gone, I get up and turn my face to the ceiling. The jumpin has stopped. The soldiers must be at the girls.

When I get upstairs though, I can account for most of the ladies with a quick scan around the room. I call Lizzy. She comes over, leans against the wall and surveys the lounge with me.

'Two soldiers just came in. Where are they?'

She points to the door. 'Way out back. With the boys.'

'Both of em?'

'Aye. Pretty keen they were too.'

'You think they'll behave themselves?'

She shrugs. 'Got a good souse on, they has. They might, they might not.'

'Maybe I'll go and put an ear to the door. Just to be sure.'

I'm walkin away when she says, 'Got me a minute to spare, if you're game for it?'

'Jesus, Lizzy.' I look around for Miss Emily as I walk away. Woman'll be the end of me.

Outside the boys' room, I eariwig in. The soldiers are on one, but it doesn't sound violent. Far as I can tell, no one's gettin hurt.

First time I've seen soldiers here. Not the infantry type, these men are officers. Clearly they know someone or they wouldn't be here. I can't say The Nightingale'll ever be within reach of the common man, but I guess it was only a matter of time before the establishment attracted a few outliers. The madam wants a certain type of man here, though, and I'm not sure army types are what she intended.

'*Go on, you little Jezebel...*'

'*Show me your fucking arse...*'

From inside the room. I walk away.

I go to the office findin it empty; Miss Emily is out on the floor. I close the door and go to the window, and open the curtain onto the boudoir. Camila is on the bed, undressed to the waist and with a man on her lap. He's suckin on her nipple. Looks like he's cryin too, while she rocks him gently. Fuck sake. What's wrong with these men, I dunno. Fellow's like a fat, overgrown wee'un at the teet. Wouldn't surprise me if he was pissin into a nappy n'all. Then this chap'll put on his hat, go outside, and tomorrow he'll be sittin in a government office somewhere overseein food exports from Ireland while the men and women in the old country die in their thousands. And this is the enemy we can't drive from our shores?

Miss Emily comes in. I turn to her and nod.

'Well... anything interestin 'app'nin?'

I turn back to the window as she comes up behind. 'Just a grown man suckin on a teet like a baby.'

'Aye,' she says, whispery and relenting. 'But ain't you all big children at the end of the day.'

'May be, but I've never tried to suck the milk out of a dry whore,' I say. 'She's not even nursin.'

'You ain't seen nuffink. Some of the things I've seen would curdle the milk from the Virgin's tit, I tell ya. Men is depraved. They's sick.'

'You are right about that.' I sigh and turn away. 'You checked on the boys?'

'Aye,' she says. 'Sounds like they're finishin up in there. Maybe have a look out in the hall and see the two gentlemen out the door. They was in a bit of a rowdy state.'

'Aye. I'll do that.'

I go out. Suddenly I feel very, very tired. Maybe the brandy then the laudanum. Mixin em's never wise. As I'm turnin the corner in the hall, one of the soldiers is comin out the boys' room, still with the leer on his face, fixin up his breeches. He gazes back into the room, smirkin, before closin the door. I've no idea where the other is, whether he's still in the room or left already. I hang back and let him pass. He stares at me aggressively as he snaps a brace over his shoulder, his jacket under his arm. I see the pistol on his waist.

'Everything alright, sir?'

He sucks the air in and walks by sayin nothin. I let him pass then follow him into the lounge to make sure he sees himself out. Down the stairs and into the bookstore. As he reaches the door, I say, 'Night, sir.'

He stops and turns around.

'Irish, are you?'

I nod. 'I am.'

'Yes,' he says, all long and slow like he's got the measure of me. He steps over quietly. His jacket on his back now, he pulls at the lapels like the cock of the walk. We're in the semi-darkness, no one else about. Then he reaches down and into his breeches, and pulls out his prick. A faint hum of shit off him, and drink. He starts pullin on his tool.

'Ever play with an Englishman's cock?' he says.

I look him in the eye. 'You'd best be gettin on, sir.'

Quick, before I can move, he pushes me back against the wall. His rancid breath in my face now, his hand grabbin at my prick. 'Never taken an Englishman's tool inside you, you dirty Irish dog, hmm? Never bent over to take it from a gent?'

I push him away and take a swing but I'm too slow. He ducks, comes up with a fist to the stomach then catches me with a hook to the jaw. I go down. He lays a kick into me.

'You fucking scum Paddy, you fucking dog... put your hand on me, would you...'

176

Another kick, and another. When he's pantin and done, he spits and stumbles towards the door. I look up. The bell tinkles. I get up and stumble to the door.

Outside, in the brisk night air, I follow him down the street.

***

Outside the window, carriages rattle over the cobbles. The clop of hooves rings out in the dense air. London sits implacable, verisimilar, a mirage against the dull watercolour of the sky. This city seems a phantasm. Only its filthy aspects give it reality: the grime, the noxious fumes, the corruption, the violence. The depravity. Buenos Aires was no utopia, but there was morality. Perhaps too much. London is the spiritual successor to Ancient Rome. The English too have their coliseums, the only difference is they're far from here, on colonial shores, where the people don't have to bear witness to the slaughter. Yes, they have an appetite for wealth but not the stomach for its accumulation. Convenient, that they do not have to see the barbarity.

I do not defend him, but my father, thirsty for power as he is, has also the stomach to seize it. That is a man. Those who pull the strings here in the imperial city of London are happy to turn their eyes from the vast destructions of empire. Perhaps this is why they come to The Nightingale nightly to suffer humiliation. They have not the heart, and they know it. Their prostration is the affirmation of their lily-liveredness. This is how they live with themselves. It's their penance.

And what does that make me? A priest? A curate of the weak and the damned? Nay. Like the vulture that picks at the insides of its prey, I will devour them piece by piece. And let no one say the vulture is a base animal. Look at the vulture in flight, or sitting atop its cragged perch. It's a thing of beauty. True, it's not majestic like the jaguar. The jaguar is a being apart. The jaguar has a greater soul than any man. Devoid of morality, it is superior in every way. It does not think, it is pure instinct.

I look down at the *caapi* in my hand. I can't hide from it any longer.

Should I keep putting it off, my fear will get the better of me. I must journey inside before the window closes. A *karai* knows when to strike. Hesitation can mean defeat.

For now, I put it back in the chest and close it up. I take a last look out the window at the fading light of day before drawing the blinds. Soon it will be dark. Right on cue, there's a rap at the door.

'Miss?' The maid holds up the candle that she may light the lamps in the room.

I nod. 'Come in.'

When she's done, she stops at the door. 'Shall I 'lert the cook, miss, that you'll be taking your dinner soon?'

'No, leave it for an hour. I'm not quite hungry yet.'

'Very well.'

When she's gone I go to my room and get into my robe. Dressing is tiresome. Sometimes I want to go like the Guaraní – a simple cotton dress is all a woman needs. How free you feel when unconstrained by layers of unnecessary clothing. Woman is a prisoner even in her vesture. Would that we were still clothed in our nakedness, as we came into this world. What sin in our raw state?

I go downstairs to seek out Constancia. She must get lonely here, all day by herself. Still I wonder if I have not done her wrong by bringing her here. She is more alone than I; at least I have my souls for company. She has no one.

I find her in the sitting room downstairs. She's at the sewing machine. She looks up and smiles when I come in.

'Mi amor...' I kiss her on the cheek. 'How are you?' I pull up a chair beside her.

'Si, bien. Como estas?'

'Well. Business is good. Here – I brought you something.'

She takes the bag and opens it. Inside is a book. She takes it out and reads the title: '*Poemas de Amor.*' The little breathy gasp that slips from her lips, and the rosy hue that assails her cheek, makes my heart flutter.

'Me encanta,' she says.

I put a hand on her arm. 'Will you read me one later?'

178

'No,' she exclaims bashfully, but I know she will. She would deny me nothing. And I so like to hear her read. Her voice is like a starling on the wing. It carries me away.

'What are you making?' I ask.

'Antimacassars,' she says. She holds one up.

'Are they for George?'

She giggles. 'For any man that may sit in our parlour.'

'Mi amor, is there something you aren't telling me?'

She knows I joke with her, and she gives me a mock scolding look. I put a hand on her arm.

'Come, sit with me for a little. I want to tell you all about my day.'

'Si, señora.'

For the first time ever, her address grates on me. It sounds cold and distant. She has never called me any different, so how indeed should she call me?

After dinner, we play a game of briscola. Constancia is competitive. She plays with a seriousness that borders on the endearing.

'Si!' She throws her cards down and claps her hands in joy when I'm routed. I smile. Do I let her win? To do so would be more cruel than I could bear.

'I give up. That's enough for one night.' I reach out to collect the cards. She grasps for them but lays her hand on mine. She pulls it away.

'We cannot! One more round...'

I look at the score sheet and smile. 'Fine. One more.'

She deals, her eyes on mine. She's going for the kill. I give her a sly look, sly but playful. A look that says, *Get ready to be mastered.* Constancia gives as good as she gets. When the cards are down, I say, 'You are competitive like a man.'

She doesn't balk. 'You are more man than any man I know.'

I raise my eyebrows. My hand hangs motionless over the cards. 'Why do you say that?'

'You are your father's daughter.'

I don't know what to say. She has never been so forthright. And the look in her eye is one I've never seen before. Like she's goading me.

I shake my head and put down a card. I almost scold her. I'm not her mistress anymore. We are more. We are sisters.

'I should have been born a man,' I say. 'My life would not have the complications it does now. It should have been much easier than it has been. A man has a simple, boring and uncomplicated life. A woman's has far too many layers. If a woman is a complex and rich cake, a man is... a pancake.'

Hearing the idiocy of my words, I put down my cards. We break into laughter.

'I am not a cake,' Constancia says. 'I am *dulce de leche*.'

'My sweet Constancia, you are a tonic. I don't know what I would do without you.' I pick up my cards. 'Play.'

'It was your mother taught me how to play,' she says, placing a card on the table.

'I know. I remember.'

'I learned a lot from your mother. She was a good teacher. She was also...'

'What?'

'Ruthless. Like you.'

'You surprise me tonight. I have never heard you talk like this.' A flush comes on her cheek. 'I know sometimes you hate me for bringing you here. But I know you love me too, and that you forgive me. I couldn't bear it if you detested me.'

She puts down a Jack. I play a three. She looks at me with a flash of resentment. Then she stands up and goes to the window.

'Constancia...'

I leave the table and go to her. I stand behind her and put a hand on her arm. Her body is stiff.

'Tell me you don't hate me, please...'

Her demeanour cold, she looks out the window. Her fits I'm familiar with, but this one is harsh. I feel it in my stomach as a physical pain.

She stares outside into the empty, silent London street. The flicker of the lamps makes it seem the room is breathing. I move closer to her, put a hand on her waist.

'Mi amor...'

My body pressed against hers, our hearts beat together. I cannot abide this – we are sisters. There is no distance between souls such as ours. I put my other hand on her waist and slide them around her body until my hands clasp her belly. I feel her shaking now. I too am trembling. I'm aware of the quickness of my breath on her skin; I see the fine hairs on the back of her neck shiver. Closing my eyes, I place my head against hers.

'Mi amor, tell me you don't hate me... I could not bear it. I would rather die...'

The tremble in her body changes to a shudder as my hand rises to her breast and I kiss her neck as if I were kissing something sacred. She gasps, a sudden intake of breath. Then she clasps my hand.

'No...' she whispers.

She breaks from me and runs from the room.

'Constancia,' I say. But she has flown.

Oh God forgive me...

I lay awake in bed, my stomach tight, my heart aching. What have I done? Have I ruined everything? All this way across the world to start a new life, and to alienate, perhaps irrevocably, the only person in the world I trust, a person I would happily give my life for...

I turn to face the wall. In the darkness, shadows writhe. I feel I'm being attacked. Unseen demons encroach on me, I feel the touch on my skin as they flit over the bed. I can't stay here. I must go to her. I shall die tonight if I don't.

I turn back the covers of the bed and get out. Quietly, I go down the hall to where she lays. Does she sleep? Or does she lie awake as I do, in torment? If I had any faith in god I should pray to him now. The door is closed, but I turn the handle and open it. The room is still, but tense. She's awake, I'm sure of it. Silently, I go to the side of the bed. She lies facing the window but I see the rise and fall of her breathing. Does it quicken?

'Mi amor?' I whisper. She doesn't answer. I know she hears me.

Dios, tengo miedo. I pull back the cover and slip in. Her body shifts. I lift the cover over us and slide close to her.

'Mi amor,' I whisper, 'I cannot bear your silence. Talk to me. Please.'

The heat of her body, the scent of her hair. I rest a hand on her shoulder. When she does not pull away, I let a finger graze her skin. I fold myself unto her. My sex aches. I want her. And I have never known it until this moment.

'Te amo, mi amor. Te amo...'

I brush the hair from her neck and kiss her there. I feel her skin prickle. A suppressed sigh. Her body twists, pushing at once into me and away. My hand comes to rest on her hips.

'Te quiero...'

I kiss her again: her neck, her shoulder. Her hand finds mine and squeezes. A remonstration.

I pull up her nightdress until my hand is on the warm outside of her thigh.

'No,' she whispers. But desire is in that word. Unmistakably and irrefutably planted there, swollen and replete. I have educed the word from her, and it tells me what my body wants to hear.

My heart is pounding now. My hand shakes as it drifts between her legs.

'Es pecado,' she whispers, her voice filled with a fearful urgency.

But she is wet. 'No, mi amor. No...'

I turn her face to mine. She looks me in the eye. A look of Christian terror. But it is pregnant too. It is that which must be unspoken, and it is overpowering.

'It is just what we want,' I say.

I close my eyes and put my lips to hers as I let my fingers drift to her sex.

In her I will lose myself.

it was not a dream

I am no killer, but I've killed. No man knows he can kill til the time comes, til the haze comes over him. And when it happens, it's the only thing he can do. Times like that the fire's in a man, burn him clean through 'less he acts. And let it be said, inaction can be as destructive as doing what needs doin.

First time was in Buenos Aires. One of Rosas's thugs. S'why I left the country in a hurry with the madam – couldn't stick around when there was a chance they'd catch up with me. Them boys was savage. I've seen some savages in my time, and I'll tell ya, they don't go about in face paint and loincloth. They're draped in finery, with top hats and fine jackets, and with the mark of respectability about em. To your face they'll have the chin up, but when your back's turned the knife'll be at your throat. I never saw men for the knife like those fellas. For them it was sport.

One fine southern night I came out the taverna lit on rum. One of those nights you have the world in ya, a heart fulla kingdoms. Goin back to my room, sails in my step, when I came across him in a side street. He'd a woman on the ground, fittin to defile her. Would have killed her after, of course, there was no mercy from those fellas. Be done with it and leave no trace, that was the way of em. In truth they were no men. They were animals. I came up with a rock in my hand. The fire in me kept the aim straight and it struck him on the temple before he even seen me behind him. I bashed his head in as the poor girl watched – a poor German girl with no word of English. I picked her up and told her to get off. At first she wouldn't let go of me, maybe she'd nowhere to go, I dunno. I had to shove her away to get her movin. When she'd disappeared I took the blade from the thug and slit his throat just to be sure. Then I stripped him. Took the clothes from his back, 'specially the overcoat, the burgundy they wore that signed em as Rosas's men, and after I'd bundled his clothes and was fittin to run, I figured I couldn't leave him like he was. I took the knife and sliced up his face so they couldn't fix his identity. His clothes I weighed down with a rock and dropped in the river. I stripped myself too and washed there on the banks til I was clean of blood.

When I woke up in the mornin, I felt I'd woken from a dream. I knew it was no dream, but part of me was happy to leave it seem so. Still feels like I mighta dreamt it. A continental dream soaked in the blood of a savage.

A man who lives like an animal has no right to go on livin.

Sittin on the bed, I turn the officer's gun over in my hand. This time too feels like a dream. And it wasn't just the laudanum in my veins. Killin a man has an unreality to it. At the very moment someone ceases to exist, a vacuum is created. Where once there was somethin, suddenly nothin. That emptiness does not belong in the world. It's of another order.

I killed a man and it was not a dream. But I won't lose any sleep over it. None.

I wrap the gun in the cloth and open the window, and reach up to push it into a small alcove below the eaves of the roof. Better it isn't found if they come lookin. And come lookin they might.

When there's a knock on the door at five in the mornin, the heart on me stops. I lift the head from the bed and listen.

'Oi, Paddy...'

'Jesus fucking Christ,' I mutter.

I get up and go to the door. Lizzy's there, holdin up her skirts.

'Could do with some cleanin out here, Paddy,' she says.

'What – you're lady of the manor all of a sudden, are ya?' She nips in. I close the door. 'Anyone know you left?'

She shakes her head. 'Madam don't come in til late in the morning. George is snoring, he's out for the count in the lounge. Don't worry, no one's the wiser.'

I shake my head. 'This ain't no good, Lizzy. No good at all. We can't be gettin in the habit. She'll fucken get wise to it, I'm tellin ya.'

She pulls off her dress, then sits down and starts takin off her boots. I just stare. Then she looks up at me and says, 'Well what in the blazes is you waitin for?'

I strip to the raw. The lad pokin up already. When I get into bed she takes my prick and squeezes it. She puts the lips on me. I pull away.

'Jesus, Lizzy, I can still taste the auld fellas on ya.'

'Oh fuck sake...'

She rolls over on her belly. 'Go on then...'

I climb up on her back, put the tool between the fat cheeks of her arse. Slide it in. 'Oh fuck...'

'Aw, sweet mother, go on, give it to me...'

I bite her neck as I ease in and out of her. Mornins, it's nice and slow like. I slide in and out, already bracin against the threatenin climax.

'Fuck, Lizzy, you're wetter than a London spring mornin...'

'Aren't you the poet...' She reaches up and grabs my hair. I bite her shoulder. In seconds, I empty into her.

She moans and pushes back on me. I lie there, spent and pantin.

When I roll off, she turns and takes my cock in hand. 'Don't you even think about goin off to sleep.' She pulls the mickey. 'Another shot or two, then I'll be gettin off...'

I wake up, she's gone. The bed's in all disarray and I'm still in the raw, clean stuck to the sheets. The woman doesn't half leak. I get up and heat some potato from the day before. Once I've somethin in my stomach I've a quick clean and get dressed. Before I can get to the door, there's another rap. It's George.

'Fuck are you doin here, big fella, at this time of the day?'

'There's a couple of soldiers at the club, Paddy. They's asking questions.'

'About what?' I say, liftin the jacket from the back of the door. But I know what.

'Seems one of their fellas is gone missin.'

'The madam there?'

He nods. 'Yes she is.'

'Fuck.'

I close the door behind me. 'Let's get on then.'

Big Georgie's feet clap on the wooden floorboards. No words goin down the stairs. Out in the street, Georgie looks at the ground as we walk.

'Time is it, big fella?'

''Bout eleven.'

'Aye.' I take the pouch outta my pocket and roll a cigarette. Georgie to his credit, doesn't ask me fuck all. We walk silently to The Nightingale. Upstairs, a few of the girls lounge in recliners. Camila's sittin in her undergarments. Lizzy eyes me queerly as I pass. I wink, and rough up a smile. Probably she thinks I'm here cause the madam knows about us. There's a crease of worry around her eyes.

We go on back to the office and go in. Miss Emily sits at the desk. The camera's been stashed away. No sign of the madam. It's like I feel her, though. *In the shadows.*

Standing watchin us as we enter are two soldiers. One of em I recognise.

'Morning Mr. Ryan,' Miss Emily says. She gestures to the soldiers. 'This is Officer Poole and Lieutenant Davies. Lieutenant Davies was 'ere several nights ago, with a fellow of his unit, do you 'member?'

I nod. 'I do, miss, I mind them well.'

'Well, it seems summink might've 'appened when his friend left.'

'Oh?' I turn to the two men. The officer steps forward. One finger is hooked in his belt, the other held aloft as if he's holdin a pipe.

'One of my men was here two nights ago, fellow. Lieutenant Geach left before Lieutenant Davies here. He did not return to his posting. We are trying to ascertain where he went after he left, and his current whereabouts.'

The officer reached into his pocket, his hand emerging with his pipe. A plug of tobacco follows, which he pushes into the bowl. He turns to Miss Emily and raises an eyebrow. She nods. He lifts the candle on her desk and puffs til the pipe glows.

'So,' he says, 'Mr. Ryan?' I nod. 'Might you have seen our Lieutenant Geach?'

'I did. Saw him come in, saw him leave.'

'Oh?' The officer takes the pipe from his mouth and spits out a speck of tobacco.

'Like you say. He left before his friend here. I saw him go out the door, and that's all I can tell you. Wasn't nothin strange to see. I didn't take no note of it, anyway.' I glance at the other Lieutenant. He doesn't look comfortable. Ain't no mystery why.

Officer Poole takes the pipe from his mouth and puts out his right foot. He examines his boot. Turns it to see what he might have trampled on on the way here. He looks at me. 'Did you happen to see what way Lieutenant Geach went when he left here?'

I nod. 'Yeah, I walked him down the stairs. He went out and took himself down Chadwick Street in the direction of Horseferry Road. Can't tell you more than that.'

'Strange.' He turns to Lieutenant Davies. Davies is sweatin now.

'It's very strange, sir. Very strange.' Davies shakes his head.

Poole watches him for a second then turns back to Miss Emily. 'We fear some mischief has befallen him, ma'am. We're still not sure what has happened, but we'll get to the bottom of it, I promise you.' He puffs on the pipe and turns to look at me and George for a second. Then he turns back to her. 'I wasn't familiar with your establishment, ma'am, until Lieutenant Davies here brought it to my attention. You are very discreet. I gather you want to remain that way. If any new information comes to you, I trust you'll share it with me.'

Miss Emily's unruffled. Steady as a rock. She sits forward in the chair, looks Poole dead in the eye. 'I can assure you, sir, if there was anyfink else we knew, then you would've 'eard it already. We run a very tight ship 'ere. Our girls are honest and these two men 'ere straight as they come. I only hope you find out what 'appened after he left. You know, when men go on a carouse, things can turn ugly. Things can turn real ugly.' She turns to me. 'Only a short time ago, Mr. Ryan here took a knife to the belly while walking 'ome. And for what? For a piece of silver. Yes, there are bad men out there, Officer Poole. And I ain't saying your fellow has 'ad a run-in with one of em – for all I know, he's sittin in the corner of a tavern somewhere. Yes, that's the most likely explanation, don't you fink?'

The officer turns red. His foot lifts off the floor, like he's about to stamp it. Then he clamps his pipe between his teeth and turns to Davies, gestures with a tilt of his head towards the door.

'Ma'am, we thank you for your time. We trust we haven't disturbed you too much. Like you say, our man will likely show up eventually. We'll just have to wait and see.'

Miss Emily stands and comes over. She walks the officer to the door. 'We've shared all we can with you, Officer Poole. But I promise you, should anyfink else come to our knowledge, we'll come find you at the barracks.'

'Thank you.'

She turns to George. 'Will you see the gentlemen out, please?'

'Yes, miss.'

When they're gone, Miss Emily says, 'You better sit down. The madam wants a word.'

My heart drops into my stomach. I nod. 'Yeah, sure.'

She puts a hand on my shoulder and gives it a squeeze. 'She'll be in soon as the men are gone.'

Miss Emily goes out. I don't have the heart to sit. I go and stand by the window. The curtains are pulled. A few minutes later, I hear her footsteps comin down the hall. The door opens and she comes in.

'Miss,' I say. I walk towards the table. She meets me in the middle of the floor.

'Tell me what happened, Mr. Ryan.'

Her gaze leaves no room for deception. I stutter out a reply. 'I killed him, miss. I killed the fellow.'

'Mierda.' The flash in her eyes leaves me momentarily struck. I see murder there. A lightning flash, then it's gone. 'Will they find him?'

'He may surface upriver in a day or two.'

She goes around the table and stands with her back to me. I don't plead, don't try to explain. I stay silent. I look at the curve of her shoulders, wondering how a creature so fine, so elegant, can hold such violent impossibilities within her. When she speaks again, there's a kind of terminality in her voice.

'You are becoming somewhat of a liability, Mr. Ryan.'

***

Miss Emily puts the hand-written note in my hand, and waits there as I read it. She's as curious as I. As soon as I begin reading, I recognise the handwriting. I smile. Miss Emily raises her eyebrows questioningly.

'See the boys are ready at three. We've a client wishes to pay a visit. Utmost discretion. See what you can do.'

'Oh my... sounds very mysterious. Who do you think it is?'

'I have my suspicions.' I fold the note. 'Let's just wait and see.'

'What if someone comes in the meantime, wants to see the boys?'

'You tell them they're unavailable.'

'Certainly, ma'am.' She lifts her skirts and goes out the door. When it closes behind her, I take the note and go to the drawer where the pictures are stored. I take out the box.

My collection expands. Not only do I have a growing assortment of pictures of the men who come here in every kind of compromising posture, but other things I also gather. Notes that have been relieved from the *porte-monnaie* of gentlemen. Or a love note that a politician has scribbled to one of our whores. Pornographic materials carried surreptitiously in pockets, and articles pertaining to matters that have no place in a whorehouse: legal documents, matters of court, matters of parliament. All these things I've begun to amass. I take the note and file it among my other peculiarities. *Currency.* A safeguard. In this land, in this city, among these people, I must do whatever necessary to protect myself.

I close the drawer and lock it.

I hear giggling from the room next door. I go to the curtain and open it. Inside, on the bed, Mary lies draped in the arms of Luara. They are indulging in some silliness. I watch them, a smile creeping onto my lips. Such tenderness that may exist only between two women. I think of Constancia and feel my entire body flush. I have discovered an intimacy, a sweetness, a joy and passion I have never known with any man. Her gentleness, her naivety, even her trepidation... such things cause a furore to awaken within me. To think of our night makes me quiver with excitement. She was like a child in her innocence, yet embraced me with full abandon. I watch the two girls: Luara's hand in Mary's hair, her lips against her temple, an arm slung lazily over her naked belly... Suddenly, and with blind desire, I want Constancia. I want to lay her down and press myself against her naked body and hear the breath leave her. I want to fill the vacuum within. I want to invade and consume her. Taste her skin. Feel her tremble beneath me. Feel myself tremble at her innocent terror. I want to make her whole.

I look at the clock. It's almost twelve. If I rush home now, I can certainly be back by three.

I go outside and find Miss Emily. 'I'm running out on an errand. I'll be back in an hour or two.'

She looks at me quizzically, but nods.

I pause and whisper to her: 'Make sure the cameras are set up and ready to go.'

I hurry down the stairs.

I blow softly in her ear and watch her shiver. A tiny smile plays on her face. She pushes me away but I hold her tighter.

'No, I shan't let you go,' I say. I present her my ear. 'Go on, do it to me...'

She giggles. I feel her hot breath. My toes curl. I wrap my arms around her waist and caress her belly, and run the tip of my finger around her bellybutton. I press my lips to her temple and run my hands through her hair. Such endless pleasure one woman may experience with another. What pronouncements of passion may I bestow on her? Can I convey the joy she has stirred in me?

I place a hand between her wet thighs. Instinctively, she clamps them tight. I force my hand towards her sex, she moans and buries her face in my neck. She can't bear to look at me when I touch her. Instead, her lips tell of her sweet distress. They pepper my neck with reckless, greedy kisses. I pull her tighter. Our bodies are hot and heaving, our breath laboured. Our breasts press together and our limbs shudder with a nervous, frantic electricity. The press of her breasts against mine fills me with gentle devastation. Tiny parts of me effervesce and float away at every trembling touch of her fingers and lips. I whisper in her ear: 'Tú eres mía, mi amor. Siempre.'

She moans. I push back her hair and kiss her neck. My hands grope blindly at her body. I'm overcome with a sensual fury. Pushing her back on the bed, I kiss her breasts, her nipples, her belly. Then I slip down between her thighs. She gasps in horror.

'No, por dios, señora, *no...*'

I put my mouth to her sex as her thighs clamp around my head. Driven to new heights of insane desire.

After, we lie in deep embrace. Constancia has her head buried in my shoulder.

'You don't need to be ashamed, mi amor,' I say. I kiss her on the forehead. 'There's no sin if two people love each other. And you love me, don't you?'

She doesn't answer. I feel her silence in my very core.

'Tell me you love me, I beg you... you're killing me.'

Her hands betray a clawing hunger. 'Te amo,' she whispers.

I raise her face to mine and look her in the eye. 'I love you,' I say, and kiss her on the lips. A tear rolls down her cheek. I catch it with my finger and put it to my lips. Caressing her, I feel her breath on my face.

'Never be ashamed of something that makes you happy.'

I squeeze her tight until her body and mine are as one. And yet, and yet... there's something, a vulnerability, something, that still exists between us. Another tear wets my shoulder. What can I say, what can I do, to reassure her?

I glance at the clock. It has just gone two. I push my hands into her hair and kiss her neck, and prepare to break away. But her arms hold me tight, tighter than I've ever been held.

After a long and teeming silence, she says, 'What shall become of us?'

I cover her face with kisses, taking on my lips the tears that still wet her face. 'We shall love each other and be happy.'

'Is he here yet?' I put my bag on the desk in the office and take off my gloves.

Miss Emily shakes her head.

'And the camera? Is it set up?'

'Yes miss. Ready to go.'

'Come and show me.'

We go out of the office and down the hall to the small box room. The camera has been arranged by the mirror. Beyond, an empty room. The boys must be in the lounge with the girls.

'Where's George?'

'He's around somewhere, miss. Shall I fetch him?'

'Yes. Go on.'

She goes out. I check through the viewing lens of the camera. This is what I built this place for. To have pictures of the country's highest politicians caught raw in their illicit pursuits. My hands are shaking with anticipation. It's not the money that's the drug, it's power. Power is the goal. And with leverage like this, it'll be mine simply to reach out and take. Should I wish to turn the tide of events in Argentina, I might simply pull the levers. Who knows what I may accomplish.

Miss Emily returns with George. George nods respectfully. He really is a good man. Perhaps too good to be working here. It may be that I have to find other employment for him.

'George, there's an important dignitary on his way here, and he has asked for the utmost discretion. He's here to meet our young fellows, so I want you to ensure he gets in here without seeing anyone. If there's someone in the shop below when he comes, you'll need to bring him in the back. Maybe it's better you do that anyway. And take him straight here, to the boys' room.'

'Very well, miss.'

'George, you look nervous. Are you alright?'

'Just fine, miss. Only, you don't need me to, you know...' He points at the camera.

'Does it trouble you, George?'

He shakes his head. 'It's just, I don't like to see that, miss, if you get me. You know, with the little boys 'n that.'

'The boys are not so "little", George. And they like their work.'

'All the same, miss. If you don't mind...'

I wave a hand. 'Don't worry, George. Miss Emily will take care of it.'

'Thank you. It's just—'

'You don't need to explain, George. Go wait downstairs for our guest to arrive.'

He nods politely and goes out. Miss Emily moves close and lowers her voice.

'So do you know who it is comin, ma'am?' Her face ages in the very asking of the question, so taut it is with intrigue.

'Yes.' I leave the answer hanging.

'So is you gonna share it with me or no?'

I smile. 'When he comes through the door it won't be a secret anymore.' I sigh and glance through the viewing lens one more time. 'It's the Foreign Minister, Miss Emily.'

'Of Britain?'

'Yes.'

'Oh my.' She falls silent as she takes this in.

'Know the man who comes here sometimes, calls himself Vallans?'

'Vaughan's his real name, innit? A right nonce, that one.'

'Yes. Well, they have some connection. I think Vaughan was here to get a feel for the place ahead of a visit by the Foreign Minister. They're in cahoots, I believe.'

She takes out her pipe and stuffs it with a plug of tobacco, her face full of a kind of childish excitement. 'Oh I do say, ma'am, you never can tell, can you. The Foreign Minister. Palmerston's his name, innit?' She shakes her head. 'They're all at it. They's a right bunch of dirty buggers, all of em.'

The pipe in hand, she takes a puff, still shaking her head. Then she looks at me, as if reading my mind.

'I'll go get the boys, shall I?'

'Yes, let's bring them in.'

She nods and goes out. I take a final look around then go to the office, leaving the door ajar so I can hear when he arrives. Miss Emily bustles the boys down the hall. They sound in light spirits. I pace the floor nervously. Why I feel this way I do not know. I've conquered better men than Palmerston. Reaching into my bosom, I take out the kerchief that I lifted from Constancia's dresser before I left. I put it to my nose and inhale. My head is filled with her perfume. I feel my heart race. Is this mere folly? Have I lost my mind?

I put the kerchief back in my bosom. I can't get distracted, not now. I go to the door and listen outside. The sound of footsteps on the back stairs. George, huffing as he climbs. A second footfall. He's here. I wait until I hear a knock on the boys' door. After a time, it closes again.

When I've waited for a minute, I go out. I walk calmly down the hall to the back room, going inside and closing the door with great care. Miss Emily is at the mirror, watching events inside. She turns to me and puts a finger to her lips. I come up beside her to see the spectacle. The excitement bristles between us.

Inside, Palmerston stands by the bed, while the two boys peel off their clothes.

'I have you,' I whisper.

***

I'm in the habit of taking the gun down from its hiding spot and holdin it. I like the feel of it in my hand. Its heavier than it appears; perhaps it's the weight of all the souls it has claimed. I imagine firin it into a human body. I've fought with knives before but never a gun. And a man can't help but wonder. I hold it out in front of me, take aim along the barrel. I flick it up as I mouth the sound of it firin. Who should I shoot? Should I track down Officer Poole and put a bullet in his head? What would be the point in that? Perhaps a politician instead. The next fucken lord that says a sideways word to me. Do it outside parliament. That'd make the papers. They'd execute me. I'd be hanged for sure. But at least I'd have done somethin before I died.

I roll up the gun and stash it back in the eaves. Then I take my jacket and go off to work.

'All alright here, Georgie?'

He dons his hat and nods. 'All is right, Paddy. No trouble.'

'Go on home with ye and see the missus. How's the bairn doin?'

A rash grin crosses the big man's face. 'Aw, she's a little diamond, she is. A diamond, I tell ya. I swear, when I walk in the door and she sees me, her little face lights up. And I take her from the missus and hold her in my arm, and there's this baby smell off her little head that makes me all warm inside.'

'You're a big teddybear, Georgie.' I slap him on the arm. 'Give my regards to the missus.'

Off he goes, a jaunt in his step. Funny what'll make some men happy.

Upstairs, Lizzy winks at me as I pass through the lounge. I nod back. Gotta stay away from that woman. I'm in enough shit with the madam as is.

The madam's in the office, sortin through her war chest. Pictures and what have you. She's a collector. I'd hate to become part of her collection.

'Evenin, miss.'

'Good evening, Mr. Ryan. Is George away?'

'He is.'

'Good. Mr. Ryan, are you disposed to do something for me this evening?'

'Somethin outside of my duties here, miss?' A dread feelin comes over me.

'Yes. It would be something of a more unsavoury nature. Like before.'

I don't feel I've a choice in the matter. 'When I came here to work for you, miss, I didn't foresee that it would involve so many, you know, dark doings.'

She nods, all slow and sleeked. 'I'm aware of that. I didn't either. But this is the last time I'll ask such a thing of you. I promise.'

I scratch my head. 'Alright then. What is it?'

At nine o'clock I'm at 17 Eccleston Square, just like the madam said. Never driven a carriage before. Not a bad old trick. If things turn at The Nightingale, maybe I'll seek out employment as a cabbie. Things look different from up above. Gives a man another perspective.

I get down from the cab and go up the steps. The street's quiet. Fog-laden, the lamps flicker from the mist and disappear in the night's sodden maw. I knock the door. It's answered.

'I'm here for Mister Terrero,' I say to the lady.

'Wait here please,' she says unceremoniously and closes the door. While I'm waitin there on the steps, I realise: *I don't wanna do this.*

When the door opens, he's standin there. He looks at me and scratches his chin.

'Mister Terrero?'

He nods. 'Yes.'

'My mistress has asked that you meet her. She told me to give you this.'

He opens the note and eyes it eagerly. 'Yes?' His face expectant. 'Now?'

'Yes sir.'

'Okay. Please, a moment.'

He closes the door and goes back inside. Seems like a genteel enough fellow. Not at all like the madam described him. Still, she's not the lyin type, is she?

When he comes back, he's with the overcoat on and hat in hand. He puts it on his head as we go down the steps. I open the door of the carriage.

'We are going to her residence, yes?'

'No sir,' I say. 'She's asked that you meet her at the port. She's at a gathering with some acquaintances.'

'On a boat? This time of evening?'

'London is a strange city, sir.'

After a pause, he climbs in. I close the door and hop into the cab. 'Come on then boy. Off ya go.' The gelding takes off at a trot.

Somethin about the sound of a horse on the hoof. Puts a man at ease. Makes him homesick, too. Hardly been up on a horse since I left home. Wasn't much of a man for ridin, anyway. The way things was, a man went one of two ways, and if he took to the sea, he didn't have much time for horses and the like. Still, there's a good solid feelin about the beasts. They're a dumb animal but reliable. I give the rein a crack as we turn onto St. George's Road. The horse is goin at a good clop. It's late and the road is quiet, only a few cabbies out searchin a bit of late-night trade. Air heavy with coal. We cross Lupus Street and head down Claverton onto Grosvenor Road. Now we're by the river. Seems she'll never let me be. She flows moraine-heavy through the city, morose and judgemental. River be damned. I reach into the inside of my jacket where the billy club sits. Hand on the hilt, I test the weight of it.

As we pull up to Pimlico Pier, the sounds of revelry from the Rosetta reaches us. I turn off the road and roll the carriage down towards the jetty. It clambers to a halt. I look at the boat moored up by the pier, festooned with lamps and with the sound of music within. I glance around to see who's about, seein no one. Dark here. From here to the boat, a hundred yards or so. Before I can get down from the cab, the door of the carriage is opening.

'Sir...' I get down. He looks about him.

'Where is she? What are we doing here?' he says.

'Sir...' I point to the boat. '...the madam is entertaining. She asked that you join her. She apologises for the late invitation. It was a surprise, you see.'

'A surprise?'

'Please, you'll have to ask her. I know nothin more.' He puts on his hat. I point down the pier. 'I'll take you to her.'

When he turns and walks towards the jetty, I take the billy club from my pocket and hold it close to my thigh. I don't know how, or where the feelin comes from, but from nowhere I get a surge of anger, a bristling, a sudden reversal. Now I want to do this. I wanna clobber him. I want to hurt him. I wanna break his head open and watch him bleed. The feelin frightens me. When he steps onto the end of the jetty, I take a last look around. Then I swing. The club catches him on the back of the neck and he drops. The hat rolls off his head and over the side.

'Shit,' I mutter. Too late. It'll have to be left. I roll him on his back and reach into his pocket, takin out the letter. I crumple it and push it into my trouser pocket. Then I roll him to the edge and over. He falls with a heavy, sick thud into the skiff below. Something cracks. The drop has probably killed him.

I hurry down the steps and hop in. Cover him with the tarp. Then I untie the skiff and push off.

A peace comes over me. The night savant curls and bursts with the swell of the river; the water and the sky, both black and imperturbable, meld and create a union of the elements. If a man sits still enough, he can feel the earth in him. I feel it now, the riled effluence of water and air, silver-spun eddies that whirl inside me. Even with the weight of a dead man in the boat, the skiff skims the water, aloft in the London night. London could be New York, could be Buenos Aires, the river stink the same no matter here or there. I put a hand over the edge of the skiff to tease the water. The hand disappears into the murk, I take it up cold and bristling; my head tingles from the sheer elation of it. Before I forget, I take the billy club from my pocket and drop it into the water. It floats away. Some child will lift it perchance, or some docker. It'll disappear into a jacket pocket and find itself in some unremarkable Limehouse home. Perhaps it'll split someone else's skull a year, or ten years, from now. Do things have a memory, like the river? Do they recall events? The river knows all – all who've sailed on her, all that live through her and all those that've died too. Know how the river remembers? Drop a core into the bed below and bring it back up... in it, a record of the years and centuries. The river doesn't forget. Maybe it'll remember my deeds. But it won't hold em against me. The river doesn't judge. The river is not concerned with the things of men.

Winchester Wharf, Phoenix Wharf, Cox's Quay. Billingsgate, Pickle Herring Stairs. Traitor's Gate, Jerusalem Wharf. Fountain Dock, Cherry Garden Pier.

Elephant Wharf. The Tristram is sitting idle, her captain smokin, one foot restin on the gunwale. He takes the pipe from his mouth as I draw up alongside him, taps it on the side of the boat and puts it in his pocket.

'Ryan, is it?'

'Aye.'

Our exchange complete, I lift the tarp, take the gentleman under the arms and lift him. The old sailor drags him onto the tug.

With a nod, our business is concluded. The only sound I hear as I turn the skiff downriver is the shuck of the man's shovel as it slings into the pile of coal on his deck. I look once over my shoulder to see him toss a shovel-load over his lumpen cargo.

Elephantine, my dreams. Dreams abhor a vacuum.

The pipe bestows on me the far ken of my reveries.

Chandoo Charlie gives me a bed and a pipe. My dream tonight is of all London. I encompass the city like a great suffocating cloud. The smog of Ryan. I embrace the city, hear my children whisper, hear their dreams and sorrows. Little sisters they sing to me and mothers weep, and the dead of the city sough and cause the river to tremble. I breathe new life into the river, the arteries of the great sooty sprawl. My breath is filled with continental serenades and Amazonian terror, the raw hum of guana and opium tonic, and Hindoo alms and Irish seas, and the first nights of the dead and the holy laments of the living. *Sonnets, sonnets, in the embryonic hum of the night's fog-laden echo. I am echo. I am the sonnet. I am the first demise of day and the onset of the great fell darkening. But do not fear, there is music to be heard yet.* I disperse and pour into every lane and gutter, every chimney and sewer and lock, every back alley, sweep under every door until London is silent entire, silent ever. I have eaten every whisper. Every howl, every sigh, every scutter. Until, there in the midst of the city, alone and imperial, I hear the padding of its steps on the cobbles. A rattle in its throat, a deep, sonorous reverberating rattle. Then a hollow rasp. Unmistakeable: It is prowling. On the hunt. Alien here in the city yet it fears nothing.

I find myself alone on the cold street. Barefoot, gun in hand. No longer embodying the vast fog of my dreams, now it is I beheld. It's the Jaguar holding the city in its vast ken, stranger here yet its instincts are unchanged. Instinctively, I crouch. When the animal's larynx rattles once again, I feel it around me. Inside me. In my very body. I grip the pistol tighter.

I am hunted.

Hunted, there's only one escape; I too must hunt. I must turn and face it, this night predator, this outsider, one come among us to fill the night with trepidation. *What does it want? Is its only purpose to kill?*

No, I know there's more. Souls are what it seeks. I feel the hunger, the need for souls, a vast unconquerable hunger for souls. Mine too, that only moments before soared beyond the limits of the city, but which now with this hunter upon us retracts and shrivels faster than water at the turn of tide. I take to the shadows, a man afraid for his own soul.

The throaty rattle echoes over my shoulder. I freeze, pistol clasped to my chest. The blood pounding in my ears betokens my end. Slowly, I turn. But there's only darkness. I cannot die here in the withering shadow of my own soul. Darkness will be my sure defeat.

I must face it. In the open.

I move out of shadow and into the streets. Now in Limehouse, now Piccadilly. Westminster. Gravitating to the heart of London, a mad array of starred boulevards. The city where civilisation begins and ends. Beasts lurk here. Once there were many. Now there is only one.

I prowl barefoot, the coat heavy on me. I shake it off, finding then the shirt on my back too much. I cast it off too. Thus divested, I am at ease, on a par with the beast that hunts me. The throaty growl more insistent now, becoming a soft roar. The feet pad the undergrowth, in the park now (*Kensington?*) it keeps to the shadow, the dark recesses, feet crisp on dry leaves, it has the cover of night and the trees but I am no stranger to these, the murky corners of the night. My palm sweats against the handle of the gun. I grip it tighter. Sweat in my eyes too. I look down at my feet in the mud of the earth. The beast does not hear me approach.

Is it something holy, that which I hunt? I catch a glimpse of it, the raven sparkle of its coat under starlight, the aquiline arch of its neck, the grace of its step as it weaves illuded through the illiterate night.

It hits me, then: demise is inescapable. The only victory is submission. I know it certain as a rock in the gut.

Assured, the Jaguar meanders into the open. Stops. Raises its head and purrs. Then sits, regally and yawns. In its maw, vast captive worlds.

A man like me never had much sense. I step out from behind the tree and fire wildly.

***

'Why do I feel like this?' Constancia whispers.

I stroke her golden hair. 'Because you love me.' After a pause: 'Because we love each other.'

She takes my hand and kisses my fingers, one after the other. 'Then why do I feel like I'm dying?'

I turn her face to mine and kiss her on the mouth. 'I don't know, but isn't that what love entails, the death of a part of ourselves? The ego, maybe? I feel it too. It's scary, but don't you feel free?'

She turns her head away, takes my arm, wraps it around her and presses her mouth to my wrist. I feel the beat of my vein against her lips. I have not been honest with her. I don't feel free. What I feel for her terrifies me. I feel I'm losing myself, and I hate it. Not all of us are made for love. I was not built to love. That is not the way I'm made. And yet, the way I feel for her... Can it be that people not made for love can yet fall deeply? Why now, why here? After all these years together? I came here to be free, yet suddenly I'm entangled in this suffocating web. Do I love her? With all my heart, yes. And yet, as she says – *Why do I feel like I'm dying?*

Last night after I fell asleep, I awoke to hear her pray quietly as she lay next to me. I know her. Her sensibilities are irretrievably Christian. She fears she's committing a mortal sin by lying with me, as if two people who love each other can commit sin by sharing a bed. I despise Christianity. I reject it. It's true I have more of my *abuela* than my mother in me. My mother was lost to that same indulgence as Constancia, and I despised her for it. I couldn't bear to see her on her knees. To get on one's knees is the most insipid, servile state a woman can put herself in. Be it for god or man.

I slide my thigh between my lover's and pull her into me, wrapping my arms around her. 'Mi amor. My little hummingbird,' I whisper to her. She smiles, a smile torn with sadness. I kiss her violently on the lips. Still with a trace of resistance in her embrace, yet she relents and lets me take her.

After breakfast, she brings me a note and places it in my hand.

I glance at the handwriting. 'From the sodomite,' I mutter, my head in other places.

'The *what*?' Constancia's voice is tainted with confusion.

'Oh... sorry, I'm rambling. It's probably nothing.' Yet I know she won't leave until I've read the note. I open it. Palmerston has summoned me to his residence this afternoon at four. I'm tempted not to go, yet there are still too many unknowns for me to shirk this meeting. I will have to attend.

'What does he want?' Constancia asks.

'He wants to see me today.'

'About what?'

I shrug and sigh, and put down the note. 'I have no idea. It's probably not important. I'll go, just to humour him.'

As she goes to move away, I take her hand and pull her to me. She looks around furtively for the maid, her face tinged with panic.

'Mi amor, what are you worried about – we are in our own home. No one can judge us under our own roof.' She relents and lets me pull her close. 'You know no one can take anything away from us, don't you? Nor will anyone separate us. I promise you. I told you I'd always protect you, and I will.'

She nods, yet doesn't display the reassurance I'm so desperately trying to instil in her. I feel a momentary flush of anger. Constancia sees it and tries to pull away. I grip her wrist tighter.

'You're hurting me... let me go.'

I push her away with force, and regret it immediately. I get up from the chair. 'Dios, mi amor... I'm sorry. Please, don't you see, I'm only trying to protect you.'

'I am not a child!' she shouts, and turns and hurries from the room. I start to go after her but stop. I cannot, now. I will talk to her later. I'll hold her and whisper sweet words to her and tell her everything is alright. Everything will be well. All will be well.

I wait longer than I care for in Palmerston's sitting room. His wife doesn't even come to greet me. Instead, I sit with the untouched cup of tea that grows cold, my impatience rising. This insult does not bode well for our meeting. It's a message. He's grandstanding. For what reasons, I can't yet guess.

When I'm eventually invited into his study, the smug look on his face tells me I've guessed right. I've come to have my face rubbed in something.

'Miss Azul... please, come and sit down. We have much to discuss.'

'Do we?' Reluctantly, I sit.

'Tea?'

'No.'

My curtness surprises him, yet he smiles and waves away his footman. The door closes. The Foreign Minister decides to work up to his little announcement.

'So, Ms. Azul, how are you? How is Old Blighty treating you?'

'Why don't you tell me why you've invited me here,' I say.

'Yes, rather. Well...' He lifts a cigar from a box on his desk and takes his time lighting it. When he's done, he resumes. 'Well, it seems there has been some development in our affairs with your home country, and your father. Just last night we hammered out a treaty with the so-called Argentine Republic. The signing of it, as well as the terms, will be announced in parliament today. It seems, after all, that your father has finally seen sense.'

He sits back in his chair, entirely pleased with himself.

'And are you going to share the terms of this treaty with me?'

He smiles. 'Well, for one, Argentina has ceded all rights to the Falkland Islands. Henceforth, the islands shall be enshrined in international law as British territory, in perpetuity.'

My fingers tighten around my bag. 'You got your little piece of rock, Lord Palmerston. Well done.'

'But m'lady, the Falkland Islands is no mere piece of rock. It is, and always has been, a part of the Great British Empire. And now we have the paper to prove it.'

'Little pieces of paper.' I sigh. 'I guess this is what empire comes down to. Signatures inveigled from people with a gun to the temple. But of course – it's all legitimate in the name of empire. Because nothing can stop the unrelenting force of civilisation, isn't that right, Lord Viscount?'

He doesn't reply, simply eyes me through the fog of cigar smoke.

'Let me tell you what has actually happened, Lord Palmerston. Oh yes, I do read and keep up to date on current affairs from my homeland. Truth is not contained solely in *The Times*. Here is what has transpired, sir – your ships have gone against my father, and yes, you may have won somewhat of a *victory*, but your Great British navy got such a slap in the face that they were forced to sit at anchor for six weeks while the ships were restored, and when they sailed downriver again, they still came under fire from my father's forces.' I pause. A little tremble has taken hold of his hand. I let him simmer for a moment, before finishing. 'Great Britain has been driven from Argentina by force, sir, by the force of its cannons and its soldiers. My father will never back down and your commanders know it. You have sued for peace, and it has been granted. And if you got your little piece of rock as a consolation prize, it is only to keep the bankers happy. That is the truth of it, *sir*.'

By the time I'm done, he's white with anger. He puts the cigar in the ashtray and stands up.

'I invited you here today, madam, to extend a hand of friendship across the Atlantic, and to put our troubles behind us. I might have expected a southern man to speak with such a foul mouth, but not a lady. Your insults will not be tolerated.' He rings a bell and the door opens. 'Let us consider our business concluded, *Ms. Rosas*. I see no further advantage in our maintaining an acquaintance.'

'You are right,' I say. I get up to go. 'But let us not part on bad terms, Lord Palmerston. Who knows when we may be of service to each other in the future?'

He waves at the footman. '*Never*, is the answer, m'lady. Now good day.'

I am dismissed. No longer of use. Banished from the kingdom. Never mind. He's of little concern to me anyway. But let us hope, for his sake, that he doesn't try to make life difficult for me. He'll soon find out how ruthless a woman without British 'civilising values' can be. I will destroy him.

*

The time has come. I'm no longer afraid, or at least, I'm prepared to overcome my fear. I understand now that to kill fear one must die. I must face my mortal enemy and let him tear me apart. Devour me. In eating me, I will in turn destroy all fear. That is the way he must be defeated. I know now.

At the dinner table, I watch Constancia. She sits with the newspaper, devouring every inch. The story of the treaty has broken. She's momentarily consumed. Since coming here, I've watched her change. Before, in Buenos Aires, she had no interest in politics or world affairs. Now, lifted from her old existence and planted here in the heart of the British Empire, she longs to be informed. She needs the reassurance of information. I like it. I like to see her curious, and desirous of expanding her mind. Yet now, at this very moment, the pursuit of knowledge only serves to fill her with fear and uncertainty.

She looks up from the paper, her face fraught. 'But what does it all mean?'

I am tired of politics. I want only the comfort of souls. 'Nada, mi amor. Nada.'

'Are we still safe?'

I get up and cross the table, and kneel by her side. 'Always.' I say.

My assertion does not reassure her. Perhaps she'll never feel safe. Perhaps she will always be searching for something more. Perhaps I have made a terrible mistake. As I rise to my feet, I see it in her eyes, the awful, stinging look of reproach. Even ire. Part of her does hate me. Part of her despises what I've done to her. In her eyes, in her glare, I feel it: *I am a monster*.

I back away from her. 'I... I must go to my study for a bit. Please leave me alone for a few hours, mi amor. I have something I must do.'

I turn and leave the room.

Upstairs, I lock my study and go to the chest, and take out the *caapi*. I must venture further than I ever have before. The beast must be confronted. He must be faced down and silenced. I must surrender to him. Like this, finally I'll be free. Free to be a monster, if that is what I must be.

The brew takes time. I spend hours in preparation. While I do, I meditate to slow my heart rate and quiet my mind. When the brew ready, I take it to the middle of the room where I sit on the rug and drink. It doesn't go down easy. It's heavy on the stomach. The urge to vomit comes on but I conquer the impulse. When the cramps have passed, I open my eyes.

It is night and the sky is purple. I lie at the foot of a jacaranda tree. The jungle moves and sways, alive. Whispers assail me from the undergrowth. Eyes that do not see mark my presence. They have learned of my coming and now they cower. Souls, innumerable souls, move silently in the deep congress of my being.

I hold up a hand and point: —You there, come out...

Out steps a man in black. A priest. I remember him well.

—It's you, he says.

—You remember me. But do you remember who you are?

—My name is Carmichael, he says.

—And who were you before that?

—I was nothing before that.

He takes off his Jesuit hat and sits in front of me, and places the hat on the ground. —I'm searching for someone...

—Who are you searching for?

—For a woman... I think...

Fool. He cannot remember. He will never remember. His being has been subsumed into mine. For all that his fickle soul is worth.

—I'm also searching for someone, I say. Tell me, priest, have you seen Teyú Yaguá?

The priest turns his head and points into the jungle. —He is back there. Hiding from you.

I pick myself up from the jungle floor. —You are all hiding from me.

The priest looks up at me morosely. —It is enough to die once. Here we die every day, yet never pass.

—You fool. Now you are immortal. A wise man would rejoice.

—Immortal, but prisoners.

I kneel and look him in the eye. —You don't see? I set you free. Free from the earthly prison of your bodies. Now you are like angels.

I put a hand on his shoulder. Then I turn and walk away.

—Not angels – ghosts, he shouts after me.

The fool knows nothing. It's a shame I can't rid myself of some of these souls. They are nothing but baggage. Yet I am entwined with them all.

I come to a stream. It flows gentle and silver through the warm night. I step into it. My footsteps cause a shimmer in the water, like a thousand tiny particles suddenly take life. I put a hand in; small fish dart between my fingers. I sip from the river and quench the fire in my belly. Then I step to the other side.

From the other bank, I see the glow of a dying fire. I can tell he is near by the stench of meat. I go quietly to the edge of the clearing. He's there, alone, staring into the fire. The sky above him has a different hue; it is almost green.

The beast does not roar as I step out of the trees and into the clearing. When I reach the fire, I sit down with my back to its warmth. I reach out a hand to touch the snout of Teyú Yaguá.

—Great beast, why do you not speak?

Still he is silent. I do not like to make demands of the gods, but sometimes it is necessary.

—Open your mouth, Old One.

The beast Teyú Yaguá opens his mouth. Inside is a hummingbird. It will speak for him.

—Tell me, little one, of Yaguareté.

The hummingbird shakes itself and opens its mouth, and a great song comes out:

—Baipú ground the manioc. Baipú tended the fire. Baipú harvested the yerba maté and Baipú kept the wolves from the door. One day Baipú went into the forest to collect kindling for the fire. All alone, Baipú had nothing but her knife and her guile. It was dawn and Baipú was tracked by Yaguareté, who stalked the jungle after a long and silent night. Baipú was hunted. Stopping to eat a little manioc cake she carried with her, she sat down under the jacaranda to rest. Yaguareté saw his chance and leapt. Baipú, with the knife in hand, raised her hand to protect herself. The knife went into the beast's throat and she was washed in the blood of Yaguareté. —*Why shouldn't I eat this beast?* thought Baipú, and she cut a portion of Yaguareté's flank and cooked it on the fire. Thus with belly filled, she finished her task and went home. Baipú, with the flesh of Yaguareté inside her, became swollen as with child, and the children were the Sun and Moon, which grew inside her. When the village people saw she was pregnant after her encounter in the jungle, they cast her out. She wandered, and wandered, still with the young inside her, but now the kin of Yaguareté hunted her. They tracked her too and killed her, but were not able to slay the Sun and Moon. A great battle ensued, and the Jaguar mauled the Sun and ate the Moon, and yet the very next night the Moon was in the sky again. So the Jaguar relented and instead raised the Sun and Moon as his own, until they had taken their unassailable position in the sky. And when it was time for the jaguar to leave, the Sun uttered:

Noisome being, sleep and awake;
Being who renders noisome
the springs and the banks of the genuine waters,
fall asleep.
Then awake.

—Yaguareté awoke by the side of a stream. He looked at the sky and saw Sun, and saw Moon, and knew it was time to return to the jungle. For he that sleeps will always awake, and he that dies will always live, for only the Sun and Moon are eternal.

The hummingbird falls silent, and the mouth of the great Teyú Yaguá closes. I put my hand on his snout.

—Thank you, Old One.

I get up and turn to leave the clearing. As I go, the great beast deigns to speak: —The Sun cannot be defeated.

I glance at him across the fire. —It can. And it will.

I leave, still with the heat of the fire at my back.

I wander deep into the jungle, deeper than I've ever gone. Here no birds sing. Here no light enters. Here where the Sun and Moon have no dominion. The abode of Yaguareté.

I am naked. I come here alone, exposed, clothed only in my fears and desires. He shall see me, and he shall know. The humidity increases. The jungle encloses itself around me. Vines grasp at my ankles, the ivy twists my hair. I force myself deeper, deeper...

Until I arrive. Before I see them, I smell the scent of their union. In the clearing, they lie in illicit embrace. When I see her, my heart crumbles.

Constancia, no...

She lies entwined with the beast, limbs a-grasp, their bodies pressed together. They sleep after the agonies of lovemaking. They are bound to each other.

—No...

Gods forgive me, I cannot...

But it must be so. Through my torment, I see there is only one way: Yaguareté must be defeated by destroying the Sun.

The Daughter of Wahari, the Death of the Sun

I am the sage darkness, I shun the light. Night finds me in the recesses of the earth's dusk. Day finds me where the hunter cannot. The godly hour is the dawn of Jaguar, whose heart knows no time nor obeys its call. I eschew the strength of man. I am on guard for the wrath of woman. Children I take from their beds, their souls returned to the source. The mother awaits me, the father awaits me. Both shall be devoured.

The hearth of the old woman is cold and the old man's wineskin is dry. Strength has left the world of men, their souls lost. One has come to take back the soul, the firstborn, the primaeval. Many men have tried to kill the Sun, none have succeeded. Now a woman comes, a daughter of Wahari. Her intent is destruction. Does she know who birthed the Sun and Moon, and raised them, and escorted them to the sky, and through whose mercy they live?

But what mercy? Yaguareté does not know mercy. Yaguareté does or does not, kills or kills not. Yaguareté's soul is clean, not cluttered and corrupt like the souls of men and women. Yaguareté is rage-sharp, a tenebrous edge. Clarity and purpose are one in Yaguareté. He does not waver.

The daughter of Wahari came for the Sun. Like those before her, unaware of the limits of her sex. She did not know that to destroy the

Sun is to destroy that which one cherishes above all. But she learned. Through fortitude and relentless will, she learned. She learned knowledge was not in books, wisdom not in others, not even in the sage learning of old *karai*. She came to the knowledge by will and violence. Violence and will, these are man's only weapons. And woman's. And forever was it true that woman has greater will than man.

In the middle of the night, the woman rose from the rug on which she lay. Newly astir from her union with the medicine, her face was wet with tears and wraught of anguish. See the weakness of the human? Yet she tore her dress and let it fall to the floor, naked in the cold night she took her knife, the knife with the handle of silver and jade. She pressed the tip to her hand. Blood pooled in her palm yet she did not baulk. Now she pressed her palm to her lips and washed her mouth in blood.

So adorned, she left the room and went down the hall to where her beloved lay. Quietly she went in. Softly she closed the door. Her beloved, as always, feigned sleep. The daughter of Wahari climbed into the bed next to her. Her beloved stirred, turned to look at the face of her lover in the moonlight. *Mi amor... Que pasa?* She took the face of the daughter of Wahari in her hands, the face streaked with blood and tears. The daughter of Wahari shook her head, stroked the cheek of her beloved and kissed her like the warm air of spring. Her beloved pulled away. *No entiendo... dime, qué ha pasado?* She wiped the tears from the face of her lover, her own face now wracked with fear. *Dime...*

Te amo, mi amor, te amo siempre... ¿Lo sabes? Siempre, mi amor, siempre... No entiendo, no entiendo...

The daughter of Wahari, face fraught, raised the knife and put it to her beloved's chest. Her tears fell like raindrops on the face of the Sun as she plunged the knife into her heart. Broken, confused and betrayed, the light in her beloved's eyes dimmed. The daughter of Wahari pulled out the knife; distraught, she tried to stem the flow of blood. Yet the light in her beloved's eyes had already died. The daughter of Wahari screamed.

I am the piercing cry in the night, the darkness that pierces the darkness. I am the dying of the dawn. I am the first light of the thousand-night eclipse, I am he who raised the Moon. I am the first, and I am the last. I am the song of the shadow and the nightly shade. I am the one who prowls. I am the death of the hummingbird.

The Sun is dead. Yaguareté lives.

Part Three

London, November 1850

like the deep fathoms of harried seas

The rattle of boots on cold stone. Keys. A grunt. He spits in disgust, appearing at the bars.

'Oi...'

I'm already sittin up.

'Stand up, you facking scum.' I stand and turn to face the door. A plate of soup is tossed through the grill onto the floor. 'Here. Eat.' He tilts his head and spits again for good measure. Turns back to me and points a finger. 'And if I catch you sittin down again, scum, I'll beat you black and facking blue.'

When he walks away, I kneel on the floor and lift a bit of potato from the mess and swallow it, and a piece of carrot. The rats will soon be on the scent. I scrape what else I can from the ground then slide into a squat by the wall.

Such a degenerate, rank hole no man has ever conceived of. They gave me the filthiest cell in the Tower. When the river rises, my cell fills with a foot of water, overspill from the sewers comin up with the rising tide.

With the water come the rats. Those who put me here think me a rat too. Lower than a rat.

At the whiff of food, my cellmates show themselves. They crawl from the wall, black and slick and heavy, run between my feet, not a care in the world for me. They attack the gruel on the floor. And when it's gone, they retreat to their hole with not a look in my direction. Zero heed. What am I to them, anyway? We fight over the same scraps is all. We're kin, me and the rodents.

I cough and spit. Everything damp. It's in my lungs now. Last night I was spittin blood. That could be the beatins n'all though. They tan me raw when the bloodlust comes on em, and the bloodlust comes on em regular. I've teeth missin. Holes in my skull. Big lumps where big lumps should not be. The only reason I'm more or less in one piece is cause they need me whole for the trial. If I make it, that is. Could be they take it too far one night and I don't wake up. Or maybe they'll kill me anyway. Make a show of it. Put the Irish in their place.

Outside the door, I hear scrapin. It's the simpleton with the whack leg. The sound of his boot draggin on the floor. He likes to beat his stick off the walls and doors. This he does as he advances down the corridor towards my cell. When he appears, he's got that strange grin on his lug that looks like it was beat into him as a child. He grips the bars and pushes his nose through.

'Oi, Paddy...'

He's alright. He only beats me when the others are around. I look up.

'Oi, you made the papers again. Wanna see?' He holds up the paper.

And yes, I'm curious. I get up and go to the door. But as I draw near, he spits at me and pulls away. Howlin that twisted fucken laugh of his. Draggin his feet to the next door to see what amusement he can extract.

I go to the corner and try to piss in the bucket. I can't. They've fucked my insides up. My pipes are all twisted up, the organs gone to shit. They've fucked me, truly and honest-to-god fucked me.

Know a man can sleep standin up? He can. I've done it. I taught myself. Head against the cold stone, I can close my eyes and sleep for twenty minutes, maybe a half hour. I do this through the day so they don't have a reason to come in and kick the livin shit outta me. It's outta one such reverie I hear footsteps comin down the hall again, this time two sets. But without the swearin and the clamour of violence. A nervous cough this time. No spittin.

When they arrive at the cell, head warder takes up his keys and opens the door.

'Visitor,' he says.

I think it's a ruse and they're gonna step in one after the other and go to work on me, then he steps aside and the madam steps into the cell. Like an unearthly vision. Dressed head to toe in jade green, an unearthly dryad.

'Miss?'

She appears different somehow. Her face sharper. More taut. Her eyes have a darkness, a blackness to em they didn't before. She turns to the warder.

He looks at me with violence. 'You want me to chain him, madam?'

'No. No need.'

He nods and gives me the look. *Mess about and we'll tan your facking hide proper.* Then he goes out. Closes the door. They walk away.

I shake my head. 'What are you doin here?'

She looks around the cell. Does her best to hide the revulsion. Only a twinge at the corner of the mouth gives it away.

'Fine mess you've got yourself into, Mr. Ryan.'

'Aye.' I sit down on the bed. I must grimace with the pain, because she notices.

'I see they've been treatin you harshly.' I nod. 'Can't say I'm surprised. Quite a reckless thing you did.'

'Aye.' I nod and look at the floor. We remain in silence for a while. 'Don't suppose you've come to get me out of here, then?'

She doesn't quite smile, but the intent is there. 'You tried to shoot Queen Victoria, Mr. Ryan. You're never getting out of here.' She watches me with deep interest. 'So why did you do it?'

I return her gaze. 'I felt *compelled* to it.'

'Hmm.' She turns away. 'How amused I was to find you're only the fourth man this century to attempt it. I wonder if the world would be at all improved if one of you'd succeeded.' After a moment she adds, 'Probably not.'

'Aye, well. I tried, fuck sake. I tried.'

She sighs and looks over her shoulder at the door. When she turns back to me, she slides a hand into her sleeve.

'I don't suppose you smuggled me in a bit of food?' I say.

She doesn't answer, but takes out a small glass vial and hands it to me.

'What's this?'

'You know what that is, Mr. Ryan. We both know you're not getting out of here. If you get to trial, it'll just be the death penalty. But you probably won't make it that far, will you?'

I look at the thing in my hand. A nothing thing. When I look up at her, her eyes are like fire.

'You do what you must. I'm just sorry you've ended up like this. You're a good man. You simply were not able to control your excesses.'

'Never had much luck at that I guess, miss.'

She nods. 'Goodbye, Mr. Ryan.'

As she turns to go out the door, I call her back. 'Do you know what's it like? Death, I mean?'

She looks at me, tongue darting to the edge of her mouth. 'How would I know that?'

'You seem like a woman who knows things.'

Tucking a whisp of hair behind her ear, she says, 'Dying is easy. Once it is done.'

I nod. Out she goes, the dress, green like the deep fathoms of harried seas, the last thing I see. It is burned into my mind, and it is the last thing I shall see before I die.

Epilogue

I arrived in London on just such a night: a heavy fog-laden night that enfolds one like some terrible harbinger. The London night does not comfort as nights do in Buenos Aires. A summer night there holds one in its arms. One feels the embrace and lies into it. Swims away. Here there's no such comfort, and yet this is where I've come in exile. But this city will not contain me. This continent will not contain me. With three establishments already open here, it's time to spread my wings. Miss Emily can run business here while I venture across the water to pursue possibilities there – first Paris, then Rome, and after perhaps even Germany and Holland. I can have houses in every major city in Europe within a couple of years. I'll build a network that spans a continent, giving me access to every major institution in every country. Vice will never go away. It's the Achilles heel that will forever be exposed. And I am the knife, braced.

'We're here,' Miss Emily says.

The boat pulls up at the pier and the captain ties off. He aids us off the boat. At the top of the pier, two Oriental gentlemen are waiting. Without a word, they bid us enter a carriage. When we are inside, they climb into the cab and we depart.

'I suppose you would not do business with em if you didn't have to,' Miss Emily says.

'They're probably infinitely more trustworthy than the English,' I say. And after a moment, add, 'I had a contact here in London but he appears to be out of the country. Either that or he's been instructed on the quiet not to do business with me. Never mind. A guarantee from the Chinese will be much safer than one from the British side. Public opinion here on the opium trade is swinging. It's jeopardising British control. We need to expand.'

Miss Emily nods. She is simple but savvy. I did well hiring her. She'll keep a firm rein on things while I'm gone.

We pull up at a warehouse on Black Eagle Wharf. The two men escort us from the cabin and into the warehouse, leading us through it and out the back. Here we enter a house. It is decrepit and candlelit. Heavy with the aroma of opium. In the back room, we enter an office where a large Oriental sits at a desk. One of our escorts introduces him.

'Miss Azul, Joon Sing.'

He nods. I nod. We get down to business.

When we are concluded, I instruct the gentlemen to bring the silver from the carriage. It's carried in and put on the desk. Mr. Sing inspects it and nods. Then it is taken away.

All of this, with barely a word spoken.

'Mr. Sing is very happy with our arrangement,' one of his aides says. 'He expects a long and fruitful partnership.'

I turn to the Oriental. 'I, too, Mr. Sing.'

Joon Sing nods. 'Big business, Ma'am 'zu,' he says, butchering my name.

I smile. 'Big business.'

When we're back on the boat and sailing back down the Thames, Miss Emily lights her pipe and wraps the shawl around her shoulders. She looks content. Perhaps even excited for the future.

'So what now, Madam Zu?'

I smile. I like it. It has a charming sound. If I need to disappear behind a thousand veils, I should perhaps take a new name. Perhaps.

'Now we are ready.'

The boat steals softly downriver as London buries us in fog, the river's tumult putting our hearts to quiet, and we disappear into a nightstory of myth on interminable waters that whisper a forgotten song of sorrows, of sorrows.

Word is, there's a woman from back of Macau
ordained on Meru in the waters of the lake,
wandered forth like a daughter of the Sun
and killed her way across the land
with a knife of green in her delicate hand.
She built a garden of bamboo and damask
and her bed was the dirge of the last ones,
the ones who saw that they were the last and no more would follow
because there was no more need for flesh.
All were filled because she was sated,
and all we needed was burgundy perfume
which was her scent;
damask and bamboo and burgundy perfume
was all we needed now.
She gave it to us.
Her name was Madam Zhu.

Many thanks to Kindra Ferriabough.

Epigraphs from, 1. *The Cannibalist Manifesto,* by Oswald de Andrade, and 2. *Beyond Good and Evil,* by Friedrich Nietzsche.

Meat

In the murky wake of the financial crisis a string of establishments pop up across Europe catering to a hedonistic underground, its clientele beholden to a strange, hallucinatory meat. Stoked by the fleshy and charismatic Hugo and fuelled by voracious consumption of ecstasy, the craze spreads from the heart of Europe all the way to the Mediterranean, where in Athens the financial elite begin to turn on each other. Murder, barbecue and apocalyptic raving ensues, culminating in the most savage party Mykonos has ever seen. Follow the story to its destructive end, where consumption eats itself alive.

Notes from a Cannibalist

1847. Assuming the identity of a dead Jesuit priest, a survivor of the famine in Ireland travels to South America where he is tasked with rebuilding the missions among the natives. Inducted into local life, Father James Carmichael finds love with a native woman and becomes acquainted with the ways of the Guaraní, discovering ayahuasca and ritualism. In a battle with his own gods and demons, the priest fights for the life he envisions, his own self the ultimate stake of the struggle. Worlds are shattered, realities crumbled, lives destroyed. His soul victim to the crucible of the New World, what is tempered in the chaos will be outside his control.

A Whore's Song

Hidden away in the backstreets of Amsterdam is a secretive whorehouse, open only to those in the know, where torture, pain and extreme sexual sport are the vehicle to understanding and self-knowledge. Run by the obscure Madame Zhu, the establishment is a magnet to the city's elite and mad soul-seekers alike. Two lives collide in a chaotic downward spiral brought about by psychoactives and sexual torture when, over the course of a day, a whore recounts her life as a destroyer of egos and one man is forced to face his deepest demons. Cast out into the far reaches of his mind, will he make it back from the other side?

In a world where the weak become prey and strength means brutality, living may come at the cost of dying first.

LITTLE SWINE

A small basement cell. A dirty bed. A chair.

These are the confines of Little Swine's world. Prisoner of Momma and subject to the tortures of Boy, her life is a living hell.

Momma is a disturbed woman. Her plan is simple: Momma wants a baby so that she may redeem the sins of her past. This is Little Swine's purpose. And when Momma has what she wants, Little Swine will be discarded.

But violence gives way to violence and blood begets blood, and many will die before the devil has his quota. One can never underestimate the power of retribution.

THE COTTAGE

Men are men until they encounter evil. And after, they are compelled to do evil itself.

Turning their backs on New York, John and Katie Mears purchase their dream home in colonial Connecticut, the place they hope to raise their firstborn and build life as a family. But the cradle of the American nation has a haunting past, and they find themselves swallowed by a dark history, one of blood and anguish, a specter of the country's painful birth in the slaughter of pilgrim times. The dark crucible of the nation is yet manifest. Blood debt is eternal, and sooner or later history calls for retribution. It is the blood of innocents that pays for the sins of the father.

THE SISTEMA SERIES

There is a company that provides a deeply sinister service for shady clients: subconscious torture for political or corporate manipulation. Vangelis Zervas is an agent of Vathos and does his job with zero qualms. But when a young boy is killed over a highly coveted piece of software that may have been produced by the company, the boy's mother goes in search of her son's killers. Meeting a group of disparate rebels with their own hostility toward Vathos, they join forces to bring down the company. Vangelis Zervas is on their radar, but will he see his way to help them and go rogue, or stay true to the devil inside? Sistema is a dystopian/cyberpunk horror that journeys into hell itself in exploration of man's search for power and control.

www.ingramcontent.com/pod-product-compliance
Lightning Source LLC
Chambersburg PA
CBHW050614190726
48283CB00007B/2411

9 781914 147265